THE
CORYSTON FAMILY

A Novel

MRS. HUMPHRY WARD

1st WORLD
LIBRARY
Literary Society

The Coryston Family

Mrs. Humphry Ward

© 1st World Library, 2006
PO Box 2211
Fairfield, IA 52556
www.1stworldlibrary.com
First Edition

LCCN: 2006937830

Softcover ISBN: 978-1-4218-3354-5
Hardcover ISBN: 978-1-4218-3254-8
eBook ISBN: 978-1-4218-3454-2

Purchase *"The Coryston Family"*
as a traditional bound book at:
www.1stWorldLibrary.com/purchase.asp?ISBN=978-1-4218-3354-5

1ˢᵗ World Library Literary Society

Giving Back to the World

"If you want to work on the core problem, it's early school literacy."

- James Barksdale, former CEO of Netscape

"No skill is more crucial to the future of a child, or to a democratic and prosperous society, than literacy."

- Los Angeles Times

Literacy... means far more than learning how to read and write... The aim is to transmit... knowledge and promote social participation."

- UNESCO

"Literacy is not a luxury, it is a right and a responsibility. If our world is to meet the challenges of the twenty-first century we must harness the energy and creativity of all our citizens."

- President Bill Clinton

"Parents should be encouraged to read to their children, and teachers should be equipped with all available techniques for teaching literacy, so the varying needs and capacities of individual kids can be taken into account."

- Hugh Mackay

TO

G.M.T. AND J.P.T.

BOOK I

LADY CORYSTON

[Greek: turannon einai moria kai tonthelein.]

CHAPTER I

The hands of the clock on the front of the Strangers' Gallery were nearing six. The long-expected introductory speech of the Minister in charge of the new Land Bill was over, and the leader of the Opposition was on his feet. The House of Commons was full and excited. The side galleries were no less crowded than the benches below, and round the entrance-door stood a compact throng of members for whom no seats were available. With every sentence, almost, the speaker addressing the House struck from it assent or protest; cheers and counter-cheers ran through its ranks; while below the gangway a few passionate figures on either side, the freebooters of the two great parties, watched one another angrily, sitting on the very edge of their seats, like arrows drawn to the string.

Within that privileged section of the Ladies' Gallery to which only the Speaker's order admits, there was no less agitation than on the floor below, though the signs of it were less evident. Some half a dozen chairs placed close against the grille were filled by dusky forms invisible, save as a dim patchwork, to the House beneath them—women with their faces pressed against the lattice-work which divided them from the Chamber, endeavoring to hear and see, in spite of all the difficulties placed in their way by a graceless Commons. Behind them stood other women, bending forward sometimes over the heads of those in front, in the feverish effort to catch the words of the speech. It was so dark in the little room that no inmate of it could be sure of the identity of any other unless she was close beside her; and it was pervaded by a constant soft *frou-frou* of silk and satin, as persons from an inner room moved in and out, or some lady silently gave up her seat to a new-comer, or one of those in front bent over to whisper to a friend behind. The background of all seemed filled with a shadowy medley of plumed hats, from which sometimes a face emerged as a shaft of faint light from the illumined ceiling of the House struck upon it.

The atmosphere was very hot, and heavy with the scent of violets, which seemed to come from a large bunch worn by a slim standing girl. In front of the girl sat a lady who was evidently absorbed in the scene below. She rarely moved, except occasionally to put up an eyeglass the better to enable her to identify some face on the Parliamentary benches, or the author of some interruption to the speaker. Meanwhile the girl held her hands upon the back of the lady's chair, and once or twice stooped to speak to her.

Next to this pair, but in a corner of the gallery, and occupying what seemed to be a privileged and habitual seat, was a woman of uncouth figure and strange headgear. Since the Opposition leader had risen, her attention had wholly wandered. She yawned perpetually, and talked a great deal to a lady behind her. Once or twice her neighbor threw her an angry glance. But it was too dark for her to see it; though if she had seen it she would have paid no attention.

"Lady Coryston!" said a subdued voice. The lady sitting in front of the girl turned and saw an attendant beckoning.

The girl moved toward him, and returned.

"What is it, Marcia?"

"A note from Arthur, mamma."

A slip of paper was handed to Lady Coryston, who read it in the gloom with difficulty. Then she whispered to her daughter:

"He hopes to get his chance about seven; if not then, after dinner."

"I really don't think I can stay so long," said the girl, plaintively. "It's dreadfully tiring."

"Go when you like," said her mother, indifferently. "Send the car back for me."

She resumed her intent listening just as a smart sally from the speaker below sent a tumultuous wave of cheers and counter-cheers through his audience.

"He can be such a buffoon, can't he?" said the stout lady in the corner to her companion, as she yawned again. She had scarcely tried to lower her voice. Her remark was, at any rate, quite audible to her next-door neighbor, who again threw her a swift, stabbing look, of no more avail, however, than its predecessors.

"Who is that lady in the corner—do you mind telling me?"

The query was timidly whispered in the ear of Marcia Coryston by a veiled lady, who on the departure of some other persons had come to stand beside her.

"She is Mrs. Prideaux." said Miss Coryston, stiffly.

"The wife of the Prime Minister!" The voice showed emotion.

Marcia Coryston looked down upon the speaker with an air that said, "A country cousin, I suppose."

But she whispered, civilly enough: "Yes. She always sits in that corner. Weren't you here when he was speaking?"

"No—I've not long come in."

The conversation dropped, just as the voice of the orator standing on the left of the Speaker rose to his peroration.

It was a peroration of considerable eloquence, subtly graduated through a rising series of rhetorical questions, till it finally culminated and broke in the ringing sentences:

"Destroy the ordered hierarchy of English land, and you will sweep away a growth of centuries which would not be where it is if it did not in the main answer to the needs and reflect the character of Englishmen. Reform and develop it if you will; bring in modern knowledge to work upon it; change, expand, without breaking it; appeal to the sense of property, while enormously diffusing property; help the peasant without slaying the landlord; in other words, put aside rash, meddlesome revolution, and set yourselves to build on the ancient foundations of our country what may yet serve the new time! Then you will have an *English*, a national policy. It happens to be the Tory policy. Every principle of it is violated by the monstrous bill you have just brought in. We shall oppose it by every means and every device in our power!"

The speaker sat down amid an ovation from his own side. Three men on the Liberal side jumped up, hat in hand, simultaneously. Two of them subsided at once. The third began to speak.

A sigh of boredom ran through the latticed gallery above, and several persons rose and prepared to vacate their places. The lady in the corner addressed some further remarks on the subject of the speech which had just concluded to an acquaintance who came up to greet her. "Childish!—positively childish!"

Lady Coryston caught the words, and as Mrs. Prideaux rose

with alacrity to go into the Speaker's private house for a belated cup of tea, her Tory neighbor beckoned to her daughter Marcia to take the vacant chair.

"Intolerable woman!" she said, drawing a long breath. "And they're in for years! Heaven knows what we shall all have to go through."

"Horrible!" said the girl, fervently. "She always behaves like that. Yet of course she knew perfectly who you were."

"Arthur will probably follow this man," murmured Lady Coryston, returning to her watch.

"Go and have some tea, mother, and come back."

"No. I might miss his getting up."

There was silence a little. The House was thinning rapidly, and half the occupants of the Ladies' Galleries had adjourned to the tearooms on the farther side of the corridor. Marcia could now see her mother's face more distinctly as Lady Coryston sat in a brown study, not listening, evidently, to the very halting gentleman who was in possession of the House, though her eyes still roamed the fast-emptying benches.

It was the face of a woman on the wrong side of fifty. The complexion was extremely fair, with gray shades in it. The eyes, pale in color but singularly imperious and direct, were sunk deep under straight brows. The nose was long, prominent, and delicately sharp in the nostril. These features, together with the long upper lip and severely cut mouth and chin, the slightly hollow cheeks and the thin containing oval of the face, set in pale and still abundant hair, made a harsh yet, on the whole, handsome impression. There was at Coryston, in the gallery, a picture of Elizabeth Tudor in her later years to which Lady Coryston had been often compared; and she, who as a rule disliked any reference to her personal appearance, did not, it was sometimes remarked, resent this particular comparison. The likeness was carried further by Lady Coryston's tall and gaunt frame; by her formidable carriage and step; and by the energy of the long-fingered hands. In dress also there was some parallel between her and the Queen of many gowns. Lady Coryston seldom wore colors, but the richest of black silks and satins and the finest of laces were pressed night and day into the service of her masterful good looks. She made her own fashions. Amid the large and befeathered hats of the day, for instance, she alone wore habitually a kind of coif made of thin black lace on her fair face, the lappets of which were fastened with a diamond close beneath her chin. For the country she invented modifications of her London dress, which, while loose and comfortable, were scarcely less stately. And whatever she wore seemed always part and parcel of her formidable self.

In Marcia's eyes, her mother was a wonderful being—oppressively wonderful—whom she could never conveniently forget. Other people's mothers were, so to speak, furniture mothers. They became the chimney-corner, or the sofa; they looked well in combination, gave no trouble, and could be used for all the common purposes of life. But Lady Coryston could never be used. On the contrary, her husband—while he lived—her three sons, and her daughter, had always appeared to her in the light of so many instruments of her own ends. Those ends were not the ends of other women. But did it very much matter? Marcia would sometimes ask herself. They seemed to cause just as much friction and strife and bad blood as other people's ends.

As the girl sat silent, looking down on the bald heads of a couple of Ministers on the Front Bench, she was uneasily conscious of her mother as of some charged force ready to strike. And, indeed, given the circumstances of the family, on that particular afternoon, nothing could be more certain than blows of some kind before long....

"You see Mr. Lester?" said her mother, abruptly. "I thought Arthur would get him in."

Marcia's dreaminess departed. Her eyes ran keenly along the benches of the Strangers' Gallery opposite till they discovered the dark head of a man who was leaning forward on his elbows, closely attentive, apparently, to the debate.

"Has he just come in?"

"A minute or two ago. It means, I suppose, that Arthur told him he expected to be up about seven. When will this idiot have done!" said Lady Coryston, impatiently.

But the elderly gentleman from the Highlands, to whom she thus unkindly referred, went on humming and hawing as before, while the House lumbered or fidgeted, hats well over noses and legs stretched to infinity.

"Oh, there is Arthur!" cried Marcia, having just discovered her brother among the shadows under the gallery to the left. "I couldn't make him out before. One can see he's on wires."

For while everybody else, after the excitement of the two opening speeches, which was now running its course through the crowded lobbies outside, had sunk into somnolence within the House itself, the fair-haired youth on whom her eyes were bent was sitting erect on the edge of his seat, papers in hand, his face turned eagerly toward the speaker on the other side of the House. His attitude gave the impression of one just about to spring to his feet.

But Marcia was of opinion that he would still have to wait some time before springing. She knew the humming and hawing gentleman—had heard him often before. He was one of those plagues of debate who rise with ease and cease with difficulty. She would certainly have time to get a cup of tea and come back. So with a word to her mother she groped her way through the dark gallery across the corridor toward a tearoom. But at the door of the gallery she turned back. There through the lattice which shuts in the Ladies' Gallery, right across the House, she saw the Strangers' Gallery at the other end. The man whose head had been propped on his hands when she first discovered his presence was now sitting upright, and seemed to be looking straight at herself, though she knew well that no one in the Ladies' Gallery was really visible from any other part of the House. His face was a mere black-and-white patch in the distance. But she imagined the clear, critical eyes, their sudden frown or smile.

"I wonder what *he*'ll think of Arthur's speech—and whether he's seen Coryston. I wonder whether he knows there's going to be an awful row to-night. Coryston's mad!"

Coryston was her eldest brother, and she was very fond of him. But the way he had been behaving!—the way he had been defying mamma!—it was really ridiculous. What could he expect?

She seemed to be talking to the distant face, defending her mother and herself with a kind of unwilling deference.

"After all, do I really care what he thinks?"

She turned and went her way to the tearoom. As she entered it she saw some acquaintances at the farther end, who waved their hands to her, beckoning her to join them. She hastened across the room, much observed by the way, and conscious of the eyes upon her. It was a relief to find herself among a group of chattering people.

Meanwhile at the other end of the room three ladies were finishing their tea. Two of them were the wives of Liberal Ministers—by name, Mrs. Verity and Mrs. Frant. The third was already a well-known figure in London society and in the precincts of the House of Commons—the Ladies' Gallery, the Terrace, the dining-rooms—though she was but an unmarried girl of two-and-twenty. Quite apart, however, from her own qualities and claims, Enid Glenwilliam was conspicuous as the only daughter of the most vigorously hated and ardently followed man of the moment—the North Country miner's agent, who was now England's Finance Minister.

"You saw who that young lady was?" said Mrs. Frant to Miss Glenwilliam. "I thought you knew her."

"Marcia Coryston? I have just been introduced to her. But she isn't allowed to know me!" The laugh that accompanied the words had a pleasant childish chuckle in it.

Mrs. Frant laughed also.

"Girls, I suppose, have to do what they're told," she said, dryly. "But it *was* Arthur Coryston, wasn't it, who sent you that extra order for to-day, Enid?"

"Yes," laughed the girl again; "but I am quite certain he didn't tell his mother! We must really be civil and go back to hear him speak. His mother will think it magnificent, anyway. She probably wrote it for him. He's quite a nice boy—but—"

She shook her head over him, softly smiling to herself. The face which smiled had no very clear title to beauty, but it was arresting and expressive, and it had beautiful points. Like the girl's figure and dress, it suggested a self-conscious, fastidious personality: egotism, with charm for its weapon.

"I wonder what Lady Coryston thinks of her eldest son's performances in the papers this morning!" said lively little Mrs. Frant, throwing up hands and eyes.

Mrs. Verity, a soft, faded woman, smiled responsively.

"They can't be exactly dull in that family," she said. "I'm told they all talk at once; and none of them listens to a word the others say."

"I think I'll bet that Lady Coryston will make Lord Coryston listen to a few remarks on that speech!" laughed Enid Glenwilliam. "Is there such a thing as *matria potestas*? I've forgotten all the Latin I learned at Cambridge, so I don't know. But if there is, that's what Lady Coryston stands for. How splendid—to stand for anything—nowadays!"

The three fell into an animated discussion of the Coryston family and their characteristics. Enid Glenwilliam canvassed them all at least as freely as her neighbors. But every now and then little Mrs. Frant threw her an odd look, as much as to say, "Am I really taken in?"

*   *   *   *   *

Meanwhile a very substantial old lady, scarcely less deliberate and finely finished, in spite of her size, than Lady Coryston herself, had taken a chair beside her in the gallery, which was still very empty.

"My dear," she said, panting a little and grasping Lady Coryston's wrist, with a plump hand on which the rings sparkled—"My dear! I came to bring you a word of sympathy."

Lady Coryston looked at her coldly.

"Are you speaking of Coryston?"

"Naturally. The only logical result of those proceedings last night would be, of course, the guillotine at Hyde Park Corner. Coryston wants our heads! There's nothing else to be said. I took the speeches for young men's nonsense—just midsummer madness, but I find people very angry. *Your* son! one of *us*!"

"I thought the speeches very clever," said Lady Coryston.

"I'm rejoiced you take it so philosophically, my dear Emilia!"—the tone was a little snappish—"I confess I thought you would have been much distressed."

"What's the good of being distressed? I have known Coryston's opinions for a long time. One has to *act*—of course," the speaker added, with deliberation.

"Act? I don't understand."

Lady Coryston did not enlighten her. Indeed, she did not hear her. She was bending forward eagerly. The fair-haired youth on the back benches, who had been so long waiting his turn, was up at last.

It was a maiden speech, and a good one, as such things go. There was enough nervousness and not too much; enough assurance and not too much. The facts and figures in it had been well arranged. A modest jest or two tripped pleasantly out; and the general remarks at the end had been well chosen from the current stock, and were not unduly prolonged. Altogether a creditable effort, much assisted by the young man's presence and manner. He had no particular good looks, indeed; his nose ascended, his chin satisfied no one; but he had been a well-known bat in the Oxford eleven of his day, and was now a Yeomanry officer; he held himself with soldierly erectness, and his slender body, cased in a becoming pale waistcoat under his tail coat, carried a well-shaped head covered with thick and tumbling hair.

The House filled up a little to hear him. His father had been a member of Parliament for twenty years, and a popular member. There was some curiosity to know what his son would make of his first speech. And springing from the good feeling which always animates the House of Commons on such occasions, there was a fair amount of friendly applause from both sides when he sat down.

"Features the father, and takes after the mother!" said a white-haired listener in the Strangers' Gallery to himself, as the young man ceased speaking. "She's drilled him! Well, now I suppose I must go and congratulate her." He rose from his seat and began to make his way out. In the passage outside the Gallery he overtook and recognized the man whose entrance into the House Lady Coryston and her daughter had noticed about an hour earlier.

"Well, what did you think of it, Lester?"

The other smiled good-humoredly.

"Capital! Everybody must make a beginning. He's taken a lot of pains."

"It's a beastly audience!" said Sir Wilfrid Bury, in reply. "Don't I know it! Well, I'm off to congratulate. How does the catalogue get on?"

"Oh, very well. I sha'n't finish till the summer. There's a good deal still to do at Coryston. Some of the things are really too precious to move about."

"How do you get on with her ladyship?" asked the old man, gaily, lowering his voice.

The young man smiled discreetly.

"Oh, very well. I don't see very much of her."

"I suppose she's pressed you into the service—makes you help Arthur?"

"I looked out a few things for his speech to-day. But he has his own secretary."

"You're not staying for the rest of the debate?"

"No, I'm going back to St. James's Square. I have a heap of arrears to get through."

"Do they put you up there? I know it's a huge house."

"Yes. I have a bedroom and sitting-room there when I want

them, and my own arrangements."

"Ta-ta."

Sir Wilfrid nodded pleasantly, and vanished into a side passage leading to the Ladies' Gallery. The young man, Reginald Lester, to whom he had been chatting, was in some sort a protege of his own. It was Sir Wilfrid, indeed, who had introduced him, immediately after he had won an Oxford historical fellowship, to Lady Coryston, as librarian, for the highly paid work of cataloguing a superb collection of MSS. belonging to the Corystons. A generation earlier, Lester's father had been a brother officer of Sir Wilfrid's, in days when the Lester family was still rich, and before the crashing failure of the great banking-house of the name.

Meanwhile, at the other end of the House of Commons, Lady Coryston had been sitting pleasantly absorbed, watching her son, who lay now like a man relieved, lolling on the half-empty bench, chatting to a friend beside him. His voice was still in her ears: mingled with the memory of other voices from old, buried times. For more than twenty years how familiar had she been with this political scene!—these galleries and benches, crowded or listless; these opposing Cabinets—the Ins and Outs—on either side of the historic table; the glitter of the Mace at its farther end; the books, the old morocco boxes, the tops of the official wigs, the ugly light which bathed it all; the exhausted air, the dreariness, the boredom! all worth while, these last, just for the moments, the crises, the play of personalities, the conflict of giants, of which they were the inevitable conditions. There, on the second bench above the gangway on the Tory side, her husband, before he succeeded to the title, had sat through four Parliaments. And from the same point of vantage above she had watched him year after year, coming in and out, speaking occasionally, never eloquent or brilliant, but always respected; a good, worthy, steady-going fellow with whom no one had any fault to find, least of all his wife, to whom he had very easily given up the management of their common life, while he represented her political opinions in Parliament much more than his own.

Until—until?

Well, until in an evil hour, a great question, the only political question on which he differed and had always differed from his wife, on which he felt he *must* speak for himself and stand on his own feet, arose to divide them. There, in that Gallery, she had sat, with rage and defeat in her heart, watching him pass along, behind the Speaker's chair, toward the wrong division lobby, his head doggedly held down, as though he knew and felt her eyes upon him, but must do his duty all the same. On this one matter he had voted against her, spoken against her, openly flouted and disavowed her. And it had broken down their whole relation, poisoned their whole life. "Women are natural tyrants," he had said to her once, bitterly—"no man could torment me as you do." And then had come his death— his swift last illness, with those tired eyes still alive in the dumb face, after speech and movement were no longer possible—eyes which were apt to close when she came near.

And yet, after all—the will!—the will which all his relations and friends had taken as the final expression of his life's weakness, his miserable failure to play the man in his own household, and in which *she*, his wife, had recognized with a secret triumph his last effort to propitiate her, his last surrender to her. Everything left to her, both land and personalty, everything! save for a thousand a year to each of the children, and fifteen hundred a year to Coryston, his heir. The great Irish, the great Devonshire properties, the accumulated savings of a lifetime, they were all hers—hers absolutely. Her husband had stood last in the entail; and with a view to her own power, she had never allowed him to renew it.

Coryston had been furiously angry when the terms of his father's will were revealed. She could never think without shivering of certain scenes, with Coryston in the past—of a certain other scene that was still to come. Well, it had been a duel between them; and after apparently sore defeat, she had

Mrs. Humphry Ward

won, so far as influence over his father was concerned. And since his father's death she had given him every chance. He had only to hold his tongue, to keep his monstrous, *sans-culotte* opinions to himself, at least, if he could not give them up; and she would have restored him his inheritance, would have dealt with him not only justly, but generously. He had chosen; he had deliberately chosen. Well, now then it was for her—as she had said to old Lady Frensham—it was for her to reply, but not in words only.

She fell back upon the thought of Arthur, Arthur, her darling; so manly, and yet so docile; so willing to be guided! Where was he, that she might praise him for his speech? She turned, searching the dark doorway with her eyes. But there was no Arthur, only the white head and smiling countenance of her old friend, Sir Wilfrid Bury, who was beckoning to her. She hurriedly bade Marcia, who had just returned to the Gallery, to keep her seat for her, and went out into the corridor to speak to him.

"Well, not bad, was it? These youngsters have got the trick! I thought it capital. But I dare say you'll have all sorts of fault to find, you most exacting of women!"

"No, no; it was good," she said, eagerly. "And he's improving fast."

"Well then"—the wise old eyes beside her laughed kindly into hers—"be content, and don't take Coryston's escapades too hardly!"

She drew back, and her long face and haughty mouth stiffened in the way he knew.

"Are you coming to see me on Sunday?" she said, quietly.

He took his snubbing without resentment.

"I suppose so. I don't often miss, do I? Well, I hear Marcia was the beauty at the Shrewsbury House ball, and that—" he whispered something, laughing in her ear.

Lady Coryston looked a little impatient.

"Oh, I dare say. And if it's not he, it will be some one else. She'll marry directly. I always expected it. Well, now I must go. Have you seen Arthur?"

"Mother! Hullo, Sir Wilfrid!"

There was the young orator, flushed and radiant. But his mother could say very little to him, for the magnificent person in charge of the Gallery and its approaches intervened. "No talking allowed here, sir, please." Even Lady Coryston must obey. All she could add to her hurried congratulations was:

"You're coming in to-night, remember, Arthur?—nine-thirty."

"Yes, I've paired. I'm coming. But what on earth's up, mother?"

Her lips shut closely.

"Remember, nine-thirty!" She turned and went back into the darkness of the Gallery.

Arthur hesitated a moment in the passage outside. Then he turned back toward the little entrance-room opposite the entrance to the ordinary Ladies' Gallery, where he found another attendant.

"Is Miss Glenwilliam here?" he inquired, carelessly.

"Yes, sir, in the front row, with Mrs. Verity and Mrs. Frant. Do you wish to speak to her, sir? The Gallery's pretty empty."

Arthur Coryston went in. The benches sloped upward, and on

the lowest one, nearest the grille, he saw the lady of his quest, and was presently bending over her.

"Well," he said, flushing, "I suppose you thought it all bosh!"

"Not at all! That's what you have to say. What else can you say? You did it excellently."

Her lightly mocking eyes looked into his. His flush deepened.

"Are you going to be at the Frenshams' dance?" he asked her, presently.

"We're not invited. They're too savage with father. But we shall be at the Opera to-morrow night."

His face lightened. But no more talk was possible. A Minister was up, and people were crowding back into the Gallery. He hurriedly pressed her hand and departed.

CHAPTER II

Lady Coryston and her daughter had made a rapid and silent meal. Marcia noticed that her mother was unusually pale, and attributed it partly to the fatigue and bad air of the House of Commons, partly to the doings of her eldest brother. What were they all going to meet for after dinner—her mother, her three brothers, and herself? They had each received a formal summons. Their mother "wished to speak to them on important business." So Arthur—evidently puzzled—had paired for the evening, and would return from the House at nine-thirty; James had written to say he would come, and Coryston had wired an hour before dinner—"Inconvenient, but will turn up."

What was it all about? Some business matter clearly. Marcia knew very well that the family circumstances were abnormal. Mothers in Lady Coryston's position, when their husbands expire, generally retire to a dower-house, on a jointure; leaving their former splendors—the family mansion and the family income—behind them. They step down from their pedestal, and efface themselves; their son becomes the head of the family, and the daughter-in-law reigns in place of the wife. Nobody for many years past could ever have expected Lady Coryston to step down from anything. Although she had brought but a very modest dowry, such from earliest days had been the strength and dominance of her character, that her divine right of rule in the family had never been seriously questioned by any of her children except Coryston; although James, who had inherited money from his grandmother, was entirely independent of her, and by the help of a detached and humorous mind could often make his mother feel the stings of criticism, when others were powerless. And as for Coryston, who had become a quasi-Socialist at Cambridge, and had ever since refused to suit his opinions in the slightest degree to his mother's, his long absences abroad after taking his degree had for some years reduced the personal friction between them; and it was only since his father's death, which had occurred while he himself was in Japan, and since the terms of his father's will had been known, that Coryston had become openly and angrily hostile.

Why should Coryston, a gentleman who denounced property, and was all for taxing land and landlords into the Bankruptcy Court, resent so bitterly his temporary exclusion from the family estates? Marcia could not see that there was any logical answer. If landlordism was the curse of England, why be angry that you were not asked to be a landlord?

And really—of late—his behavior! Never coming to see his mother—writing the most outrageous things in support of the Government—speaking for Radical candidates in their very own county—denouncing by name some of their relations and old family friends: he had really been impossible!

Meanwhile Lady Coryston gave her daughter no light on the situation. She went silently up-stairs, followed by Marcia. The girl, a slight figure in white, mounted unwillingly. The big, gloomy house oppressed her as she passed through it. The classical staircase with its stone-colored paint and its niches holding bronze urns had always appeared to her since her childhood as the very top of dreariness; and she particularly disliked the equestrian portrait of her great-grandfather by an early Victorian artist, which fronted her as she ascended, in the gallery at the top of the staircase, all the more that she had been supposed from her childhood to be like the portrait. Brought up as she had been in the belief that family and heredity are the master forces of life, she resented this teasing association with the weak, silly fellow on the ill-balanced rocking-horse whose double chin, button nose, and receding forehead not even the evident flattery of the artist had been able to disguise. Her hatred of the picture often led her to make a half-protesting pause in front of the long Chippendale mirror which hung close to it. She made it to-night.

Indeed, the dim reflection in the glass might well have reassured her. Dark eyes and hair, a brunette complexion, grace, health, physical strength—she certainly owed none of these qualities or possessions to her ancestor. The face reminded one of ripe fruit—so rich was the downy bloom on the delicate cheeks, so vivid the hazel of the wide black-fringed eyes. A touch of something heavy and undecided in the lower part of the face made it perhaps less than beautiful. But any man who fell in love with her would see in this defect only the hesitancy of first youth, with its brooding prophecy of passion, of things dormant and powerful. Face and form were rich—quite unconsciously—in that magic of sex which belongs to only a minority of women, but that, a minority drawn from all ranks and occupations. Marcia Coryston believed herself to be interested in many things—in books, in the Suffrage, in the girls' debating society of which she was the secretary, in politics, and in modern poetry. In reality her whole being hung like some chained Andromeda at the edge of the sea of life, expecting Perseus. Her heart listened for him perpetually—the unknown!—yearning for his call, his command....

There were many people—witness Sir Wilfrid Bury's remark to her mother—who had already felt this magic in her. Without any conscious effort of her own she had found herself possessed, in the course of three seasons since her coming out, of a remarkable place in her own circle and set. She was surrounded by a court of young people, men and women; she received without effort all the most coveted invitations; she was watched, copied, talked about; and rumor declared that she had already refused—or made her mother refuse for her—one or more of the men whom all other mothers desired to capture. This quasi-celebrity had been achieved no one quite knew how, least of all Marcia herself. It had not, apparently, turned her head, though those who knew her best were aware of a vein of natural arrogance in her character. But in manner she remained *nonchalant* and dreamy as before, with just those occasional leaps to the surface of passionate, or scornful, or chivalrous feeling which made her interesting. Her devotion to her mother was plain. She espoused all her mother's opinions with vehemence, and would defend her actions, in the family or out of it, through thick and thin. But there were those who wondered how long the subservience would last, supposing the girl's marriage were delayed.

As to the gossip repeated by Sir Wilfrid Bury, it referred to the latest of Marcia's adventures. Her thoughts played with the matter, especially with certain incidents of the Shrewsbury House ball, as she walked slowly into the drawing-room in her mother's wake.

The drawing-room seemed to her dark and airless. Taste was not the Coryston strong point, and this high, oblong room was covered with large Italian pictures, some good, some indifferent, heavily framed, and hung on wine-colored damask. A feebly false Guido Reni, "The Sacrifice of Isaac," held the center of one wall, making vehement claim to be just as well worth looking at as the famous Titian opposite. The Guido had hung there since 1820, and what was good enough for the Corystons of that date was good enough for their descendants, who were not going to admit that their ancestors were now discredited—laughed out of court—as collectors, owing to the labors of a few middle-aged intellectuals. The floor was held by a number of gilt chairs and sofas covered also in wine-colored damask, or by tables holding *objets d'art* of the same mixed quality as the pictures. Even the flowers, the stands of splendid azaleas and early roses with which the room was lavishly adorned, hardly produced an impression of beauty. Marcia, looking slowly round her with critical eyes, thought suddenly of a bare room she knew in a Roman palace, some faded hangings in dull gold upon the walls, spaces of light and shadow on the empty matted floor, and a great branch of Judas tree in blossom lighting up a corner. The memory provoked in her a thrill of sensuous pleasure.

Meanwhile Lady Coryston was walking slowly up and down, her hands behind her. She looked very thin and abnormally tall; and Marcia saw her profile, sharply white, against the darkness of the wall. A vague alarm struck through the daughter's mind. What was her mother about to say or do? Till now Marcia had rather lazily assumed that the meeting would concern some matter of family property—some selling or buying transaction—which a mother, even in the abnormally independent position Lady Coryston, might well desire to communicate to her children. There had been a family meeting in the preceding year when the Dorsetshire property had been sold under a recent Act of Parliament. Coryston wouldn't come. "I take no interest in the estates "—he had written to his mother. "They're your responsibility, not mine."

And yet of course Coryston would inherit some day. That was taken for granted among them. What were Tory principles worth if they did not some time, at some stage, secure an eldest son, and an orthodox succession? Corry was still in the position of heir, when he should normally have become owner. It was very trying for him, no doubt. But exceptional women make exceptional circumstances. And they were all agreed that their mother was an exceptional woman.

But whatever the business, they would hardly get through without a scene, and during the past week there had been a number of mysterious interviews with lawyers going on.... What was it all about? To distract her thoughts she struck up conversation.

"Did you see Enid Glenwilliam, mother, in Palace Yard?"

"I just noticed her," said Lady Coryston, indifferently. "One can't help it, she dresses so outrageously."

"Oh, mother, she dresses very well! Of course nobody else

could wear that kind of thing."

Lady Coryston lifted her eyebrows.

"That's where the ill-breeding comes in—that a young girl should make herself so conspicuous."

"Well, it seems to pay," laughed Marcia. "She has tremendous success. People on our side—people you'd never think—will do anything to get her for their parties. They say she makes things go. She doesn't care what she says."

"That I can quite believe! Yes—I saw she was at Shrewsbury House the other day—dining—when the Royalties were there. The daughter of that *man*!"

Lady Coryston's left foot gave a sharp push to a footstool lying in her path, as though it were Glenwilliam himself.

Marcia laughed.

"And she's very devoted to him, too. She told some one who told me, that he was so much more interesting than any other man she knew, that she hadn't the least wish to marry! I suppose you wouldn't like it if I were to make a friend of her?" The girl's tone had a certain slight defiance in it.

"Do what you like when I'm gone, my dear," said Lady Coryston, quietly.

Marcia flushed, and would have replied, but for the sudden and distant sound of the hall-door bell. Lady Coryston instantly stopped her pacing and took her seat beside a table on which, as Marcia now noticed, certain large envelopes had been laid. The girl threw herself into a low chair behind her mother, conscious of a distress, a fear, she could not analyze. There was a small fire in the grate, for the May evening was chilly, but on the other side of the room a window was open to the twilight, and in a luminous sky cut by the black boughs of a plane tree, and the roofs of a tall building, Marcia saw a bright star shining. The heavy drawing-room, with its gilt furniture and its electric lights, seemed for a moment blotted out. That patch of sky suggested strange, alien, inexorable things; while all the time the sound of mounting footsteps on the stairs grew nearer.

In they came, her three brothers, laughing and talking. Coryston first, then James, then Arthur. Lady Coryston rose to meet them, and they all kissed their mother. Then Coryston, with his hands on his sides, stood in front of her, examining her face with hard, amused eyes, as much as to say, "Now, then, for the scene. Let's get it over!" He was the only one of the three men who was not in evening dress. He wore, indeed, a shabby greenish-gray suit, and a flannel shirt. Marcia noticed it with indignation. "It's not respectful to mother!" she thought, angrily. "It's all very well to be a Socialist and a Bohemian. But there are decencies!"

In spite, however, of the shabby suit and the flannel shirt, in spite also of the fact that he was short and very slight, while his brothers were both of them over six feet and broadly built men, there could be no doubt that, as soon as he entered, Coryston held the stage. He was one of the mercurial men who exist in order to keep the human tide in movement. Their opinions matter principally because without them the opinions of other men would not exist. Their function is to provoke. And from the time he was a babe in the nursery Coryston had fulfilled it to perfection.

He himself would have told you he was simply the reaction from his mother. And indeed, although from the time he had achieved trousers their joint lives had been one scene of combat, they were no sooner in presence of each other than the strange links between them made themselves felt no less than the irreconcilable differences.

Now, indeed, as, after a few bantering remarks to his mother on his recent political escapades—remarks which she took in complete silence—he settled himself in a high chair in front of her to listen to what she had to say, no subtle observer of the scene but must have perceived the likeness—through all contrast—between mother and son. Lady Coryston was tall, large-boned, thin to emaciation, imposing—a Lady Macbeth of the drawing-room. Coryston was small, delicately finished, a whimsical snippet of a man—on wires—never at ease—the piled fair hair overbalancing the face and the small, sarcastic chin. And yet the essential note of both physiognomies, of both aspects, was the same. *Will*—carried to extremes, absorbing and swallowing up the rest of the personality. Lady Coryston had handed on the disease of her own character to her son, and it was in virtue of what she had given him that she had made him her enemy.

Her agitation in his presence, in spite of her proud bearing, was indeed evident, at least to Marcia. Marcia read her; had indeed been compelled to read her mother—the movements of hand and brow, the tricks of expression—from childhood up. And she detected, from various signs of nervousness, that Lady Coryston expected a rough time.

She led the way to it, however, with deliberation. She took no notice of Coryston's, "Well, mother, what's up? Somebody to be tried and executed?" but, waving to him to take a particular chair, she asked the others to sit, and placed herself beside the table which held the sheets of folded foolscap. The ugly electric light from overhead fell full upon the pallid oval of her face, on her lace cap, and shimmering black dress. Only Marcia noticed that the hand which took up the foolscap shook a little. It was an old hand, delicately white, with large finger-joints.

"I can't pretend to make a jest of what I'm going to say," she said, with a look at Coryston. "I wanted to speak to you all on a matter of business—not very agreeable business, but necessary. I am sure you will hear me out, and believe that I am doing my best, according to my lights, by the family—the estates—and the country."

At the last slowly spoken words Lady Coryston drew herself up. Especially when she said "the country," it was as though she mentioned something peculiarly her own, something attacked which fled to her for protection.

Marcia looked round on her three brothers: Coryston sunk in a big gilt chair, one leg cocked over the other, his fingers lightly crossed above his head; James with his open brow, his snub nose, his charming expression; and Arthur, who had coaxed Lady Coryston's spaniel on to his lap and was pulling his ears. He looked, she thought, bored and only half attentive. And yet she was tolerably certain that he knew no more than she did what Was going to happen.

"I am quite aware," said Lady Coryston, resuming after a pause, "that in leaving his estates and the bulk of his fortune to myself your dear father did an unusual thing, and one for which many persons have blamed him—"

Coryston's cocked leg descended abruptly to the ground. Marcia turned an anxious eye upon him; but nothing more happened, and the voice speaking went on:

"He did it, as I believe you have all recognized, because he desired that in these difficult times, when everything is being called in question, and all our institutions, together with the ideas which support them, are in danger, I should, during my lifetime, continue to support and carry out his ideas—the ideas he and I had held in common—and should remain the guardian of all those customs and traditions on his estates which he had inherited—and in which he believed—"

Coryston suddenly sat up, shook down his coat vehemently, and putting his elbows on his knees, propped his face on them, the better to observe his mother. James was fingering his watch-chain, with downcast eyes, the slightest smile on his gently twitching mouth; Arthur was measuring one ear of the spaniel against the other.

"Two years," said Lady Coryston, "have now passed since your father's death. I have done my best with my trust, though of course I realize that I cannot have satisfied *all* my children." She paused a moment. "I have not wasted any of your father's money in personal luxury—that none of you can say. The old establishment, the old ways, have been kept up—nothing more. And I have certainly *wished*"—she laid a heavy emphasis on the word—"to act for the good of all of you. You, James, have your own fortune, but I think you know that if you had wanted money at any time, for any reasonable purpose, you had only to ask for it. Marcia also has her own money; but when it comes to her marriage, I desire nothing better than to provide for her amply. And now, as to Coryston—"

She turned to him, facing him magnificently, though not, as Marcia was certain, without trepidation. Coryston flung back his head with a laugh.

"Ah, now we come to it!" he said. "The rest was all 'but leather and prunella.'"

James murmured, "Corry—old man?" Marcia flushed angrily.

"Coryston also knows very well," said Lady Coryston, coldly, "that everything he could possibly have claimed—"

"Short of the estates—which were my right," put in Coryston, quietly, with an amused look.

His mother went on without noticing the interruption:

"—would have been his—either now or in due time—if he would only have made certain concessions—"

"Sold my soul and held my tongue?—quite right!" said Coryston. "I have scores of your letters, my dear mother, to that effect."

Lady Coryston slightly raised her voice, and for the first time it betrayed emotion.

"If he would, in simple decent respect to his father's memory and consideration of his mother's feelings, have refrained from attacking his father's convictions—"

"What!—you think he still has them—in the upper regions?"

Coryston flung an audacious hand toward the ceiling. Lady Coryston grew pale. Marcia looked fiercely at her brother, and, coming to her mother's side, she took her hand.

"Your brothers and sister, Coryston, will not allow you, I think, to insult your father's memory!" The voice audibly shook.

Coryston sprang up impetuously and came to stand over his mother, his hands on his sides.

"Now look here, mother. Let's come to business. You've been plotting something more against me, and I want to know what it is. Have you been dishing me altogether?—cutting me finally out of the estates? Is that what you mean? Let's have it!"

Lady Coryston's face stiffened anew into a gray obstinacy.

"I prefer, Coryston, to tell my story in my own words and in my own way—"

"Yes—but please *tell* it!" said Coryston, sharply. "Is it fair to keep us on tenter-hooks? What is that paper, for instance? Extracts, I guess, from your will—which concern me—and the rest of them"—he waved his hand toward the other three. "For God's sake let's have them, and get done with it."

"I will read them, if you will sit down, Coryston."

With a whimsical shake of the head Coryston returned to his chair. Lady Coryston took up the folded paper.

"Coryston guessed rightly. These are the passages from my will which concern the estates. I should like to have explained before reading them, in a way as considerate to my eldest son as possible" she looked steadily at Coryston—"the reasons which have led me to take this course. But—"

"No, no! Business first and pleasure afterward!" interrupted the eldest son. "Disinherit me and then pitch into me. You get at me unfairly while I'm speculating as to what's coming."

"I think," said Marcia, in a tone trembling with indignation, "that Coryston is behaving abominably."

But her brothers did not respond, and Coryston looked at his sister with lifted brows. "Go it, Marcia!" he said, indulgently.

Lady Coryston began to read.

Before she had come to the end of her first paragraph Coryston was pacing the drawing-room, twisting his lips into all sorts of shapes, as was his custom when the brain was active. And with the beginning of the second, Arthur sprang to his feet.

"I say, mother!"

"Let me finish?" asked Lady Coryston with a hard patience.

She read to the end of the paper. And with the last words Arthur broke out:

"I won't have it, mother! It's not fair on Corry. It's beastly unfair!"

Lady Coryston made no reply. She sat quietly staring into Arthur's face, her hands, on which the rings sparkled, lightly clasped over the paper which lay upon her knee. James's expression was one of distress. Marcia sat dumfounded.

James approached his mother.

"I think, mother, you will hardly maintain these provisions."

She turned toward him.

"Yes, James, I shall maintain them."

Meanwhile Arthur, deeply flushed, stood running his hand through his fair hair as though in bewilderment.

"I sha'n't take it, mother! I give you full warning. Whenever it comes to me I shall hand it back to Corry."

"It won't come to you, except as a life interest. The estates will be in trust," said Lady Coryston.

Coryston gave a loud, sudden laugh, and stood looking at his mother from a little distance.

"How long have you been concocting this, mother? I suppose my last speeches have contributed?"

"They have made me finally certain that your father could never have intrusted you with the estates."

"How do you know? He meant me to have the property if I survived you. The letter which he left for me said as much."

"He gave me absolute discretion," said Lady Coryston, firmly.

"At least you have taken it!" said Coryston, with emphasis. "Now let's see how things stand."

He paused, a thin, wiry figure, under the electric light, checking off the items on his fingers. "On the ground of my political opinion—you cut me out of the succession. Arthur is to have the estates. And you propose to buy me off by an immediate gift of seven thousand a year in addition to my present fortune—the whole income from the land and the tin-mines being, I understand, about ten times that; and you

Mrs. Humphry Ward

intend to sell certain outlying properties in order to do this. That's your proposal. Well, now, here's mine. I won't take your seven thousand a year! I will have all—all, that is, which would have normally come to me—or *nothing!*"

He stood gazing intently at his mother's face, his small features sparkling.

"I will have all—or nothing!" he repeated. "Of course I don't deny it for a moment, if the property had come to me I should have made all sorts of risky experiments with it. I should have cut it up into small holdings. I should have pulled down the house or made it into a county hospital."

"You make it your business to wound, Coryston."

"No, I simply tell you what I should have done. And I should have been *absolutely in my right!*" He brought his hand down with passion on the chair beside him. "My father had his way. In justice I—the next generation—ought to have mine. These lands were not yours. You have no moral rights over them whatever. They come from my father, and his father. There is always something to be said for property, so long as each generation is free to make its own experiments upon it. But if property is to be locked in the dead hand, so that the living can't get at it, *then* it is what the Frenchman called it, *theft!*— or worse.... Well, I'm not going to take this quietly, I warn you. I refuse the seven thousand a year! and if I can't possess the property—well!—I'm going to a large extent to manage it!"

Lady Coryston started.

"Cony!" cried Marcia, passionately.

"I have a responsibility toward my father's property," said Coryston, calmly. "And I intend to settle down upon it, and try and drum a few sound ideas into the minds of our farmers and laborers. Owing to my absurd title I can't stand for our parliamentary division—but I shall look out for somebody who suits me, and run him. You'll find me a nuisance, mother, I'm afraid. But you've done your best for your principles. Don't quarrel with me if I do the best for mine. Of course I know it's hard for you. You would always have liked to manage me. But I never could be managed—least of all by a woman."

Lady Coryston rose from her seat.

"James!—Arthur!—" The voice had regained all its strength. "You will understand, I think, that it is better for me to leave you. I do not wish that either Coryston or I should say things we should afterward find it hard to forgive. I had a public duty to do. I have performed it. Try and understand me. Good night."

"You will let me come and see you to-morrow?" said James, anxiously.

She made no reply. Then James and Arthur kissed her, Marcia threw an arm round her and went with her, the girl's troubled, indignant eyes holding Coryston at bay the while.

As Lady Coryston approached the door her eldest son made a sudden rush and opened it for her.

"Good night, mother. We'll play a great game, you and I—but we'll play fair."

Lady Coryston swept past him without a word. The door closed on her and Marcia. Then Coryston turned, laughing, to his brother Arthur, and punched him in the ribs.

"I say, Arthur, old boy, you talked a jolly lot of nonsense this afternoon! I slipped into the Gallery a little to hear you."

Arthur grew red.

"Of course it was nonsense to you!"

"What did Miss Glenwilliam say to you?"

"Nothing that matters to you, Corry."

"Arthur, my son, you'll be in trouble, too, before you know where you are!"

"Do hold your tongue, Corry!"

"Why should I? I back you strongly. But you'll have to stick to her. Mother will fight you for all she's worth."

"I'm no more to be managed than you, if it comes to that."

"Aren't you? You're the darling, at present. I don't grudge you the estates, Arthur."

"I never lifted a finger to get them," said Arthur, moodily. "And I shall find a way of getting out of them—the greater part of them, anyway. All the same, Corry, if I do—you'll have to give guarantees."

"Don't you wish you may get them! Well now"—Coryston gave a great stretch—"can't we have a drink? You're the master here, Arthur. Just order it. James, did you open your mouth while mother was here? I don't remember. You looked unutterable things. But nobody could be as wise as you look. I tell you, though you are a philosopher and a man of peace, you'll have to take sides in this family row, whether you like it or not. Ah! Here's the whisky. Give us a cigar. Now then, we'll sit on this precious paper!"

He took up the roll his mother had left behind her and was soon sipping and puffing in the highest good humor, while he parodied and mocked at the legal phraseology of the document which had just stripped him of seventy thousand a year.

Half an hour later the brothers had dispersed, Coryston and James to their bachelor quarters, Arthur to the House of

Commons. The front door was no sooner shut than a slender figure in white emerged from the shadows of the landing overhead. It was Marcia, carrying a book.

She came to the balustrade and looked over into the hall below. Nothing to be heard or seen. Her brothers, she perceived, had not left the house from the drawing-room. They must have adjourned to the library, the large ground-floor room at the back.

"Then Mr. Lester knows," she thought, indignantly. "Just like Corry!" And her pride revolted against the notion of her brothers discussing her mother's actions, her mother's decisions, with this stranger in the house. It was quite true that Mr. Lester had been a friend both of Arthur and of Coryston at Oxford, and that Arthur in particular was devoted to him. But that did not excuse the indiscretion, the disloyalty, of bringing him into the family counsels at such a juncture. Should she go down? She was certain she would never get to sleep after these excitements, and she wanted the second volume of *Diana of the Crossways*. Why not? It was only just eleven. None of the lights had yet been put out. Probably Mr. Lester had gone to bed.

She ran down lightly, and along the passage leading to the library. As she opened the door, what had been light just before became suddenly darkness, and she heard some one moving about.

"Who is that?" said a voice. "Wait a moment."

A little fumbling; and then a powerful reading-lamp, standing on a desk heaped with books midway down the large room, was relit. The light flashed toward the figure at the door.

"Miss Coryston! I beg your pardon! I was just knocking off work. Can I do anything for you?"

The young librarian came toward her. In the illumination

from the passage behind her she saw his dark Cornish face, its red-brown color, broad brow, and blue eyes.

"I came for a book," said Marcia, rather hurriedly, as she entered. "I know where to find it. Please don't trouble." She went to the shelves, found her volume, and turned abruptly. The temptation which possessed her proved too strong.

"I suppose my brothers have been here?"

Lester's pleasant face showed a certain embarrassment.

"They have only just gone—at least, Arthur and Lord Coryston. James went some time ago."

Marcia threw her head back defiantly against the latticed bookcase.

"I suppose Corry has been attacking my mother?"

Lester hesitated; then spoke with grave sincerity: "I assure you, he did nothing of the kind. I should not have let him." He smiled.

"But they've told you—he and Arthur—they've told you what's happened?"

"Yes," he said, reluctantly. "I tried to stop them."

"As if anything could stop Corry!" cried Marcia—"when he wants to do something he knows he oughtn't to do. And he's told you his precious plan?—of coming to settle down at Coryston—in our very pockets—in order to make mother's life a burden to her?"

"A perfectly mad whim!" said Lester, smiling again. "I don't believe he'll do it."

"Oh yes, he will," said Marcia; "he'll do anything that suits his ideas. He calls it following his conscience. Other people's ideas and other people's consciences don't matter a bit."

Lester made no answer. His eyes were on the ground. She broke out impetuously:

"You think he's been badly treated?"

"I had rather not express an opinion. I have no right to one."

"Mayn't women care for politics just as strongly as men?" cried the girl, as though arguing the question with herself. "I think it's *splendid* my mother should care as she does! Corry ought to respect her for it."

Lester made a pretense of gathering up some papers on his desk, by way of covering his silence. Marcia observed him, with red cheeks.

"But of course you don't, you can't, feel with us, Mr. Lester. You're a Liberal."

"No!" he protested mildly, raising his eyes in surprise. "I really don't agree with Coryston at all. I don't intend to label myself just yet, but if I'm anything I think I'm a Conservative."

"But you think other things matter more than politics?"

"Ah yes," he said, smiling, "that I do. Especially—" He stopped.

"Especially—for women?" The breaking of Marcia's delightful smile answered his. "You see, I guessed what you meant to say. What things? I think I know."

"Beauty—poetry—sympathy. Wouldn't you put those first?"

He spoke the words shyly, looking down upon her.

There was something in the mere sound of them that thrilled, that made a music in the girl's ears. She drew a long breath, and suddenly, as he raised his eyes, he saw her as a white vision, lit up, Rembrandt-like, in the darkness, by the solitary light—the lines of her young form, the delicate softness of cheek and brow, the eager eyes.

She held out her hand.

"Good night. I shall see what Meredith has to say about it!"

She held up her volume, ran to the door, and disappeared.

CHAPTER III

"Her ladyship says she would like to see you, Miss, before you go."

The speaker was Lady Coryston's maid. She stood just within the doorway of the room where Marcia was dressing for the Opera, delivering her message mechanically, but really absorbed in the spectacle presented by the young girl before her. Sewell was an artist in her own sphere, and secretly envious of the greater range of combination which Marcia's youth and beauty made possible for the persons who dressed her, as compared with Lady Coryston. There are all kinds of subtle variants, no doubt, in "black," such as Lady Coryston habitually wore; and the costliness of them left nothing to be desired. But when she saw Marcia clothed in a new Worth or Paquin, Sewell was sorely tempted to desert her elderly mistress and go in search of a young one.

"Come in, Sewell," cried Marcia. "What do you think of it?"

The woman eagerly obeyed her. Marcia's little maid, Bellows, did the honors, and the two experts, in an ecstasy, chattered the language of their craft, while Marcia, amid her shimmering white and pink, submitted good-humoredly to being pulled about and twisted round, till after endless final touches, she was at last pronounced the perfect thing.

Then she ran across the passage to her mother's sitting-room. Lady Coryston had complained of illness during the day and

Mrs. Humphry Ward

had not been down-stairs. But Marcia's experience was that when her mother was ill she was not less, but more active than usual, and that withdrawal to her sitting-room generally meant a concentration of energy.

Lady Coryston was sitting with a writing-board on her knee, and a reading-lamp beside her, lighting a table covered with correspondence. Within her reach was a deep cupboard in the wall containing estate and business letters, elaborately labeled and subdivided. A revolving bookcase near carried a number of books of reference, and at her elbow, with the paper-knife inside it, lay a copy of the *Quarterly Review*. The walls of the room were covered with books—a fine collection of county histories, and a large number of historical memoirs and biographies. In a corner, specially lit, a large bust of the late Lord Coryston conveyed to a younger generation the troubled, interrogative look which in later life had been the normal look of the original. His portrait by Holl hung over the mantelpiece, flanked on either side by water-color pictures of his sons and daughter in their childhood.

There was only one comfortable chair in the room, and Lady Coryston never sat in it. She objected to flowers as being in the way; and there was not a sign anywhere of the photographs and small knick-knacks which generally belitter a woman's sitting—room. Altogether, an ugly room, but characteristic, businesslike, and not without a dignity of its own.

"Mother!—why don't you rest a little?" cried Marcia, eying the black-robed figure and the long pale face, marked by very evident fatigue. "You've been writing letters or seeing people all day. How long did James stay?"

"About an hour."

"And Mr. Page?" Mr. Page was the agent of the main Coryston estate.

"Some time. There was a great deal to settle."

"Did you"—the girl fidgeted—"did you tell him about Coryston?"

"Certainly. He says there is only one house in the neighborhood he could take—"

"He has taken it." Marcia opened her right hand, in which she crushed a telegram. "Bellows has just brought me this."

Lady Coryston opened and read it.

"Have taken Knatchett for three years. Tell mother." Lady Coryston's lips stiffened.

"He has lost no time. He can vex and distress us, of course. We shall have to bear it."

"Vex and distress us! I should think he can!" cried Marcia. "Has James been talking to him?"

"I dare say," said Lady Coryston, adding, with a slight, sarcastic laugh, "James is a little too sure of being always in the right."

From which Marcia guessed that James had not only been talking to Coryston, but also remonstrating with his mother, which no doubt accounted for Lady Coryston's worn-out looks. James had more effect upon her than most people; though never quite effect enough.

Marcia stood with one foot on the fender, her gaze fixed on her mother in a frowning abstraction. And suddenly Lady Coryston, lifting her eyes, realized her daughter, and the vision that she made.

"You look very well, Marcia. Have I seen that dress before?"

"No. I designed it last week. Ah!"—the sound of a distant gong made itself heard—"there's the motor. Well, good night, mother. Take care of yourself and do go to bed soon."

She stooped to kiss her mother.

"Who's going with you?"

"Waggin and James. Arthur may come in. He thinks the House will be up early. And I asked Mr. Lester. But he can't come for the first part."

Her mother held her sleeve and looked up, smiling. Lady Coryston's smiles were scarcely less formidable than her frowns.

"You expect to see Edward Newbury?"

"I dare say. They have their box, as usual."

"Well!—run off and enjoy yourself. Give my love to Miss Wagstaffe."

"Waggin" was waiting in the hall for Marcia. She had been Miss Coryston's governess for five years, and was now in retirement on a small income, partly supplied by a pension from Lady Coryston. It was understood that when she was wanted to act duenna, she came—at a moment's notice. And she was very willing to come. She lived in an Earl's Court lodging, and these occasional expeditions with Marcia represented for her the gilt on her modest gingerbread. She was a small, refined woman, with a figure still slender, gray hair, and a quiet face. Her dresses were years old, but she had a wonderful knack of bringing them up-to-date, and she never did Marcia any discredit. She adored Marcia, and indeed all the family. Lady Coryston called her "Miss Wagstaffe"—but to the others, sons and daughter, she was only "Waggin." There were very few things about the Coryston family she did not know; but her discretion was absolute.

As she saw Marcia running down-stairs her face lit up.

"My dear, what a lovely gown!—and how sweet you look!"

"Don't talk nonsense, Waggin!—and put on this rose I've brought for you!"

Waggin submitted while Marcia adorned her and gave various pats and pulls to her hair.

"There!—you look ten years younger," said the girl, with her bright look, stepping back. "But where is James?"

The butler stepped forward.

"Mr. James will meet you at the Opera."

"Oh, good!" murmured Marcia in her companion's ear. "Now we can croon."

And croon they did through the long crowded way to Covent Garden. By the time the motor reached St. Martin's Lane, Waggin was in possession of all that had happened. She had long expected it, having shrewdly noted many signs of Lady Coryston's accumulating wrath. But now that "Corry," her dear "Corry," with whom she had fought so many a schoolroom fight in the days of his Eton jackets, was really disinherited, her concern was great. Tears stood in her kind eyes. "Poor Corry!" alternated in her mouth with "Your poor mother!" Sinner and judge appealed equally to her pity.

Marcia meanwhile sat erect and fierce.

"What else could he expect? Father *did* leave the estates to mother—just because Corry had taken up such views—so that she might keep us straight."

"But *afterward*! My dear, he is so young! And young men change."

Lady Coryston's death was not, of course, to be mentioned—except with this awe and vagueness—scarcely to be thought of. But hotter revolutionists than Corry have turned Tories by forty. Waggin harped on this theme.

Marcia shook her head.

"He won't change. Mother did not ask it. All she asked was—for her sake and father's—that he should hold his tongue."

A flush sprang to Waggin's faded cheek.

"A *man*!—a grown man!" she said, wondering—"forbid him to speak out—speak freely?"

Marcia looked anxiously at her companion. It was very seldom that Waggin betrayed so much heat.

"I know," said the girl, gloomily—"'Your money or your life'—for I suppose it sounds like that. Corry would say his convictions are his life. But why 'a man,' Waggin?" She straightened her pretty shoulders. "I don't believe you'd mind if it were a woman. You don't believe in a *woman* having convictions!"

Waggin looked a little bewildered.

"I'm old-fashioned, I suppose—but—"

Marcia laughed triumphantly.

"Why shouldn't Corry respect his mother's convictions? She wants to prove that women oughtn't to shrink from fighting for what they believe, even—"

"Even with their sons?" said Waggin, tremulously. "Lady Coryston is so splendid—so splendid!"

"Even with their sons!" cried Marcia, vehemently. "You take it for granted, Waggin, that they trample on their daughters!"

Waggin protested, and slipped her thin hand into the girl's. The note of storm in Marcia's mood struck her sharply. She tried, for a moment, to change the subject. Who, she asked, was a tall, fair girl whom she had seen with Mr. Arthur, "a week ago" at the National Gallery? "I took my little niece—and suddenly I turned, and there at the end of the room were Mr. Arthur—and this lady. Such a remarkable-looking young woman!—not exactly handsome—but you couldn't possibly pass her over."

"Enid Glenwilliam!" exclaimed Marcia, with a startled voice. "But of course, Waggin, they weren't alone?"

"Oh no—probably not!—though—though I didn't see any one else. They seemed so full of talk—I didn't speak to Mr. Arthur. *Who* do you say she was?" repeated Waggin, innocently.

Marcia turned upon her.

"The daughter of the man mother hates most in the world! It's too bad of Arthur! It's abominable! It would kill mother if she knew! I've heard things said sometimes—but I never believed them for a moment. Oh, Waggin!—you *didn't* see them alone?"

The voice changed into what was almost a wail of indignation. "Of course Enid Glenwilliam would never consider appearances for a moment. She does exactly what suits her. She never bothers about chaperons, unless she absolutely must. When she sees what she wants she takes it. But *Arthur*!"

Marcia leaned back in the car, and as in the crush of the traffic they passed under a lamp Waggin saw a countenance of genuine distress.

"Oh, my dear, I'm so sorry to have worried you. How stupid

of me to mention it! I'm sure there's nothing in it."

"I've half suspected it for the last month," said Marcia with low-toned emphasis. "But I wouldn't believe it!—I shall tell Arthur what I think of him! Though, mind you, I admire Enid Glenwilliam myself enormously; but that's quite another thing. It's as though mother were never to have any pleasure in any of us! Nothing but worry and opposition!—behind her back, too."

"My dear!—it was probably nothing! Girls do just as they like nowadays, and who notices!" said Waggin, disingenuously. "And as to pleasing your mother, I know somebody who has only to put out her hand—"

"To please mother—and somebody else?" said Marcia, turning toward her with perfect composure. "You're thinking of Edward Newbury?"

"Who else should I be thinking of!—after all you told me last week?"

"Oh yes—I like Edward Newbury"—the tone betrayed a curious irritation—"and apparently he likes me. But if he tries to make me answer him too soon I shall say No, Waggin, and there will be an end of it!"

"Marcia—dearest!—don't be cruel to him!"

"No—but he mustn't press me! I've given him hints—and he won't take them. I can't make up my mind, Waggin. I can't! It's not only marrying him—it's the relations. Yesterday a girl I know described a week-end to me—at Hoddon Grey. A large, smart party—evening prayers in the private chapel, *before dinner!*—nobody allowed to breakfast in bed—everybody driven off to church—and such a *fuss* about Lent! It made me shiver. I'm not that sort, Waggin—I never shall be."

And as again a stream of light from a music-hall facade poured into the carriage, Waggin was aware of a flushed, rebellious countenance, and dark eyes full of some passionate feeling, not very easy to understand.

"He is at your feet, dear goose!" murmured the little gray-haired lady—"make your own conditions!"

"No, no!—never. Not with Edward Newbury! He seems the softest, kindest—and underneath—*iron*! Most people are taken in. I'm not."

There was silence in the car. Waggin was uneasily pondering. Nothing—she knew it—would be more acceptable to Lady Coryston than this match, though she was in no sense a scheming mother, and had never taken any special pains on Marcia's behalf. Her mind was too full of other things. Still undoubtedly this would suit her. Old family—the young man himself heir presumptive to a marquisate money—high character—everything that mortal mother could desire. And Marcia was attracted—Waggin was certain of it. The mingled feeling with which she spoke of him proved it to the hilt. And yet—let not Mr. Newbury suppose that she was to be easily run to earth! In Waggin's opinion he had his work cut out for him.

Covent Garden filled from floor to ceiling with a great audience for an important "first night"—there is no sight in London, perhaps, that ministers more sharply to the lust of modern eyes and the pride of modern life. Women reign supreme in it. The whole object of it is to provide the most gorgeous setting possible, for a world of women—women old and young—their beauty or their jewels, their white necks and their gray heads; the roses that youth wears—divinely careless; or the diamonds wherewith age must make amends for lost bloom and vanished years.

Marcia never entered the Coryston box, which held one of the most coveted positions on the grand tier, without a vague thrill of exultation; that instinctive, overbearing delight in the goods of Vanity Fair, which the Greek called *hubris*, and which is only vile when it outlives youth. It meant in her—"I am young—I am handsome—the world is all on my side—who shall thwart or deny me?" To wealth, indeed, Marcia rarely gave a conscious thought, although an abundance of it was implied in all her actions and attitudes of mind. It would have seemed to her, at any rate, so strange to be without it, that poverty was not so much an object of compassion as of curiosity; the poverty, for instance, of such a man as Mr. Lester. But behind this ignorance there was no hardness of heart; only a narrow inexperience.

The overture had begun—in a shadowy house. But the stream of the audience was still pouring in from all sides, in spite of the indignant "Hush" of those who wanted not to lose a note of something new and difficult. Marcia sat in the front of the box, conscious of being much looked at, and raising her own opera-glass from time to time, especially to watch the filling up of two rows of chairs on the floor, just below the lower tier of boxes. It was there that Mr. Newbury had told her to look for him. James, who had joined them at the entrance of the theater and was now hanging on the music, observed her once or twice uneasily. Presently he bent over.

"Marcia—you vandal!—listen!"

The girl started and blushed.

"I don't understand the music, James!—it's so strange and barbarous."

"Well, it isn't Glueck, certainly," said James, smiling.

Marcia turned her face toward it. And as she did so there rose from the crash of its opening tumult, like a hovering bird in a clear space of sky, a floating song of extraordinary loveliness. It rose and fell—winds caught it—snatches of tempest over-powered it—shrieking demons rushed upon it and silenced it. But it persisted; passing finally into a processional march, through which it was still dimly, mysteriously traceable to the end.

"The song of Iphigenia!" said James. And as the curtain rose, "And here are the gulfs of Aulis, and the Greek host."

The opera, by a young Bavarian of genius, a follower of Strauss, who had but recently captured Munich and Berlin, was based on the great play of Euripides, freely treated by a translator who had known, a hundred and fifty years after Glueck, how to make it speak, through music, to more modern ears. It was carried through without any lowering of the curtain, and the splendid story unfolded itself through a music at once sensuous and heroic, with a swiftness and a passion which had soon gripped Covent Garden.

There, in a thousand ships, bound motionless by unrelenting winds, lies the allied host that is to conquer Troy and bring back the stolen Helen. But at the bidding of Artemis, whose temple crowns the coast, fierce, contrary blasts keep it prisoner in the harbor. Hellas cannot avenge itself on the Phrygian barbarians who have carried off a free Greek woman. Artemis holds back the hunters from the prey. Why? Because, as goddess of the land, she claims her toll, the toll of human blood. Agamemnon, the leader of the host, distracted by fears of revolt and of the break-up of the army, has vowed to Artemis the dearest thing he possesses. The answer is, "Your daughter!—Iphigenia!"

Under pressure from the other chiefs of the host, and from the priests, the stricken father consents at last to send a letter to Clytemnestra at Argos, bidding her bring their young daughter to the camp, on the pretext that she is to become the bride of the hero Achilles. The letter is no sooner despatched than, tormented with remorse, he tries to recall it. In vain. Mother and child arrive, with the babe Orestes; the mother full of exultant joy in such a marriage, the daughter thinking only of her father, on whose neck she throws herself with fond home prattle, lifting Orestes to him to kiss, saying tender, touching things—how she has missed him—how long the time has been....

The young singer, an American, with a voice and a magic reminding many an old frequenter of Covent Garden, through all difference, of Giulia Ravogli in her prime, played this poignant scene as though the superb music in which it was clothed was her natural voice, the mere fitting breath of the soul.

Marcia sat arrested. The door of the box opened softly. A young man, smiling, stood in the doorway. Marcia, looking round, flushed deeply; but in the darkness only Waggin saw it. The girl beckoned to him. He came in noiselessly, nodded to James, bowed ceremoniously to Waggin, and took a seat beside Marcia.

He bent toward her, whispering, "I saw you weren't very full, and I wanted to hear this—with you."

"She's good!" was all that Marcia could find to whisper in return, with a motion of her face toward the Iphigenia.

"Yes—but only as part of the poem! Don't mistake it—please!—for the ordinary 'star'—business."

"But she is the play!"

"She is the *idea*! She is the immortal beauty that springs out of sorrow. Watch the contrast between the death she shrinks from—and the death she accepts; between the horror—and the greatness! Listen!—here is the dirge music beginning."

Marcia listened—with a strange tremor of pulse. Even through the stress of the music her mind went wandering over the past weeks, and those various incidents which had marked the growth of her acquaintance with the man beside her. How long had she known him? Since Christmas only? The Newburys and the Corystons were now neighbors indeed in the country; but it was not long since his father had inherited the old house of Hoddon Grey, and of the preceding three years Edward Newbury had spent nearly two in India. They had first met at a London dinner party; and their friendship, then begun, had ripened rapidly. But it was not till the Shrewsbury House ball that a note of excitement, of uncertain or thrilled expectation, had crept into what was at first a mere pleasant companionship. She had danced with him the whole night, reckless of comment; and had been since, it seemed to her, mostly engaged in trying to avoid him. But to-night there was no avoiding him. And as his murmured yet eager comments on the opera reached her, she became more and more conscious of his feelings toward her, which were thus conveyed to her, as it were, covertly, and indirectly, through the high poetry and passion of the spectacle on which they both looked. With every stage of it Newbury was revealing himself; and exploring her.

Waggin smiled to herself in the darkness of the box. James and she once exchanged glances. Marcia, to both of them, was a dim and beautiful vision, as she sat with her loosely clasped hands lying on the edge of the box, her dark head now turned toward the stage, and now toward Newbury.

*   *   *   *   *

The ghastly truth had been revealed; Iphigenia, within earshot, almost, of the baffled army clamoring for her blood, was clinging to her father's knees, imploring him to save her:

"Tears will I bring—my only cunning—all I have! Round your knees, my father, I twine this body, which my mother bare you. Slay me not, before my time! Sweet, sweet is the light!— drive me not down into the halls of death. 'Twas I first called you father—I, your firstborn. What fault have I in Paris's sin? Oh, father, why, why did he ever come—to be my death? Turn to me—give me a look—a kiss! So that at least, in dying, I may have that to remember—if you will not heed my prayers."

She takes the infant Orestes in her arms:

"Brother!—you are but a tiny helper—and yet—come, weep with me!—come, pray our father not to slay your sister. Look, father, how—silently—he implores you! Have pity! Oh, light, light, dearest of all goods to men! He is mad indeed who prays for death. Better an ill living than a noble dying!"

The music rose and fell like dashing waves upon a fearful coast—through one of the most agonizing scenes ever imagined by poet, ever expressed in art. Wonderful theme!— the terror-stricken anguish of the girl, little more than a child, startled suddenly from bridal dreams into this open-eyed vision of a hideous doom; the helpless remorse of the father; the misery of the mother; and behind it all the pitiless fate—the savage creed—the blood-thirst of the goddess—and the maddened army howling for its prey.

Marcia covered her eyes a moment. "Horrible!" she said, shivering, "too horrible!"

Newbury shook his head, smiling.

"No! You'll see. She carries in her hands the fate of her race— of the Hellenic, the nobler world, threatened by the barbarian, the baser world. She dies, to live. It's the motive of all great art—all religion. Ah—here is Achilles!"

There followed the strangest, pitifulest love scene. Achilles, roused to fury by the foul use made of his great name in the plot against the girl, adopts the shrinking, lovely creature as his own. She has been called his bride; she shall be his bride; and he will fight for her—die for her—if need be. And suddenly, amid the clashing horror of the story, there springs up for an instant the red flower of love. Iphigenia stands dumb in the background, while her mother wails, and Achilles, the goddess-born, puts on his armor and his golden-crested helmet. An exultant sword-song rises from the orchestra. There is a gleam of hope; and the girl, as she looks at her champion, loves him.

The music sank into tenderness, flowing like a stream in summer. And the whole vast audience seemed to hold its breath.

"Marvelous!" The word was Newbury's.

He turned to look at his companion, and the mere energy of his feeling compelled Marcia's eyes to his. Involuntarily, she smiled an answer.

But the golden moment dies!—forever. Shrieking and crashing, the vulture-forces of destruction sweep upon it. Messengers rush in, announcing blow on blow. Achilles' own Myrmidons have turned against him. Agamemnon is threatened—Achilles—Argos! The murderous cries of the army fill the distance like the roar of an uncaged beast.

Iphigenia raises her head. The savage, inexorable music still surges and thunders round her. And just as Achilles is about to leave her, in order to throw himself on the spears of his own men, her trance breaks.

"Mother!—we cannot fight with gods. I die!—I die! But let me die gloriously—unafraid. Hellas calls to me!—Hellas, my country. I alone can give her what she asks—fair sailing, and fair victory. You bore me for the good of Hellas—not for your own joy only, mother! Shall men brave all for women and their fatherland?—and shall one life, one little life, stand in their way? Nay! I give my self to Hellas! Slay me!—pull down the towers of Troy! This through all time shall be sung of me— this be my glory!—this, child and husband both. Hellas, through me, shall conquer. It is meet that Hellenes should rule barbarians, and not barbarians Hellenes. For they are slave-folk—and *we* are free!"

Achilles cries out in mingled adoration and despair. Now he knows her for what she is—now that he has "looked into her soul"—must he lose her?—is it all over? He pleads again that he may fight and die for her.

But she puts him gently aside.

"Die not for me, kind stranger. Slay no man for me! Let it be *my* boon to save Hellas, if I may."

And under her sternly sweet command he goes, telling her that he will await her beside the altar of Artemis, there to give his life for her still, if she calls to him—even at the last moment.

But she, tenderly embracing her mother, and the child Orestes, forbidding all thought of vengeance, silencing all clamor of grief—she lifts the song of glorious death, as she slowly passes from view, on her way to the place of sacrifice, the Greek women chanting round her.

"Hail, Hellas, Mother-land! Hail, light-giving Day—torch of Zeus!"

"To another life, and an unknown fate, I go! Farewell, dear light!—farewell!"

"That," said Newbury, gently, to Marcia only, as the music died away, "is the death—*she accepts!*" The tears stood in the girl's eyes. The exaltation of great passion, great poetry, had touched her; mingled strangely with the spell, the resisted spell, of youth and sex. Newbury's dark, expressive face, its proud refinement, its sensitive feeling; the growing realization in her of his strong, exacting personality; the struggle of her weaker will against an advancing master; fascination—revolt; of all these things she was conscious as they both sat drowned in the passion of applause which was swelling through the Opera House, and her eyes were still vaguely following that white figure on the stage, with the bouquets at its feet....

Bright eyes sought her own; a hand reached out, caught hers, and pressed it. She recoiled—released herself sharply. Then she saw that Edward Newbury had risen, and that at the door of the box stood Sir Wilfrid Bury.

*   *   *   *   *

Edward Newbury gave up his seat to Sir Wilfrid, and stood against the back of the box talking to Waggin. But she could not flatter herself he paid much attention to her remarks. Marcia could not see him; but his eyes were on her perpetually. A wonderfully handsome fellow, thought Waggin. The profile and brow perfect, the head fine, the eyes full—too full!—of consciousness, as though the personality behind burnt with too intense a flame. Waggin liked him, and was in some sort afraid of him. Never did her small talk seem to her so small as when she launched it at Edward Newbury. And yet no one among the young men of Marcia's acquaintance showed so much courtesy to Marcia's "companion."

"Oh, very fine! very fine!" said Sir Wilfrid; "but I wanted a big fight—Achilles and his Myrmidons going for the other fellows—and somebody having the decency to burn the temple of that hag Artemis! I say!" He spoke, smiling, in Marcia's ear. "Your brother Arthur's in very bad company! Do you see where he is? Look at the box opposite."

Marcia raised her opera-glass, and saw Enid Glenwilliam sitting in front of the box to which Sir Wilfrid pointed her. The Chancellor's daughter was bending her white neck back to talk to a man behind her, who was clearly Arthur Coryston. Behind her also, with his hands in his pockets, and showing a vast expanse of shirt-front, was a big, burly man, who stood looking out on the animated spectacle which the Opera House presented, in this interval between the opera and the ballet, with a look half contemptuous, half dreamy. It was a figure wholly out of keeping—in spite of its conformity in dress—with the splendid opera-house, and the bejeweled crowd which filled it. In some symbolic group of modern statuary, it might have stood for the Third Estate—for Democracy—Labor—personified. But it was a Third Estate, as the modern world has developed it—armed with all the weapons of the other two!

            Mrs. Humphry Ward

"The Chancellor himself!" said Sir Wilfrid; "watching 'the little victims play'! I picture him figuring up all these smart people. 'How much can I get out of you?—and you?'"

Marcia abruptly put down the glass she held, and turned to Sir Wilfrid. He was her godfather, and he had been her particular friend since the days when they used to go off together to the Zoo or the Pantomime.

"Do, please, talk to Arthur!" she said, eagerly, but so as not to be heard by any one else. "Perhaps he'd listen to you. People are beginning to notice—and it's too, too dreadful. You know what mother would feel!"

"I do," said Sir Wilfrid, gravely; "if that's what you mean." His eyes rested a moment on the striking figure of the Chancellor's daughter. "Certainly—I'll put in a word. But she is a very fascinating young woman, my dear!"

"I know," said Marcia, helplessly, "I know."

There was a pause. Then Sir Wilfrid asked:

"When do you go down to Coryston?"

"Just before Whitsuntide."

He looked round with a smile, saw that Edward Newbury was still in the box, and whispered, mischievously:

"Hoddon Grey, too, I think, will not be empty?"

Marcia kept an indifferent face.

"I dare say. You're coming?" Sir Wilfrid nodded. "Oh, *have* you heard—?"

She murmured to him behind her fan. Sir Wilfrid knew all their history—had been her father's most intimate friend. She gave him a rapid account of Coryston's disinheriting. The old man rose, his humorous eyes suddenly grave.

"We'll talk of this—at Coryston. Ah, Newbury—I took your chair—I resign. Hullo, Lester—good evening. Heavens, there's the curtain going up. Good night!"

He hurried away. Newbury moved forward, his eager look on Marcia. But she turned, smiling, to the young librarian.

"You haven't seen this ballet, Mr. Lester?—Schumann's 'Carnival'? Oh, you mustn't stand so far back. We can make room, can't we?" She addressed Newbury, and before he knew what had happened, the chairs had been so manipulated that Lester sat between Marcia and Newbury, while Waggin had drawn back into the shadow. The eyes of Marcia's duenna twinkled. It pleased her that this magnificent young man, head, it was said, of the young High Church party, distinguished in many ways, and as good as he was handsome, was not to have too easy a game. Marcia had clearly lost her head a little at the Shrewsbury House ball; and was now trying to recover it.

CHAPTER IV

After one of those baffling fortnights of bitter wind and cold, which so often mark the beginning of an English May, when all that the spring has slowly gained since March seems to be confiscated afresh by returning winter, the weather had repented itself, the skies had cleared, and suddenly, under a flood of sunshine, there were blue-bells in the copses, cowslips in the fields, a tawny leaf breaking on the oaks, a new cheerfulness in the eyes and gait of the countryman.

A plain, pleasant-looking woman sat sewing out-of-doors, in front of a small verandaed cottage, perched high on a hillside which commanded a wide view of central England. The chalk down fell beneath her into a sheath of beech woods; the line of hills, slope behind slope, ran westward to the sunset, while eastward they mounted to a wooded crest beyond which the cottage could not look. Northward, beginning some six hundred feet below the cottage, stretched a wide and varied country, dotted with villages and farms, with houses and woods, till it lost itself in the haze of a dim horizon.

A man of middle age, gray-headed, spare in figure, emerged from one of the French windows of the cottage.

"Marion, when did you say that you expected Enid?"

"Between three and four, papa."

"I don't believe Glenwilliam himself will get here at all. There will be a long Cabinet this afternoon, and another to-morrow probably—Sunday or no Sunday!"

"Well then, he won't come, father," said the daughter, placidly, thrusting her hand into a sock riddled with holes, and looking at it with concern.

"Annoying! I wanted him to meet Coryston—who said he would be here to tea."

Miss Atherstone looked a little startled.

"Will that do, father? You know Enid told me to ask Arthur Coryston, and I wrote yesterday."

"Do? Why not? Because of politics? They must have got used to that in the Coryston family! Or because of the gossip that Arthur is to have the estates? But it's not his fault. I hear the two brothers are on excellent terms. They say that Arthur has warned his mother that he means to make it up to Coryston somehow."

"Enid doesn't like Lord Coryston," said Miss Atherstone, slowly.

"I dare say. He finds out her weak points. She has a good many. And he's not a ladies' man. Between ourselves, my dear, she poses a good deal. I never know quite where to have her, though I dandled her as a baby."

"Oh, Enid's all right," said Marion Atherstone, taking a fresh needleful of brown wool. Miss Atherstone was not clever, though she lived with clever people, and her powers of expressing herself were small. Her father, a retired doctor, on the other hand, was one of the ablest Liberal organizers in the country. From his perch on the Mintern hills he commanded half the midlands, in more senses than one; knew thirty or forty constituencies by heart; was consulted in all difficulties; was better acquainted with "the pulse of the party" than its chief agent, and was never left out of count by any important Minister framing an important bill.

He had first made friends with the man who was now the powerful head of English finance, when Glenwilliam was the young check-weigher of a large Staffordshire colliery; and the friendship—little known except to an inner ring—was now an important factor in English politics. Glenwilliam did nothing without consulting Atherstone, and the cottage on the hill had been the scene of many important meetings, and some decisions which would live in history.

Marion Atherstone, on the other hand, though invaluable to her father, and much appreciated by his friends, took no intellectual part in his life. Brilliant creatures—men and women—came and went, to and from the cottage. Marion took stock of them, provided them with food and lodging, and did not much believe in any of them. Atherstone was a philosopher, a free-thinker, and a vegetarian. Marion read the *Church Family Times*, went diligently to church, and if she had possessed a vote, and cared enough about it to use it, would probably have voted Tory. All the same she and her father were on the best of terms and perfectly understood each other.

Among the brilliant creatures, however, who came and went, there was one who had conquered her. For Enid Glenwilliam, Marion felt the profound affection that often links the plain, scrupulous, conscientious woman to some one or other of the Sirens of her sex. When Enid came to the cottage Marion became her slave and served her hand and foot. But the probability is that she saw through the Siren—what there was to see through—a good deal more sharply than her father did.

Atherstone took a garden chair beside her, and lit his pipe. He had just been engaged in drafting an important Liberal manifesto. His name would probably never appear in connection with it. But that mattered nothing to him. What did vex him was that he probably would not have an opportunity of talking it over with Glenwilliam before it finally left his hands. He was pleased with it, however. The drastic, or scathing phrases of it kept running through his head. He had never felt a more thorough, a more passionate, contempt for his opponents. The Tory party must go! One more big fight, and they would smash the unclean thing. These tyrants of land, and church, and finance!—democratic England when it once got to business—and it was getting to business—would make short work of them.

As he looked out over the plain he saw many things well fitted to stir the democratic pulse. There among the woods, not a mile from the base of the hills, lay the great classic pile of Coryston, where "that woman" held sway. Farther off on its hill rose Hoddon Grey, identified in this hostile mind with Church ascendancy, just as Coryston was identified with landlord ascendancy. If there were anywhere to be found a narrower pair of bigots than Lord and Lady William Newbury, or a more poisonous reactionary than their handsome and plausible son, Atherstone didn't know where to lay hands on them.

One white dot in the plain, however, gave him unmixed satisfaction. He turned, laughing to his daughter.

"Coryston has settled in—with a laborer and his wife to look after him. He has all sorts of ructions on his hands already."

"Poor Lady Coryston!" said Marion, giving a glance at the classical cupolas emerging from the woods.

"My dear—she began it. And he is quite right—he *has* a public duty to these estates."

"Couldn't he go and stir up people somewhere else? It looks so ugly."

"Oh! women have got to get used to these things, if they play such strong parts as Lady Coryston. The old kid-glove days, as between men and women, are over."

"Even between mothers and sons?" said Marion, dubiously.

"I repeat—she began it! Monstrous, that that man should have made such a will, and that a mother should have taken advantage of it!"

"Suppose she had been a Liberal," said Marion, slyly.

Atherstone shrugged his shoulders—too honest to reply.

He ruminated over his pipe. Presently his eyes flashed.

"I hear Coryston's very servants—his man and wife—were evicted from their cottage for political reasons."

"Yes, by that Radical miller who lives at Martover," said Marion.

Atherstone stared.

"My dear!—"

"The wife told me," said Marion, calmly, rolling up her socks.

"I say, I must look into that," said Atherstone, with discomposure. "It doesn't do to have such stories going round—on our side. I wonder why Coryston chose them."

"I should think—because he hates that kind of thing on both sides." The slightest twinge of red might have been noticed on Miss Atherstone's cheek as she spoke. But her father did not notice it. He lifted his head to listen.

"I think I hear the motor."

"You look tired," said Marion to her guest. The first bout of conversation was over, and Dr. Atherstone had gone back to his letters.

Enid Glenwilliam took off her hat, accepted the cushion which her hostess was pressing upon her, and lay at ease in her cane chair.

"You wouldn't wonder, if you could reckon up my week!" she said, laughing. "Let's see—four dinners, three balls, two operas,—a week-end at Windsor, two bazars, three meetings, two concerts, and tea-parties galore! What do you expect but a rag!"

"Don't say you don't like it!"

"Oh yes, I like it. At least, if people don't ask me to things I'm insulted, and when they do—"

"You're bored?"

"It's you finished the sentence!—not I! And I've scarcely seen father this week except at breakfast. *That's* bored me horribly."

"What have you *really* been doing?"

"Inquisitor!—I have been amusing myself."

"With Arthur Coryston?"

Marion turned her large fresh-colored face and small gray eyes upon her companion.

"And others! You don't imagine I confine myself to him?"

"Has Lady Coryston found out yet?"

"That we get on? I am sure she has never imagined that Mr. Arthur could so demean himself."

"But she must find out some day."

"Oh yes, I mean her to," said Miss Glenwilliam, quietly. She reached out a long hand toward Marion's cat and stroked it. Then she turned her large eyes of pale hazel set under beautiful dark brows to her companion. "You see—Lady Coryston has not only snubbed me—she has insulted father."

"How?" exclaimed Marion, startled.

"At Chatton House the other day. She refused to go down to dinner with him. She positively did. The table had to be rearranged, and little Lady Chatton nearly had hysterics."

The girl lay looking at her friend, her large but finely cut mouth faintly smiling. But there was something dangerous in her eyes.

"And one day at lunch she refused to be introduced to me. I saw it happen quite plainly. Oh, she didn't exactly mean to be insolent. But she thinks society is too tolerant—of people like father and me."

"What a foolish woman!" said Marion Atherstone, rather helplessly.

"Not at all! She knows quite well that my whole existence is a fight—so far as London is concerned. She wants to make the fight a little harder—that's all."

"Your 'whole existence a fight,'" repeated Marion, with a touch of scorn, "after that list of parties!"

"It's a good fight at present," said the girl, coolly, "and a successful one. But Lady Coryston gets all she wants without fighting. When father goes out of office I shall be nobody. *She* will be always at the top of the tree."

"I am no wiser than before as to whether you really like Arthur Coryston or not. You have heard, of course, the gossip about the estates?"

"Heard?" The speaker smiled. "I know not only the gossip—but the facts—by heart! I am drowned—smothered in them. At present Arthur is the darling—the spotless one. But when she knows about me!"—Miss Glenwilliam threw up her hands.

"You think she will change her mind again?"

The girl took up a stalk of grass and nibbled it in laughing meditation.

"Perhaps I oughtn't to risk his chances?" she said, looking sidelong.

"Don't think about 'chances,'" said Marion Atherstone, indignantly—"think about whether you care for each other!"

"What a *bourgeois* point of view! Well, honestly—I don't know. Arthur Coryston is not at all clever. He has the most absurd opinions. We have only known each other a few months. If he were *very* rich—By the way, is he coming this afternoon? And may I have a cigarette?"

Marion handed cigarettes. The click of a garden gate in the distance caught her ear.

"Here they are—he and Lord Coryston."

Enid Glenwilliam lit her cigarette, and made no move. Her slender, long-limbed body, as it lay at ease in the deep garden chair, the pale masses of her hair, and the confident quiet face beneath it, made a charming impression of graceful repose. As Arthur Coryston reached her she held out a welcoming hand, and her eyes greeted him—a gay, significant look.

Coryston, having shaken hands with Miss Atherstone, hastily approached her companion.

"I didn't know you smoked," he said, abruptly, standing before her with his hands on his sides.

As always, Coryston made an odd figure. His worn, ill-fitting clothes, with their bulging pockets, the grasshopper slimness of his legs and arms, the peering, glancing look of his eternally restless eyes, were all of them displeasing to Enid Glenwilliam as she surveyed him. But she answered him with a smile.

"Mayn't I?"

He looked down on her, frowning.

"Why should women set up a new want—a new slavery—that costs money?"

The color flew to her cheeks.

"Why shouldn't they? Go and preach to your own sex."

"No good!" He shrugged his shoulders. "But women are supposed to have consciences. And—especially—*Liberal* women," he added, slowly, as his eyes traveled over her dress.

"And pray why should Liberal women be ascetics any more than any other kind of women?" she asked him, quietly.

"Why?" His voice grew suddenly loud. "Because there are thousands of people in this country perishing for lack of proper food and clothing—and it is the function of Liberals to bring it home to the other thousands."

Arthur Coryston broke out indignantly:

"I say, Cony, do hold your tongue! You do talk such stuff!"

The young man, sitting where the whole careless grace of Miss Glenwilliam's person was delightfully visible to him, showed a countenance red with wrath.

Coryston faced round upon him, transformed. His frown had disappeared in a look of radiant good humor.

"Look here, Arthur, you've got the money-bags—you might leave me the talking. Has he told you what's happened?"

The question was addressed to Miss Glenwilliam, while the speaker shot an indicating thumb in his brother's direction.

The girl looked embarrassed, and Arthur Coryston again came to the rescue.

"We've no right to thrust our family affairs upon other people, Corry," he said, resolutely. "I told you so as we walked up."

"Oh, but they're so interesting," was Coryston's cool reply as he took his seat by Marion Atherstone. "I'm certain everybody here finds them so. And what on earth have I taken Knatchett for, except to blazon abroad what our dear mother has been doing?"

"I wish to heaven you hadn't taken Knatchett," said Arthur, sulkily.

"You regard me as a nuisance? Well, I meant to be. I'm finding out such lots of things," added Coryston, slowly, while his eyes, wandering over the plain, ceased their restlessness for a moment and became fixed and dreamy.

Dr. Atherstone caught the last words as he came out from his study. He approached his guests with an amused look at Coryston. But the necessary courtesies of the situation imposed themselves. So long as Arthur Coryston was present the Tory son of his Tory mother, an Opposition M.P. for a constituency, part of which was visible from the cottage garden, and a comparative stranger to the Atherstones, it was scarcely possible to let Coryston loose. The younger brother was there—Atherstone perfectly understood—simply because Miss Glenwilliam was their guest; not for his own *beaux yeux* or his daughter's. But having ventured on to hostile ground, for a fair lady's sake, he might look to being kindly treated.

Arthur, on his side, however, played his part badly. He rose indeed to greet Atherstone—whom he barely knew, and was accustomed to regard as a pestilent agitator—with the indifferent good breeding that all young Englishmen of the classes have at command; he was ready to talk of the view and the weather, and to discuss various local topics. But it was increasingly evident that he felt himself on false ground; lured there, moreover, by feelings he could hardly suppose were unsuspected by his hosts. Enid Glenwilliam watched him with secret but sympathetic laughter; and presently came to his aid. She rose from her seat.

"It's a little hot here, Marion. Shall I have time to show Mr. Coryston the view from the wood-path before tea?"

Marion assented. And the two tall figures strolled away across a little field toward a hanging wood on the edge of the hill.

"Will she have him?" said Coryston to Marion Atherstone, looking after the departing figures.

The question was disconcertingly frank. Marion laughed and colored.

"I haven't the slightest idea."

"Because there'll be the deuce to pay if she does," said Coryston, nursing his knees, and bubbling with amusement. "My unfortunate mother will have to make another will. What the lawyers have made out of her already!"

"There would be no reconciling her to the notion of such a marriage?" asked Atherstone, after a moment.

"If my son takes to him a wife of the daughters of Heth, what good shall my life be unto me?" quoted Coryston, laughing. "Good gracious, how handy the Bible comes in—for most things! I expect you're an infidel, and don't know." He looked up curiously at Atherstone.

A shade of annoyance crossed Atherstone's finely marked face.

"I was the son of a Presbyterian minister," he said, shortly. "But to return. After all, you know, Radicals and Tories do still intermarry! It hasn't quite come to that!"

"No, but it's coming to that!" cried Coryston, bringing his hand down in a slap on the tea-table. "And women like my mother are determined it shall come to it. They want to see this country divided up into two hostile camps—fighting it out—blood and thunder, and devilries galore. Ay, and"—he brought his face eagerly, triumphantly, close to Atherstone's—"so do you, too—at bottom."

The doctor drew back. "I want politics to be realities, if that's what you mean," he said, coldly. "But the peaceful methods of democracy are enough for me. Well, Lord Coryston, you say you've been finding out a lot of things in these few weeks you've been settled here. What sort?"

Coryston turned an odd, deliberate look at his questioner.

"Yes, I'm after a lot of game—in the Liberal preserves just as much as the Tory. There isn't a pin to choose between you! Now, look here!" He checked the items off on his fingers. "My mother's been refusing land for a Baptist chapel. Half the village Baptist—lots of land handy—she won't let 'em have a yard. Well, we're having meetings every week, we're sending her resolutions every week, which she puts in the waste-paper basket. And on Sundays they rig up a tent on that bit of common ground at the park gates, and sing hymns at her when she goes to church. That's No. 1. No. 2—My mother's been letting Page—her agent—evict a jolly decent fellow called Price, a smith, who's been distributing Liberal leaflets in some of the villages. All sorts of other reasons given, of course—but that's the truth. Well, I sat on Page's doorstep for two or three days—no good. Now I'm knocking up a shop and a furnace, and all the rest of the togs wanted, for Price, in my back yard at Knatchett. And we've made him Liberal agent for the

village. I can tell you he's going it! That's No. 2. No. 3—
There's a slight difficulty with the hunt I needn't trouble you
with. We've given 'em warning we're going to kill foxes
wherever we can get 'em. They've been just gorging chickens
this last year—nasty beasts! That don't matter much, however.
No. 4—Ah-ha!"—he rubbed his hands—"I'm on the track of
that old hypocrite, Burton of Martover—"

"Burton! one of the best men in the country!" cried
Atherstone, indignantly. "You're quite mistaken, Lord
Coryston!"

"Am I!" cried Coryston, with equal indignation—"not a bit of
it. Talking Liberalism through his nose at all the meetings
round here, and then doing a thing—Look here! He turned
that man and his wife—Potifer's his name—who are now
looking after me—out of their cottage and their bit of land—
why, do you think?—because *the man voted for Arthur*! Why
shouldn't he vote for Arthur? Arthur kissed his baby. Of course
he voted for Arthur. He thought Arthur was 'a real nice
gentleman'—so did his wife. Why shouldn't he vote for
Arthur? Nobody wanted to kiss Burton's baby. Hang him! You
know this kind of thing must be put a stop to!"

And, getting up, Coryston stamped up and down furiously, his
small face aflame. Atherstone watched him in silence. This
strange settlement of Lady Coryston's disinherited son—
socialist and revolutionist—as a kind of watchman, in the very
midst of the Coryston estates, at his mother's very gates, might
not after all turn out so well as the democrats of the
neighborhood had anticipated. The man was too queer—too
flighty.

"Wait a bit! I think some of your judgments may be too hasty,
Lord Coryston. There's a deal to learn in this neighborhood—
the Hoddon Grey estate, for instance—"

Coryston threw up his hands.

"The Newburys—my word, the Newburys! 'Too bright and good'—aren't they?—'for human nature's daily food.' Such churches—and schools—and villages! All the little boys patterns—and all the little girls saints. Everybody singing in choirs—and belonging to confraternities—and carrying banners. 'By the pricking of my thumbs' when I see a Newbury I feel that a mere fraction divides me from the criminal class. And I tell you, I've heard a story about that estate"—the odd figure paused beside the tea-table and rapped it vigorously for emphasis—"that's worse than any other villainy I've yet come across. You know what I mean. Betts and his wife!"

He paused, scrutinizing the faces of Atherstone and Marion with his glittering eyes.

Atherstone nodded gravely. He and Marion both knew the story. The neighborhood indeed was ringing with it. On the one hand it involved the pitiful tale of a divorced woman; on the other the unbending religious convictions of the Newbury family. There was hot championship on both sides; but on the whole the Newbury family was at the moment unpopular in their own county, because of the affair. And Edward Newbury in particular was thought to have behaved with harshness.

Coryston sat down to discuss the matter with his companions, showing a white heat of feeling. "The religious tyrant," he vowed, "is the most hideous of all tyrants!"

Marion said little. Her grave look followed her guest's vehement talk; but she scarcely betrayed her own point of view. The doctor, of course, was as angry as Coryston.

Presently Atherstone was summoned into the house, and then Coryston said, abruptly:

"My mother likes that fellow—Newbury. My sister likes him. From what I hear he might become my brother-in-law. He sha'n't—before Marcia knows this story!"

Marion looked a little embarrassed, and certainly disapproving.

"He has very warm friends down here," she said, slowly; "people who admire him enormously."

"So had Torquemada!" cried Coryston. "What does that prove? Look here!"—he put both elbows on the table, and looked sharply into Marion's plain and troubled countenance —"don't you agree with me?"

"I don't know whether I do or not—I don't know enough about it."

"You mustn't," he said, eagerly—"you mustn't disagree with me!" Then, after a pause, "Do you know that I'm always hearing about you, Miss Atherstone, down in those villages?"

Marion blushed furiously, then laughed.

"I can't imagine why."

"Oh yes, you can. I hate charity—generally. It's a beastly mess. But the things you do—are human things. Look here, if you ever want any help, anything that a fellow with not much coin, but with a pair of strong arms and a decent headpiece, can do, you come to me. Do you see?"

Marion smiled and thanked him.

Coryston rose.

"I must go. Sha'n't wait for Arthur. He seems to be better employed. But—I should like to come up here pretty often, Miss Atherstone, and talk to you. I shouldn't wonder if I agreed with you more than I do with your father. Do you see any objection?"

He stood leaning on the back of a chair, looking at her with his queer simplicity. She smiled back.

"Not the least. Come when you like."

He nodded, and without any further farewell, or any conventional message to her father, he strode away down the garden, whistling.

Marion was left alone. Her face, the face of a woman of thirty-five, relaxed; a little rose-leaf pink crept into the cheeks. This was the fourth or fifth time that she had met Lord Coryston, and each time they had seemed to understand each other a little better. She put aside all foolish notions. But life was certainly more interesting than it had been.

* * * * *

Coryston had been gone some time, when at last his brother and Miss Glenwilliam emerged from the wood. The tea-table was now spread in the shade, and they approached it. Marion tried to show nothing of the curiosity she felt.

That Arthur Coryston was in no mood for ordinary conversation at least was clear. He refused her proffered cup, and almost immediately took his leave. Enid subsided again into her long chair, and Atherstone and Marion waited upon her. She had an animated, excited look, the reflection, no doubt, of the conversation which had taken place in the wood. But when Marion and she were left alone it was a long time before she disclosed anything. At last, when the golden May light was beginning to fade from the hill, she sat up suddenly.

"I don't think I can, Marion; I don't think I *can*!"

"Can what?"

"Marry that man, my dear!" She bent forward and took her friend's hands in hers. "Do you know what I was thinking of all the time he talked?—and he's a very nice boy—and I like him very much. I was thinking of my father!"

Mrs. Humphry Ward

She threw her head back proudly. Marion looked at her in some perplexity.

"I was thinking of my father," she repeated. "My father is the greatest man I know. And I'm not only his daughter. I'm his friend. He has no one but me since my mother died. He tells me everything, and I understand him. Why should I marry a man like that, when I have my father! And yet of course he touches me—Arthur Coryston—and some day I shall want a home—and children—like other people. And there is the money, if his mother didn't strip him of it for marrying me! And there's the famous name, and the family, and the prestige. Oh yes, I see all that. It attracts me enormously. I'm no ascetic, as Coryston has discovered. And yet when I think of going from my father to that man—from my father's ideas to Arthur's ideas—it's as though some one thrust me into a cave, and rolled a stone on me. I should beat myself dead, trying to get out! I told him I couldn't make up my mind yet—for a long, long time."

"Was that kind?" said Marion, gently.

"Well, he seemed to like it better than a final No," laughed the girl, but rather drearily. "Marion! you don't know, nobody can know but me, what a man my father is!"

And sitting erect she looked absently at the plain, the clear hardness of her eyes melting to a passionate tenderness. It was to Marion as though the rugged figure of the Chancellor overshadowed them; just as, at that moment, in the political sense, it overshadowed England.

CHAPTER V

Lady Coryston's quarters at Coryston Place were not quite so devoid of all the lighter touches as her London sitting-room. The view from the windows, of the formal garden outside, with its rows of white statues, leading to a winding lake, and parklike slopes beyond it, was certainly cheerful. Coryston particularly disliked it, and had many ribald things to say about the statues, which in his mad undergraduate days he had more than once adorned with caps of liberty, pipes, mustaches, and similar impertinences. But most people were attracted by the hard brightness of the outlook; and of light and sunshine—on sunny days—there was, at any rate, no lack. Marcia had recently chosen a new chintz for the chairs and sofas, and one small group of photographs, on a table beside the fireplace, were allowed to remind the spectator that the owner of the room had once been a young mother, with a maternal pride in a bunch of fine children. Here were Coryston, aged nine, on pony-back, pompously showing off; James, dreamily affable, already a personage at seven; Arthur, fondling a cricket-bat, with a stiff mouth, hastily closed—by order—on its natural grin; and Marcia, frowning and pouting, in fancy dress as "The Strawberry Girl," just emerging, it seemed, from one battle-royal with her nurse, and about to plunge into another.

Lady Coryston had just entered the room. She was alone, and she carried a pile of letters, which she put down on the central writing-table. Then she went to one of the windows, which on this May day was open, and stood, looking out, one long

Mrs. Humphry Ward

mittened hand resting vaguely on the table that held the photographs. A commanding figure! She was in black, carrying her only ornament, an embossed silver girdle and chatelaine, the gift of her husband in their first year of marriage. As she paused, motionless, in the clear sunshine, her great height and her great thinness and flatness brought out with emphasis the masculine carriage of the shoulders and the strong markings of the face. In this moment of solitude, however, the mistress of Coryston Place and of the great domain on which she looked, allowed herself an expression which was scarcely that of an autocrat—at any rate of an autocrat at ease.

She was thinking of Coryston; and Coryston was giving her a good deal to think about. Of course she had expected annoyance; but scarcely such annoyance as Coryston, it seemed, was now bent on causing her. At bottom, she had always reckoned on her position as mother and woman. Coryston might threaten, but that he should actually carry out such iniquities as he was now engaged on, had been—she owned it—beyond her calculations.

For she had come down to find the whole neighborhood in a ferment, and many pleasant illusions, in the shelter of which she had walked for years, both before and since her husband's death, questioned, at least, and cracking, if not shattered. That the Corystons were model landlords, that they enjoyed a feudal popularity among their tenants and laborers, was for Lady Coryston one of the axioms on which life was based. She despised people who starved their estates, let their repairs go, and squeezed the last farthing out of their tenants. Nor had she any sympathy with people who owned insanitary cottages. It had been her fond belief that she at least possessed none. And now here was Coryston, her eldest son, camped in the very midst of her property, not as her friend and support, but as her enemy and critic; poking his nose into every corner of the estates, taken in by every ridiculous complaint, preaching Socialism at full blast to the laborers, and Land Acts to the farmers, stirring up the Nonconformists to such antics as the Baptists had lately been playing on Sundays at her gates;

discovering bad cottages, where none were known to exist; and, in general, holding up his mother to blame and criticism, which, as Lady Coryston most truly, sincerely, indignantly felt, was wholly undeserved.

This then was the "game" that Coryston had warned her of. He was actually playing it; though she had never believed for one moment that he would ever do so. How was she to meet it? With firmness, no doubt, and dignity. As to the firmness she had no fears; it was the dignity she was anxious about.

Lady Coryston was a woman of conscience; although no doubt she had long ago harnessed her will to her conscience, which revolved—sometimes heavily—in the rear. Still there the conscience was, and periodically she had to take account of it. Periodically, it made her uncomfortable on the subject of her eldest son. Periodically, it forced her to ask herself—as in this reverie by the window—"How is it that, bit by bit, and year by year, he and I have drifted to this pass? Who began it? Is it in any sense my fault?"

How was it, in the first place, that neither she nor his father had ever had any real influence over this incorrigible spirit; that even in Corry's childish days, when his parents had him at their mercy, they might punish, and thwart, and distress him, but could never really conquer him? Lady Coryston could recall struggles with her son, whether at home or at school, which turned her sick to think of.

Corry—for instance—at his preparatory school, taking a loathing to his head master, demanding to be withdrawn, and stubbornly refusing to say why; the master's authority upheld by Corry's parents; vindictive punishment; followed by sudden illness on the boy's part in the midst of the commotion, and his return home, white-faced, silent, indomitable. It made her shiver to remember how he had refused to be nursed by her or by any one but the old housekeeper at Coryston; how for weeks he had scarcely spoken to his father or mother. Then had come the lad's justification—a hideous cruelty charge against the head master; and on a quasi-apology from his father, Corry had consented to forgive his parents.

And again—at Cambridge—another recollection clutched at memory; Corry, taking up the case of a youth who had been sent down, according to him, unjustly—furious attacks on the college authorities—rioting in college—ending of course in the summary sending down of Coryston also. She and his father in their annoyance and disappointment had refused to listen to his explanations, to let him defend himself indeed at all. His mother could see still Corry's strange hostile look at her, on his first arrival at home, as much as to say, "Nothing to expect from *you*!" She could still hear the hall door closing behind him as he went off on wanderings abroad and in the East for what proved to be an absence of three years.

Yet there were some things she could remember on the other side, dating also from Corry's Cambridge years. When her old father died, one Easter vacation, and she, who was deeply attached to him, had arrived at Coryston after the funeral, worn out by misery and grief, there, suddenly, were Corry's arms open to her, and his—almost timid—kiss on her cheek. The thought of those few weeks when he had been so tender to her, and she had been too tired and sad for anything except to lie still and accept the kindness of her husband and sons, was embittered to her by the remembrance of all the fierce jars which had come after; but, at the moment, they were halcyon days. As she thought of them now beside the open window, she was suddenly aware of a catch in the throat, which she must instantly restrain. It was really too late for any such melting between herself and Corry!

As to the scene which had taken place in the drawing-room of the St. James's Square house on Coryston's hurried return home after his father's death, and the explanation to him of the terms of his father's will, she had expected it, and had prepared for it. But it had been none the less a terrible experience. The fierceness of Corry's anger had been indeed quietly expressed—he had evidently schooled himself; but the words and phrases used by him had bitten into her mind. His wrath had taken the form of a long summing up of the relations between himself and her since his boyhood, of a final scornful attack on her supposed "principles," and a denunciation of her love of power—unjustified, unwarranted power—as the cause of all the unhappiness in their family life. He had not said it in so many words, but she knew very well that what he meant was "You have refused to be the normal woman, and you have neither mind enough nor knowledge enough to justify you. You have sacrificed everything to politics, and you don't understand a single political problem. You have ruined your own life and ours for a barren intellectualism, and it will leave you in the end a lonely and unhappy woman."

Well, well, she had borne with him—she had not broken with him, after all that. She would have found a dozen ways of improving his position, of giving him back his inheritance, if he had shown the smallest disposition to meet her, to compromise with her. But he had gone from extravagance to extravagance, from outrage to outrage. And finally she had gathered up all her strength and struck, for the family traditions, for the party's, the country's interests. And of course she had been right—she had been abundantly right.

Drawing herself unconsciously erect, she looked out over the wide Coryston domain, the undulations of the great estate as it stretched northward to the hills. Politics! She had been in politics from her childhood; she had been absorbed in them through all her married life; and now, in her later years, she was fairly consumed by the passion of them, by the determination to win and conquer. Not for herself!—so at least her thoughts, judged in her own cause, vehemently insisted; not for any personal motive whatever, but to save the country from the break-up of all that made England great, from the incursions of a venomous rabble, bent on destroying the upper class, the landed system, the aristocracy, the Church, the Crown. Woman as she was, she would fight revolution to the last; they should find her body by the wall, when and if the fortress of the old English life went down.

Glenwilliam!—in that name all her hatreds were summed up.

For there had arisen, during these latter years, a man of the people, to lead what Lady Coryston called the "revolution"—a man who had suffered cruelties, so it was said, at the hands of the capitalist and employing class; who, as a young miner, blacklisted because of the part he had taken in a successful strike, had gone, cap in hand, to mine after mine, begging vainly for work, his wife and child tramping beside him. The first wife and her child had perished, so the legend ran, at any rate, of hardship and sheer lack of food. That insolent conspicuous girl who was now the mistress of his house was the daughter of a second wife, a middle-class woman, married when he was already in Parliament, and possessed of a small competence which had been the foundation of her husband's political position. On that modest sum he had held his ground; and upon it, while England was being stirred from end to end by his demagogue's gift, he had built up a personal independence and a formidable power which had enabled him to bargain almost on equal terms with the two great parties.

"We refused to pay his price," was the way in which Lady Coryston was accustomed to put it, "so the Liberals bought him—*dear!*"

And he was now exacting from that luckless party the very uttermost farthing! Destruction of the Church; conscription, with a view, no doubt, to turning a workman-led army, in case of need, upon the possessing class; persecution of the landed interests; criminally heavy taxation—these were Apollyon's weapons. And against such things even a weak woman must turn to bay—must fight even her own heart, in the interests of her country.

"Did I choose my post in life for myself?—its duties, its responsibilities? It was as much given to me as a soldier's place in the line of battle! Am I to shirk it because I am a woman?

The women have no more right to run away than the men—vote or no vote! Haven't we eyes to see this ruin that's coming, and minds to baffle it with? If I make Corry rich?—and help thereby to throw England to the dogs? Am I to give him what he says he hates—land and money—to use for what *I* hate—and what his father hated? Just because he is my son—my flesh and blood? He would scorn the plea himself—he has scorned it all his life. Then let him respect his mother—when she does the same."

But meanwhile the "game," as Coryston was playing it?—what was to be done as to this episode and that?

She sat down to her writing-table, still busily thinking, and reminding herself that her agent Mr. Page was to come and see her at twelve. She had hoped to get some counsel and help out of Arthur, now that the House was up for a fortnight. But Arthur had really been very inconsiderate and tiresome so far. He had arrived so late for dinner on the Saturday that there had been no time for talk, especially as there was a large party in the house. On Sunday he had taken a motor, and had been away all day, paying—he said—some constituency visits. And now this morning with the earliest train he was off to London, though there was really no occasion for him whatever to go up there. He seemed rather unlike himself. His mother wondered if he was ill. And she fell into some indignant reflections on the stuffy atmosphere and bad lighting of the House of Commons. But ever since he knew that he was to have the estates his manner seemed to have changed; not certainly in the direction of triumph or satisfaction. On the contrary, he had once or twice said irritably to his mother that the will was ridiculous and ought not to stand. She had been obliged to make it clear to him that the matter was *not* to be discussed.

Suddenly, as she sat there, distress seized her at the bare thought of any shadow between herself and Arthur—Arthur, her darling, who was upholding his father's principles and hers in Parliament with so much zeal and good feeling; who had never all his life—till these latter weeks—given her so much as a cross word. Yet now that she could no longer chase the thought quite away, she admitted, more and more frankly, that she was anxious. Was he in any money difficulties? She must get James to find out. In love? She smiled. There were very few maidens in England, whatever their pretensions, who would be likely to refuse Arthur Coryston. Let him only throw the handkerchief, and his mother would soon do the rest. And indeed it was high time he set up house for himself. There is a restlessness in a man which means—marriage; and a mother soon becomes aware of it.

* * * * *

Recalling her thoughts to the letters before her, Lady Coryston perceived among them a note from Lady William Newbury asking her and Marcia to spend a week-end at Hoddon Grey. Lady Coryston rather wearily reflected that she must no doubt accept. That young man was clearly in pursuit of Marcia. What Marcia's own views were, her mother had not yet discovered. She seemed sometimes glad to see him; sometimes entirely indifferent; and Lady Coryston thought she had observed that her daughter's vacillations tried Edward Newbury's pride sorely, at times. But it would end in a match—it was pretty certain to end in a match. Marcia was only testing her power over a strong-willed man, who would capture her in the end. That being so, Lady Coryston acknowledged that the necessary tiresome preliminaries must be gone through.

She hastily scrawled a note of acceptance, without any of the fond imaginings that would have accompanied the act in the ordinary mother. Like all imperious women she disliked staying in other people's houses, where she could not arrange her hours. And she had a particularly resentful memory of a visit which she had paid with her husband to Lord and Lady William Newbury when they were renting a house in Surrey, before they had inherited Hoddon Grey, and while Marcia was still in the schoolroom. Never in her life had she been so ordered about. The strict rules of the house had seemed to her intolerable. She was a martinet herself, and inclined to pay all due attention to the observances of religion; but they must be her own observances, or at least approved by her. To be expected to follow other people's observances set her aflame. To make such a fuss, also, about your religion seemed to her indecorous and absurd. She remembered with a satisfaction which was half ashamed, that she—who was always down at home to a half-past-eight breakfast, and was accustomed to walk a mile to church—had insisted on breakfasting in her own room, on Sunday, under the Newburys' roof, and had quite enjoyed Lady William's surprised looks when they met at luncheon.

Well, now the thing had to be done again—for the settling of Marcia. Whether the atmosphere of the family or the house would suit Marcia, her mother did not inquire. In the matters of birth and money, nothing could be more appropriate. Lady Coryston, however, was mostly concerned in getting it through quickly, lest it should stand in the way of things more important. She was fond of Marcia; but her daughter occupied, in truth, only the fringe of her thoughts.

However, she duly put up her letter, and was addressing the envelope, when the door opened to admit the head agent of the estate, Mr. Frederick Page.

Mr. Page was, in Lady Coryston's eyes, a prince of agents. Up till now she had trusted him entirely, and had been more largely governed by his advice than her pride of rule would ever have allowed her to confess. Especially had she found reason to be grateful to him for the large amount of money he had lately been able to provide her with from the savings of the Coryston estates, for political purposes. Lady Coryston was one of the largest subscribers to the party funds in the kingdom; the coming election demanded an exceptional effort, and Page's economies had made it almost easy. She greeted him with a peculiarly gracious smile, remembering perhaps the letter of thanks she had received only the day before from the party headquarters.

The agent was still a young man, not much over forty, ruddy, good-looking, inclined to be plump, and possessed of a manner calculated to win the confidence of any employer. He looked the pink of discretion and capacity, and Lady Coryston had never discovered in him the smallest flaw with regard to any of the orthodoxies she required, political or religious. He was a widower, with two girls, who had often been allowed to play with Marcia.

It was clear to Lady Coryston's eyes at once that Mr. Page was much disturbed and upset. She had expected it, of course. She herself was disturbed and upset. But she had perhaps hoped that he would reassure her—make light of the situation.

He did nothing of the kind. On the contrary, the effects of an encounter he had just had with Lord Coryston himself in the village street, before entering the park, were plainly visible in the agent's bearing. He plunged at once into the subject.

"I fear, Lady Coryston, there is great trouble brewing on this estate!"

"You will stop it," she said, confidently; "you always have stopped it before—you and I together."

He shook his head.

"Ah, but—you see what makes the difference!"

"That Coryston is my son?—and has always been regarded as my heir? Certainly that makes a difference," she admitted, unwillingly. "But his proceedings will soon disgust people—will soon recoil on himself!"

Page looked up to see her pale profile, with its marked hollows in cheek and temple, outlined on the white paneling of the room like some strong, hawkish face of the Renaissance. But, in awe of her as he always was, she seemed to him a foolish woman. Why had she driven matters to this extremity?

He poured out his budget of troubles. All the smoldering discontent which had always existed on the estate had been set alight by Lord Coryston. He was trying to form a union among the laborers, and the farmers were up in arms. He was rousing the dissenters against the Church school of the estate. He was even threatening an inquiry into the state of some of his mother's cottages.

Lady Coryston interrupted. Her voice showed annoyance. "I thought, Mr. Page, there were no insanitary cottages on this property!"

Page hemmed and hawed. He had not the courage to say that if a landowner insists on spending the reserve fund of an estate on politics, the estate suffers. He had found Lady Coryston large sums for the party war-chest; but only a fool could expect him to build new cottages, and keep up a high level of improvements, at the same time.

"I am doing what I can," he said, hurriedly. "There are certain things that must be done. I have given orders."

"My son seems to have caught us napping," said Lady Coryston, rather grimly.

The agent passed the remark by. He inquired whether her ladyship was still determined to refuse land for the Baptist chapel.

"Certainly! The minister they propose is a most mischievous person, I have no intention whatever of extending his influence."

Page acquiesced. He himself would have made the Baptists happy with a half an acre, long since, and so, in his belief, scotched a hornet's nest. But he had never breathed any suggestion of the kind to Lady Coryston.

"I have done my best—believe me—to stop the Sunday

disturbances," he said, "but in vain. They are chiefly got up, however, by people from a distance. Purely political!"

"Of course. I am not to be intimidated by them," said Lady Coryston, firmly.

The agent's inner mind let loose a thought to the effect that the increasing influence of women in politics did not seem to be likely to lead to peaceable living. But he merely remarked:

"I much regret that Lord Coryston should have addressed them himself last Sunday. I ventured to tell his lordship so when I met him just now in the village."

Lady Coryston stiffened on her chair.

"He defended himself?"

"Hotly. And I was to tell you that with your leave he will call on you himself this afternoon about the affair."

"My house is always open to my son," said Lady Coryston, quietly. But Page perceived the tremor of battle that ran through her.

"As to his support of that blacksmith from Ling, whom he is actually setting up in business at Knatchett itself—the man is turning out a perfect firebrand!—distributing Socialist leaflets over the whole neighborhood—getting up a quarrel between some of the parents here in this very village and our schoolmaster, about the punishment of a child—perfectly legitimate! —everything in order!—and enrolling more members of Mr. Glenwilliam's new Land League—within a stone's-throw of this house!—than I like to think of. I won't answer for this village, Lady Coryston, at the next election, if Lord Coryston goes on with these proceedings!"

Lady Coryston frowned. She was not accustomed to be addressed in so pessimistic a tone, and the mere mention of her arch-enemy—Glenwilliam—had put defiance into her. With some dryness, she preached energy, watchfulness, and a hopeful mind. The agent grasped the situation with the quickness born of long acquaintance with her, and adroitly shifted his ground. He remarked that at any rate Lord Coryston was making things uncomfortable all round; and he described with gusto the raids upon some of the Radical employers and small cottage-owners of the district, in the name of political liberty and decent housing, by which Coryston had been lately bewildering the Radical mind. Lady Coryston laughed; but was perhaps more annoyed than amused. To be brought down to the same level with Radical millers and grocers—and by her own son—was no consolation to a proud spirit.

"If our cottages can be reasonably attacked, they must be put in order, and at once," she said, with dignity. "You, Mr. Page, are my eyes and ears. I have been accustomed to trust you."

The agent accepted the implied reproach with outward meekness, and an inward resolve to put Lady Coryston on a much stricter financial regime for the future.

A long conversation followed, at the end of which Mr. Page rose, with the remark:

"Your ladyship will be sorry to hear that Mr. Glenwilliam is to speak at Martover next month,—and that it is already rumored Lord Coryston will be in the chair."

He had kept this bombshell to the last, and for various reasons he closely watched its effect.

Lady Coryston paled.

"We will have a Tory meeting here the same night, and my son Arthur shall speak," she said, with vivacity.

Some odd thoughts arose in the mind of Mr. Page as he met

the angry fire in the speaker's look.

"By all means. By the way, I did not know Mr. Arthur was acquainted with those strange people the Atherstones?" he said, in a tone of easy interrogation, looking for his hat.

Lady Coryston was a little surprised by the remark.

"I suppose an M.P. must be acquainted with everybody—to some extent," she said, smiling. "I know very well what his opinion of Mr. Atherstone is."

"Naturally," said Page, also smiling. "Well, good-by, Lady Coryston. I hope when you see Lord Coryston this afternoon you will be able to persuade him to give up some of these extravagances."

"I have no power with him," she said, sharply.

"Why did you give up what you had?" thought the agent, as he took his departure. His long experience of Lady Coryston, able as she was, and as he admitted her to be, in many respects, had in the end only increased in him a secret contempt for women, inbred in all but a minority of men. They seemed to him to have so little power of "playing the game"—the old, old game of success that men understand so well; through compromise, cunning, give and take, shrewd and prudent dealing. A kind of heady blundering, when caution and a few lies would have done all that was wanted—it was this he charged them with— Lady Coryston especially.

And as to that nice but rather stupid fellow Arthur, what on earth could he be doing at the Atherstones'? Had he—Page— come by chance on a secret,—dramatic and lamentable!— when, on the preceding Saturday, as he was passing along the skirts of the wood bounding the Atherstones' little property, on his way to one of the Coryston hill-farms, he had perceived in the distance—himself masked by a thin curtain of trees— two persons in the wood-path, in intimate or agitated conversation. They were Arthur Coryston and Miss Glenwilliam. He recognized the lady at once, had several times seen her on the platform when her father spoke at meetings, and the frequent presence of the Glenwilliams at the Atherstones' cottage was well known to the neighborhood.

By George!—if that *did* mean anything!

CHAPTER VI

Meanwhile on this May morning Marcia was reading in the park, not far from a footpath—a right of way—leading from the village to the high road running east and west along the northern boundary of the Coryston property. Round her the slopes were white with hawthorn under a thunderous sky of blue and piled white cloud. The dappled forms of deer glanced through the twisted hawthorn stems, and at her feet a trout-stream, entrancingly clear and clean, slipped by over its chalk bottom—the gray-green weeds swaying under the slight push of the water. There was a mist of blossom, and everywhere the fragrance of a bountiful earth, young once more.

Marcia, it must be confessed, was only pretending to read. She had some reason to think that Edward Newbury might present himself at Coryston for lunch that day. If so, and if he walked from Hoddon Grey—and, unlike most young men of his age, he was a great walker, even when there was no question of grouse or golf—he would naturally take this path. Some strong mingled impulse had placed her there, on his road. The attraction for her of his presence, his smile, his character was irresistibly increasing. There were many days when she was restless and the world was empty till he came. And yet there were other days when she was quite cold to him; when the thought of giving her life into his hands made her cry "impossible"; when it seemed to her, as she had said to Waggin, that she rather feared than loved him.

Edward Newbury indeed belonged to a type not common in

our upper class, yet always represented there, and in its main characteristics to be traced back at least to the days of Laud and the Neoplatonists. It is a spiritual, a mystical type, developed under English aristocratic conditions and shaped by them. Newbury had been brought up in a home steeped in high Anglican tradition. His grandfather, old Lord Broadstone, had been one of the first and keenest supporters of the Oxford movement, a friend of Pusey, Keble, and Newman, and later on of Liddon, Church, and Wilberforce. The boy had grown up in a religious hothouse; his father, Lord William, had been accustomed in his youth to make periodical pilgrimages to Christchurch as one of Pusey's "penitents," and his house became in later life a rallying-point for the High Anglican party in all its emergencies. Edward himself, as the result of an intense travail of mind, had abandoned habitual confession as he came to manhood, but he would not for the world have missed the week of "retreat" he spent every year, with other Anglican laymen, under the roof of the most spiritual of Anglican bishops. He was a joyous, confident, devoted son of the English church; a man governed by the most definite and rigid beliefs, held with a pure intensity of feeling, and impervious to any sort of Modernism.

At the same time his handsome person, his ardent and amiable temper, his poetic and musical tastes, made him a very general favorite even in the most miscellaneous society. The enthusiastic Christian was also a popular man of the world; and the esoteric elements in his character, though perfectly well known to all who were in any degree his intimates, were jealously hidden from the multitude, who welcomed him as a good-looking fellow and an agreeable companion. He had been four years in the Guards, and some years in India, as private secretary to his uncle, the Viceroy. He was a good shot, a passionate dancer, a keen musician; and that mysterious note in him of the unbending and the inexorable only made him— in general—the more attractive both to men and women, as it became apparent to them. Men scoffed at him, yet without ever despising him. Perhaps the time was coming when, as character hardened, and the glamour of youth dropped away, many men might hate him. Men like Coryston and Atherstone were beginning indeed to be bitterly hostile. But these were possibilities which were only just emerging.

Marcia was well aware of Newbury's distinction; and secretly very proud of his homage. But rebellion in her was still active. When, however, she asked herself, with that instinct for self-analysis bred in the woman of to-day by the plays she sees, and half the tales she reads—"Why is it he likes me?"—the half-sarcastic reply would still suggest itself—"No doubt just because I am so shapeless and so formless—because I don't know myself what I want or what I mean to be. He thinks he'll form me—he'll save my soul. Shall he?"

A footstep on the path made her look up, annoyed that she could not control a sudden burning of the cheek. But the figure she expected was not there.

"Coryston!" she cried.

Her brother approached her. He seemed to be reciting verse, and she thought she caught some words from a Shelley chorus which she knew, because he had made her learn it when she was a child in the schoolroom. He threw himself down beside her.

"Well?"

Brother and sister had only met twice since Coryston's settlement at Knatchett—once in the village street, and once when Marcia had invaded his bachelor quarters at Knatchett. On that occasion she had discharged upon him all the sarcasm and remonstrance of which she was capable. But she only succeeded in reminding herself of a bullfight of which she had once seen part at San Sebastian. Her shafts stuck glittering in the bull's hide, but the bull barely shook himself. There he stood—good-humored, and pawing.

To-day also Coryston seemed to be in high spirits. Marcia, on the other hand, gave him a look half troubled, half hostile.

"Corry!—I wanted to speak to you. Are you really going to see mother this afternoon?"

"Certainly. I met Page in the village half an hour ago and asked him to announce me."

"I don't want to talk any more about all the dreadful things you've been doing," said Marcia, with sisterly dignity. "I know it wouldn't be any good. But there's one thing I must say. I do beg of you, Corry, not to say a word to mamma about—about Arthur and Enid Glenwilliam. I know you were at the Atherstones on Saturday!"

The anxiety in the girl's face seemed to give a softer shade to its strong beauty. She went on, appealingly:

"Arthur's told me a lot. He's quite mad. I've argued—and argued with him—but it's no good. He doesn't care for anything—Parliament, mamma, the estates, anything—in comparison with that girl. At present she's playing with him, and he's getting desperate. But I'm simply in *terror* about mamma!"

Corry whistled.

"My dear, she'll have to know some time. As you say, he's in it, head over ears. No use your trying to pull him back!"

"It'll kill her!" cried Marcia, passionately; "what's left of her, after you've done!"

Coryston lifted his eyebrows and looked long and curiously at his sister. Then he slowly got up from the grass and took a seat beside her.

"Look here, Marcia, do you think—do you honestly think— that I'm the aggressor in this family row?"

"Oh, I don't know—I don't know what to think!"

Marcia covered her face with her hands. "It's all so miserable!—" she went on, in a muffled voice. "And this Glenwilliam thing has come so suddenly! Why, he hardly knew her, when he made that speech in the House six weeks ago! And now he's simply demented! Corry, you must go and argue with him—you *must*! Persuade him to give her up!"

She laid her hand on his arm imploringly.

Coryston sat silent, but his eyes laughed a little.

"I don't believe in her," he said at last, abruptly. "If I did, I'd back Arthur up through thick and thin!"

"*Corry*!—how on earth can Arthur be happy if he marries her—how can he live in that set—the son-in-law of *that man*! He'll have to give up his seat—nobody here would ever vote for him again. His friends would cut him—"

"Oh come, come, my dear, we're not as bad as that!" said Coryston, impatiently.

But Marcia wailed on:

"And it isn't as if he had ideas and theories—like you—"

"Not a principle to his back!—I know," said Coryston, cheerfully. "I tell you again, I'd not dissuade him; on the contrary, I'd shove him into it!—if she were the right sort. But she's not. She's ruined by the luxury she's been living in. I believe—if you ask me—that she'd accept Arthur for his money—but that she doesn't care one brass farthing about him. Why should she?"

"Corry!"

"He's a fool, my dear, though a jolly one—and she's not been accustomed to living with fools. She's got wits as sharp as gimlets. Well, well"—he got up from the seat—"can't talk any more now. Now what is it exactly you want me to do? I repeat—I'm coming to see mother this afternoon."

"Don't let her guess anything. Don't tell her anything. She's a little worried about Arthur already. But we must stop the madness before she knows anything. Promise!"

"Very well. For the present—I'm mum."

"And talk to him!—tell him it'll ruin him!"

"I don't mind—from my own point of view," said Coryston, surveying her with his hands on his sides. Then suddenly his face changed. A cloud overshadowed it. He gave her a queer, cold look.

"Perhaps I have something to ask you," he said, slowly.

"What?" The tone showed her startled.

"Let *me* come and talk to *you* about that man whom all the world says you're going to marry!"

She stared at him, struck dumb for the moment by the fierceness of his voice and expression. Then she said, indignantly:

"What do you mean, Corry!"

"You are deceived in him. You can't marry him!" he said, passionately. "At least let me talk to you."

She rose and stood facing him, her hands behind her, her dark face as full of energy and will as his own.

"You are thinking of the story of Mrs. Betts. I know it."

"Not as I should tell it!"

A moving figure in a distant field caught her attention. She made a great effort to master her excitement.

"You may tell me what you like. But I warn you I shall ask *him* for his version, too."

Corry's expression changed. The tension relaxed.

"That's only fair," he said, indifferently. Then, perceiving the advancing man: "Ah, I see!—here he is. I'm off. It's a bargain. I say nothing to mother—and do my best to make Arthur hang himself. And I have it out with you—my small sister!— when we next meet."

He paused, looking at her, and in his strangely penetrating eyes there dawned, suddenly, the rare expression that Marcia remembered—as of a grave yet angry tenderness. Then he turned away, walking fast, and was soon invisible among the light shadows of a beech avenue, just in leaf. Marcia was left behind, breathing quick, to watch the approach of Edward Newbury.

* * * * *

As soon as he perceived Marcia under the shade of the hawthorns Newbury quickened his pace, and he had soon thrown himself, out of breath, on the grass beside her.

"What a heavenly spot!—and what a morning! How nice of you to let me find you! I was hoping Lady Coryston would give me lunch."

Radiant, he raised his eyes to her, as he lay propped on his elbows, the spring sun, slipping through the thin blossom-laden branches overhead, dappling his bronzed face.

Marcia flushed a little—an added beauty. As she sat there in a white hat and dress, canopied by the white trees, and lit by a warm reflected light, she stirred in Newbury's senses once more a thrilling delight made all the keener perhaps by the misgiving, the doubts which invariably accompanied it. She could be so gracious; and she could be so dumb and inaccessible. Again and again he had been on the point of declaring himself during the last few weeks, and again and again he had drawn back, afraid lest the decisive word from him should draw the decisive word from her, and it should be a word of denial. Better—better infinitely—these doubts and checks, than a certainty which would divide him from her.

This morning indeed he found her all girlish gentleness and appeal. And it made his own task easier. For he also had matters on his mind. But she anticipated him.

"I want to talk to you about Corry—my brother!" she said, bending toward him.

There was a child in Marcia, and she could evoke it when she pleased. She evoked it now. The young man before her hungered, straightway, to put out his arms to her—gathering her to him caressingly as one does with the child that clings and confides. But instead he merely smiled at her with his bright conscious eyes.

"I, too, want to talk to you about Coryston," he said, nodding.

"We know he's behaving dreadfully—abominably!" laughed Marcia, but with a puckered brow.

"Mr. Lester tells me there was a great attack on Lord and Lady William yesterday in the Martover paper. Mother hasn't seen it yet—and I don't want to read it—"

"Don't!" said Newbury, smiling.

"But mother will be so ashamed, unhappy, when she knows! So am I. But I wanted to explain. We suffer just as much. He's stirring up the whole place against mother. And now that he's begun to attack you, I thought perhaps that if you and I—"

"Took counsel! Excellent!"

"We might perhaps think of some way of stopping it."

"He's much more acutely angry with us at present than with anything your mother does," said Newbury, gravely! "Has he told you?"

"No, but—he means to," said the girl, hesitating.

"It is not unfair I think I should anticipate him. You will have his version afterward. I got an extraordinary letter from him this morning. It is strange that he cannot see we also plead justice and right for what we do—that if we satisfied his conscience we should wound our own."

He rose from the grass as he spoke, and took a seat on a stone a little way from her. And as she looked at him Marcia had a strange, sudden feeling that here was quite another man from the wooer who had just been lying on the grass at her feet. *This* was the man of whom she had said to Waggin—"he seems the softest, kindest!—and underneath—*iron*!" A shade of some habitual sternness had crept over the features. A noble sternness, however; and it had begun to stir in her, intermittently, the thrill of an answering humility.

"It is difficult for me—perhaps impossible—to tell you all the story," he said, after a pause, "but I will try and tell it shortly— in its broad outlines."

"I have heard some of it."

"So I supposed. But let me tell it in order—so far as I can. It concerns a man whom a few weeks ago we all regarded—my father and mother—myself—as one of our best friends. You know how keen my father is about experimenting with the land? Well, when we set up our experimental farm here ten years ago we made this man—John Betts—the head of it. He has been my father's right hand—and he has done splendidly—made the farm, indeed, and himself, famous. And he seemed to be one with us in other respects." He paused a moment, looked keenly into her face, and then said, gravely and simply: "We looked upon him as a deeply religious man. My mother could not say enough of his influence on the estate. He took a large men's class on Sundays. He was a regular communicant; he helped our clergyman splendidly. And especially"—here again the speaker hesitated a moment. But he resumed with a gentle seriousness—"he helped us in all our attempts to make the people here live straight—like Christians—not like animals. My mother has very strict rules—she won't allow any one in our cottages who has lost their character. I know it sounds harsh. It isn't so—it's merciful. The villages were in a terrible state when we came—as to morals. I can't of course explain to you—but our priest appealed to us—we had to make changes—and my father and mother bravely faced unpopularity—"

He looked at her steadily, while his face changed, and the sudden red of some quick emotion invaded it.

"You know we are unpopular!"

"Yes," said Marcia, slowly, his perfect sincerity forbidding anything else in her.

"Especially"—there was a touch of scorn in the full voice—"owing to the attacks on my father and mother of that Liberal agitator—that man Atherstone—who lives in that cottage on the hill—your mother knows all about him. He has spread innumerable stories about us ever since we came to live here. He is a free-thinker and a republican—we are church people and Tories. He thinks that every man—or woman—is a law unto themselves. We think—but you know what we think!"

He smiled at her.

"Well—to return to Betts. This is May. Last August he had an attack of influenza, and went off to North Wales, to the sea, to recruit. He was away much longer than any one expected, and after about six weeks he wrote to my father to say that he should return to Hoddon Grey—with a wife. He had found a lady at Colwyn Bay, whom he had known as a girl. She was a widow, had just lost her father, with whom she lived, and was very miserable and forlorn. I need not say we all wrote the most friendly letters. She came, a frail, delicate creature, with one child. My mother did all she could for her, but was much baffled by her reserve and shrinking. Then—bit by bit—through some extraordinary chances and coincidences—I needn't go through it all—the true story came out."

He looked away for a moment over the reaches of the park, evidently considering with himself what he could tell, and how far.

"I can only tell you the bare facts," he said, at last. "Mrs. Betts was divorced by her first husband. She ran away with a man who was in his employment, and lived with him for two years. He never married her, and after two years he deserted her. She has had a wretched life since—with her child. Then Betts came along, whom she had known long ago. She threw herself on his pity. She is very attractive—he lost his head—and married her. Well now, what were we to do?"

"They *are* married?" said Marcia.

"Certainly—by the law. But it is a law which matters nothing to us!"

The voice had taken to itself a full challenging note.

Marcia looked up.

"Because—you think—divorce is wrong?"

"Because—'What God has joined together let no man

put asunder!'"

"But there are exceptions in the New Testament?"

The peach bloom on Marcia's cheek deepened as she bent over the daisy chain she was idly making.

"Doubtful ones! The dissolution of marriage may itself be an open question. But, for all churchmen, the remarriage of divorced persons—and trebly, when it is asked for by the person whose sin caused the divorce!—is an absolutely closed one!"

Marcia's mind was in a ferment. But her girlish senses were keenly alive to the presence beside her—the clean-cut classical face, the spiritual beauty of the eyes. Yet something in her shivered.

"Suppose she was very unhappy with her first husband?"

"Law cannot be based on hard cases. It is made to help the great multitude of suffering, sinning men and women through their lives." He paused a little, and then said, "Our Lord 'knew what was in man.'"

The low tone in which the last words were spoken affected Marcia deeply, not so much as an appeal to religion, for her own temperament was not religious, as because they revealed the inner mystical life of the man beside her. She was suddenly filled again with a strange pride that he should have singled her out—to love her.

But the rise of feeling was quickly followed by recoil.

She looked up eagerly.

"If I had been very miserable—had made a hideous mistake—and knew it—and somebody came along and offered to make me happy—give me a home—and care for me—I couldn't and

I shouldn't resist!"

"You would," he said, simply, "if God gave you strength."

Nothing so intimate had yet been said between them. There was silence. That old, old connection between the passion of religion—which is in truth a great romanticism—and the passion of sex, made itself felt; but in its most poetic form. Marcia was thrillingly conscious of the debate in herself—of the voice which said, "Teach me, govern me, love me—be my adored master and friend!" and the voice which replied, "I should be his slave—I will not!"

At last she said:

"You have dismissed Mr. Betts?"

He sighed.

"He is going in a month. My father offered all we could. If— Mrs. Betts"—the words came out with effort—"would have separated from him we should have amply provided for her and her child. The Cloan Sisters would have watched over her. She could have lived near them, and Betts could have seen her from time to time—"

"They refused?"

"Absolutely. Betts wrote my father the fiercest letters. They were married, he said, married legally and honestly—and that was an end of it. As to Mrs. Betts's former history, no one had the smallest right to pry into it. He defied my father to dismiss him. My father—on his principles—had no choice but to do so. So then—your brother came on the scene!"

"Of course—he was furious?"

"What right has he to be furious?" said Newbury, quietly. "His principles may be what he pleases. But he must allow us ours.

This is a free country."

A certain haughtiness behind the gentle manner was very perceptible. Marcia kindled for her brother.

"I suppose Corry would say, if the Church ruled us—as you wish—England wouldn't be free!"

"That's his view. We have ours. No doubt he has the present majority with him. But why attack us personally—call us names—because of what we believe?"

He spoke with vivacity, with wounded feeling. Marcia melted.

"But every one knows," she murmured, "that Corry is mad—quite mad."

And suddenly, impulsively, she put out her hand.

"Don't blame us!"

He took the hand in both his own, bent over and kissed it.

"Don't let him set you against us!"

She smiled and shook her head. Then by way of extricating herself and him from the moment of emotion—by way of preventing its going any further—she sprang to her feet.

"Mother will be waiting lunch for us."

They walked back to the house together, discussing as they went Coryston's whole campaign. Newbury's sympathy with her mother was as balm to Marcia; insensibly she rewarded him, both by an open and charming mood, and also by a docility, a readiness to listen to the Newbury view of life which she had never yet shown. The May day, meanwhile, murmured and gleamed around them. The spring wind like a riotous life leaped and rustled in the new leaf of the oaks and beeches; the sky seemed to be leaning mistily to earth; and there were strange, wild lights on the water and the grass, as though, invisible, the train of Dionysius or Apollo swept through the land. Meanwhile the relation between the young man and the girl ripened apace. Marcia's resistance faltered within her; and to Newbury the walk was enchantment.

Finally they agreed to leave the task of remonstrating with Coryston to Sir Wilfrid Bury, who was expected the following day, and was an old friend of both families.

"Corry likes him," said Marcia. "He says, 'Give me either a firebrand or a cynic!' He has no use for other sorts of people. And perhaps Sir Wilfrid will help us, too—with Arthur." Her look darkened.

"Arthur?" said Newbury, startled. "What's wrong with Arthur?"

Marcia hurriedly told him. He looked amazed and shocked.

"Oh, that can't be allowed. We must protect your mother— and persuade Arthur. Let me do what I can. He and I are old pals."

Marcia was only too glad to be helped. It had begun to seem to her, in spite of the rush of her London gaieties, and the brilliance of her London successes, that she had been very lonely at home for a long time, and here, in this strong man, were warmth and shelter.

* * * * *

Luncheon passed gaily, and Lady Coryston perceived, or thought she perceived, that Marcia's affairs were marching briskly toward their destined end. Newbury took his leave immediately afterward, saying to Lady Coryston, "So we expect you—next Sunday?" The slight emphasis he laid on the words, the pressure on her hand seemed to reveal to her the hope in the young man's mind. Well!—the sooner, the better.

Afterward Lady Coryston paid some calls in the village, and, coming home through a stately series of walled gardens ablaze with spring flowers, she gave some directions for a new herbaceous border. Then she returned to the house to await her son. Marcia meanwhile had gone to the station to meet Sir Wilfrid Bury.

Coryston duly arrived, a more disreputable figure than usual— bedraggled with rain, his shabby trousers tucked into his boots, and his cap festooned with fishing-flies; for the afternoon had turned showery, and Coryston had been pursuing the only sport which appealed to him in the trout-stream of the park. Before he did so he had formally asked leave of the agent, and had been formally granted it.

He and Lady Coryston were closeted together for nearly an hour. Had any one been sitting in the adjoining room they would have heard, save on two occasions when the raised voices clashed together, but little variation in the tones of the combatants. When the conference broke up and Coryston departed Lady Coryston was left alone for a little while. She sat motionless in her chair beside her writing-table. Animation and color faded slowly from her features; and before her trance of thought was broken by the arrival of a servant announcing that Sir Wilfrid Bury had arrived, one who knew her well would have been startled by certain subtle changes in her aspect.

Coryston, meanwhile, made his way to the great library in the north wing, looking for Lester. He found the young librarian at his desk, with a fifteenth-century MS. before him, which he was describing and cataloguing. The beautiful pages sparkling with color and gold were held open by glass weights, and the young man's face, as he bent over his task, showed the happy abstraction of the scholar. All around him rose the latticed walls of the library, holding on one side a collection of MSS., on the other of early printed books, well known to learned

Europe. Wandering gleams from the showery sky outside lit up the faded richness of the room, the pale brown and yellows of the books, the sharp black and white of the old engravings hanging among them. The windows were wide open, and occasionally a westerly gust would blow in upon the floor petals from a fruit tree in blossom just outside.

Coryston came in, looking rather flushed and excited, and took a seat on the edge of the table where Lester was working, his hands in his pockets.

"What a blessed place!" he said, glancing round him. Lester looked up and smiled absently.

"Not bad?"

Silence a moment. Then Coryston said, with sudden vehemence:

"Don't you go into politics, Lester!"

"No fear, old man. But what's up, now? You seem to have been ragging a good deal."

"I've been 'following the gleam,'" said Coryston, with a sarcastic mouth. "Or to put it in another way—there's a hot coal in me that makes me do certain things. I dignify it by calling it a sense of justice. What is it? I don't know. I say, Lester, are you a Suffragist?"

"Haven't made up my mind."

"I am—theoretically. But upon my word—politics plays the deuce with women. And sometimes I think that women will play the deuce with politics."

"You mean they're so unmeasured?" said Lester, cautiously.

Coryston shook his head vaguely, staring at the floor, but

presently broke out:

"I say, Lester, if we can't find generosity, tenderness, an open mind—among women—where the devil are we going to find them?" He stood up. "And politics kills all that kind of thing."

"Physician, heal thyself," laughed Lester.

"Ah, but it's our *business*!"—Coryston smote the table beside him—"our dusty, d—d business. We've got somehow to push and harry and drive this beastly world into some sort of decency. But the women!—oughtn't they to be in the shrine—tending the mystic fire? What if the fire goes out—if the heart of the nation dies?"

Lester's blue-gray eyes looked up quietly. There was sympathy in them, but he said nothing.

Coryston tramped half-way to the library door, then turned back.

"My mother's quite a good woman," he said, abruptly. "There are no great scandals on this estate—it's better managed than most. But because of this poison of politics, no one can call their souls their own. If she'd let them live their own lives they'd adore her."

"The trade-unions are just the same."

"I believe you!" said Coryston. "Freedom's a lost art in England—from Parliament downward. Well, well—Good-by!"

"Coryston!"

"Yes?" Lord Coryston paused with his hand on the door.

"Don't take the chair for Glenwilliam?"

"By George, I will!" Coryston's eyes flamed. And going out he noisily shut the door.

*   *   *   *   *

Lester was left to his work. But his mood had been diverted, and he presently found that he was wasting time. He walked to the window, and stood there gazing at the bright flower-beds in the formal garden, the fountain plashing in its center, the low hills and woods that closed the horizon, the villages with their church-towers, piercing the shelter of the woods. May had drawn over the whole her first veils of green. The English perfection, the English mellowness, was everywhere; the spring breathings in the air came scented with the young leaf of trees that had been planted before Blenheim was fought.

Suddenly across the farther end of the garden passed a girlish figure in white. Lester's pulses ran. It was Marcia. He saw her but seldom, and that generally at a distance. But sometimes she would come, in her pretty, friendly way, to chat to him about his work, and turn over his manuscripts.

"She has the same feeling about me that nice women have about their dogs and cats. They are conscious of them, sorry for them; they don't like them to feel themselves neglected. So she comes to see me every now and then—lest I should think myself forgotten. Her conscience pricks her for people less prosperous than herself. I see it quite plainly. But she would be angry if I were to tell her so!"

CHAPTER VII

It was a breezy June afternoon, with the young summer at its freshest and lustiest.

Lord and Lady William Newbury were strolling in the garden at Hoddon Grey. The long low line of the house rose behind them—an attractive house and an old one, but with no architectural features to speak of, except a high-pitched mossy roof, a picturesque series of dormer-windows, and a high gable and small lantern cupola at the farther end which marked the private chapel. The house was evidently roomy, but built for comfort, not display; the garden with its spreading slopes and knolls was simple and old-fashioned, in keeping thereby with the general aspect of the two people who were walking up and down the front lawn together.

Lord William Newbury was a man of sixty-five, tall and slenderly built. His pale hazel eyes, dreamily kind, were the prominent feature of his face; he had very thin flat cheeks, and his white hair—he was walking bareheaded—was blown back from a brow which, like the delicate mouth, was still young, almost boyish. Sweetness and a rather weak refinement—a stranger would probably have summed up his first impressions of Lord William, drawn from his bodily presence, in some such words. But the stranger who did so would have been singularly wide of the mark. His wife beside him looked even frailer and slighter than he. A small and mouse-like woman, dressed in gray clothes of the simplest and plainest make, and wearing a shady garden hat; her keen black eyes in her

Mrs. Humphry Ward

shriveled face gave that clear promise of strong character in which her husband's aspect, at first sight, was lacking. But Lady William knew her place. She was the most submissive and the most docile of wives; and on no other terms would life have been either possible or happy in her husband's company.

They were discussing, with some eagerness, the approaching arrival of their week-end guests—Lady Coryston and Marcia, the new dean of a neighboring cathedral, an ex-Cabinet Minister and an Oxford professor. But the talk, however it circled, had a way of returning to Marcia. It was evident that she held the field.

"It is so strange that I have scarcely seen her!" Lady William was saying in a tone which was not without its note of complaint. "I hope dear Edward has not been too hasty in his choice. As for you, William, I don't believe you would know her again, if you were to see her without her mother."

"Oh yes, I should. Her mother introduced her to me at the Archbishop's party, and I talked to her a little. A very handsome young woman. I remember thinking her talk rather too theatrical."

"About theaters, you mean," sighed Lady William. "Well, that's the way with all the young people. The fuss people make about actors and actresses is perfectly ridiculous."

"I remember she talked to me enthusiastically about Madame Froment," said Lord William, in a tone of reminiscence. "I asked her whether she knew that Madame Froment had a scandalous story, and was not fit acquaintance for a young girl. And she opened her eyes at me, as though I had propounded something absurd. 'One doesn't inquire about that!' she said— quite indignantly, I assure you! 'but only whether she can *act*.' It was curious—and rather disquieting—to see so much decision—self-assertion—in so young a woman."

"Oh, well, Edward will change all that." Lady William's voice was gently confident. "He assures me that she has excellent principles—a fine character really, though quite undeveloped. He thinks she will be readily guided by one she loves."

"I hope so, for Edward's sake—for he is very much in love. I trust he is not letting inclination run away with him. So much—to all of us—depends on his marriage!"

Lord William, frowning a little, paused a moment in his walk and turned his eyes to the house. Hoddon Grey had only become his personal property some three years before this date; but ever since his boyhood it had been associated for him with hallowed images and recollections. It had been the dower-house of his widowed mother, and after her death his brother, a widower with one crippled son, had owned it for nearly a quarter of a century. Both father and son had belonged to the straitest sect of Anglo-Catholicism; their tender devotion to each other had touched with beauty the austerity and seclusion of their lives. Yet at times Hoddon Grey had sheltered large gatherings—gatherings of the high Puseyite party in the English Church, both lay and clerical. Pusey himself had preached in the chapel; Liddon with the Italianate profile— orator and ascetic—might have been seen strolling under the trees where Lord and Lady William were strolling now; Manning, hatchet-faced, jealous and self-conscious, had made fugitive appearances there; even the great Newman himself, in his extreme old age, had once rested there on a journey, and given his Cardinal's blessing to the sons of one of his former comrades in the Oxford movement.

Every stone in the house, every alley in the garden, was sacred in Lord William's eyes. To most men the house they love represents either the dignity and pride of family, or else successful money-making, and the pleasure of indulged tastes. But to Lord William Newbury the house of Hoddon Grey stood as the symbol of a spiritual campaign in which his forebears, himself, and his son were all equally enrolled—the endless, unrelenting campaign of the Church against the world, the Christian against the unbeliever.

... His wife broke in upon his reverie.

"Are you going to say anything about Lord Coryston's letter, William?"

Lord William started.

"Say anything to his mother? Certainly not, Albinia!" He straightened his shoulders. "It is my intention to take no notice of it whatever."

"You have not even acknowledged it?" she asked, timidly.

"A line—in the third person."

"Edward thinks Lady Coryston most unwise—"

"So she is—most unwise!" cried Lord William, warmly. "Coryston has every right to complain of her."

"You think she has done wrong?"

"Certainly. A woman has no right to do such things— whatever her son may be. For a woman to take upon herself the sole direction and disposal of such properties as the Coryston properties is to step outside the bounds of her sex; it is to claim something which a woman ought not to claim— something altogether monstrous and unnatural!"

Lord William's thin features had flushed under a sudden rush of feeling. His wife could not help the sudden thought, "But if we had had an infidel or agnostic son?"

Aloud she said, "You don't think his being such a Radical, so dreadfully extreme and revolutionary, justifies her?"

"Not at all! That was God's will—the cross she had to bear. She interferes with the course of Providence—presumptuously interferes with it—doing evil that what she conceives to be good may come. A woman must persuade men by gentleness—not govern them by force. If she attempts that she is usurping what does not—what never can—belong to her."

The churchman had momentarily disappeared in the indignant stickler for male prerogative and the time-honored laws of English inheritance. Lady William acquiesced in silence. She, too, strongly disapproved of Lady Coryston's action toward her eldest son, abominable as Coryston's opinions were. Women, like minorities, must suffer; and she was glad to have her husband's word for it that it is not their business to correct or coerce their eldest sons, on the ground of political opinions, however grievous those opinions may be.

"I trust that Lady Coryston will not open on this subject to me," said Lord William, after a pause. "I am never good at concealing my opinions for politeness' sake. And of course I hold that Coryston is just as much in the wrong as she. And mad to boot! No sane man could have written the letter I received last week?"

"Do you think he will do what he threatens?"

"What—get up a subscription for Mr. and Mrs. Betts, and settle them somewhere here? I dare say! We can't help it. We can only follow our consciences."

Lord William held himself erect. At that moment no one could have thought of "sweetness" in connection with the old man's delicately white features. Every word fell from him with a quiet and steely deliberation.

His wife walked beside him a little longer. Then she left him and went into the house to see that all the last preparations for the guests were made; gathering on her way a bunch of early roses from a bed near the house. She walked slowly through the guestrooms on the garden front, looking at everything with a critical eye. The furniture of the rooms was shabby and plain. It had been scarcely changed at all since 1832, when Lord

William's widowed mother had come to live at Hoddon Grey. But everything smelt of lavender and much cleaning. The windows were open to the June air, and the house seemed pervaded by the cooing of doves from the lime walk outside; a sound which did but emphasize the quiet of the house and garden. At the end of the garden front Lady William entered a room which had a newer and fresher appearance than the rest. The walls were white; a little rosebud chintz curtained the windows and the bed. White rugs made the hearth and the dressing-table gay, and there was a muslin bedspread lined with pink and tied with knots of pink ribbon.

Lady William stood and looked at it with an intense and secret pleasure. She had been allowed to "do it up" the preceding summer, out of her own money, on which, in all her life, she had never signed a check; and she had given orders that Miss Coryston was to be put into it. Going to the dressing-table, she took from the vase there the formal three sprigs of azalea which the housemaid had arranged, and replaced them by the roses. Her small, wrinkled hands lingered upon them. She was putting them there for the girl Edward loved—who was probably to be his wife. A great tenderness filled her heart.

When she left the room, she rapidly descended a staircase just beyond it, and found herself in the vestibule of the chapel. Pushing the chapel doors open, she made her way in. The rich glooms and scents of the beautiful still place closed upon her. Kneeling before the altar, still laden with Whitsun flowers, and under the large crucifix that hung above it, she prayed for her son, that he might worthily uphold the heritage of his father, that he might be happy in his wife, and blessed with children....

* * * * *

An hour later the drawing-room and the lawns of Hoddon Grey were alive with tea and talk. Lady Coryston, superbly tall, in trailing black, was strolling with Lord William. Sir Wilfrid, the ex-Minister Sir Louis Ford, the Dean, and the Chaplain of the house were chatting and smoking round the deserted tea-table, while Lady William and the Oxford Professor poked among the flower-beds, exchanging confidences on phloxes and delphiniums.

In the distance, under the lime avenue, now in its first pale leaf, two young figures paced to and fro. They were Newbury and Marcia.

Sir Wilfrid had just thrown himself back in his chair, looking round him with a sigh of satisfaction.

"Hoddon Grey makes me feel good! Not a common effect of country-houses!"

"Enjoy them while you may!" laughed Sir Louis Ford. "Glenwilliam is after them."

"Glenwilliam!" exclaimed the Dean. "I saw him at the station, with his handsome but rather strange-looking daughter. What's he doing here?"

"Hatching mischief with a political friend of his—a 'fidus Achates'—who lives near here," said the Chaplain, Mr. Perry, in a deep and rather melancholy tone.

"From the bills I saw posted up in Martover as we came through"—Sir Louis Ford lowered his voice—"I gathered the amazing fact that Coryston—*Coryston!*—is going to take the chair at a meeting where Glenwilliam speaks some way on in next month."

Sir Wilfrid shrugged his shoulders, with a warning glance at the stately form of Coryston's mother in the distance.

"Too bad to discuss!" he said, shortly.

A slight smile played round the Dean's flexible mouth. He was

Mrs. Humphry Ward

a new-comer, and much more of an Erastian than Lord William approved. He had been invited, not for pleasure, but for tactics; that the Newburys might find out what line he was going to take in the politics of the diocese.

"We were never told," said the Dean, "that a *woman's* foes were to be those of her own household!"

The Chaplain frowned.

"Lord Coryston is making enemies in all directions," he said, hastily. "I understand that a letter Lord William received from him last week was perfectly outrageous."

"What about?" asked Sir Louis.

"A divorce case—a very painful one—on which we have found it necessary to take a strong line."

The speaker, who was largely made and gaunt, with grizzled hair and spectacles, spoke with a surprising energy. The Dean looked puzzled.

"What had Lord Coryston to do with it?"

"What indeed?—except that he is out for picking up any grievances he can."

"Who are the parties?"

The Chaplain told the story.

"They didn't ask anybody to marry them in church, did they?" asked the Dean.

"Not that I know of."

The Dean said nothing, but as he lay back in his chair, his hands behind his head, his expression was rather hostile than acquiescent.

* * * * *

Meanwhile, under the lime walk the golden evening insensibly heightened the pleasure of Newbury and Marcia in each other's society. For the sunny fusion of earth and air glorified not only field and wood, but the human beings walking in them. Nature seemed to be adapting herself to them— shedding a mystic blessing on their path. Both indeed were conscious of a secret excitement. They felt the approach of some great moment, as though a pageant or presence were about to enter. For the first time, Marcia's will was in abeyance. She was scarcely ecstatically happy; on the far horizon of life she seemed to be conscious of storm-clouds, of things threatening and unexplored. And yet she was in love; she was thrilled both physically and spiritually by the man beside her; with a certain helplessness, she confessed in him a being stronger and nobler than herself; the humility, the self-surrender of passion was rising in her, like the sap in the spring tree, and she trembled under it.

Newbury too had grown a little pale and silent. But when his eyes met hers there was that in them under which her own wavered.

"Come and see the flowers in the wood," he said, softly, and leading the way, he took her out of range of those observers in the garden; deep into a noble beech wood that rose out of the garden, climbing through a sea of wild hyacinths to a hilltop.

A mossy path offered itself, winding through the blue. And round them closed the great beech trees, in a marvel of young green, sparkling and quivering under the shafts of light that struck through the wood. The air was balm. And the low music of the wood-pigeons seemed to be there for them only; a chorus of earth's creatures, wooing them to earth's festival.

Unconsciously, in the deep heart of the wood, their footsteps

Mrs. Humphry Ward

slackened. She heard her name breathed.

"Marcia!"

She turned, submissive, and saw him looking down upon her with adoring tenderness, his lips gravely smiling.

"Yes!"

She raised her eyes to his, all her ripe beauty one flush. He put his arms round her, whispering:

"Marcia! will you come to me—will you be my wife?"

She leaned against him in a trance of happiness, hiding her face, yet not so that his lips could not find hers. So this was love?—the supreme of life?

They stood so in silence a little. Then, still holding her, he drew her within the low feathering branches of a giant tree, where was a fallen log. He placed her on it, and himself beside her.

"How wonderful that you should love me, that you should let me love you!" he said, with passionate emotion. "Oh, Marcia, am I worthy—shall I make you happy?"

"That is for me to ask!" Her mouth was trembling now, and the tears were in her eyes. "I'm not nearly as good as you, Edward. I shall often make you angry with me."

"Angry!" He laughed in scorn. "Could any one, ever, be angry with you, Marcia! Darling, I want you to help me so! We'll help each other—to live as we ought to live. Isn't God good? Isn't life wonderful?"

She pressed his hand for answer. But the intensity of his joy, as she read it in his eyes, had in it—for her—and for the moment—just a shade of painfulness. It seemed to claim something from her that she could not quite give—or that she might not be able to give. Some secret force in her cried out in protest. But the slight shrinking passed almost immediately. She threw off her hat, and lifted her beautiful brow to him in a smiling silence. He drew her to him again, and as she felt the pressure of his arm about her, heart and soul yielded utterly. She was just the young girl, loving and beloved.

"Do your father and mother really approve?" she asked at last as she disengaged herself, and her hands went up to her hot cheeks, and then to her hair, to smooth it back into something like order.

"Let us go and see." He raised her joyously to her feet.

She looked at him a little wistfully.

"I'm rather afraid of them, Edward. You must tell them not to expect too much. And I shall always—want to be myself."

"Darling! what else could they, could any one want for you— or for me!" The tone showed him a little startled, perhaps stung, by her words. And he added, with a sudden flush:

"Of course I know what Coryston will say to you. He seems to think us all hypocrites and tyrants. Well—you will judge. I won't defend my father and mother. You will soon know them. You will see what their lives are."

He spoke with feeling. She put her hand in his, responding.

"You'll write to Corry—won't you? He's a dreadful thorn in all our sides; and yet—" Her eyes filled with tears.

"You love him?" he said, gently. "That's enough for me."

"Even if he's rude and violent?" she pleaded.

"Do you think I can't keep my temper—when it's *your*

brother? Try me."

He clasped her hand warm and close in his strong fingers. And as she moved through the young green of the woodland he saw her as a spirit of delight, the dark masses of her hair, her white dress and all her slender grace flecked by the evening sun. These were moments, he knew, that could never come again; that are unique in a man's history. He tried to hold and taste them as they passed; tormented, like all lovers, by what seems, in such crises, to be the bitter inadequacy and shallowness of human feeling.

They took a more round-about path home than that which had brought them into the wood, and at one point it led them through a clearing from which there was a wide view of undulating ground scattered with houses here and there. One house, a pleasant white-walled dwelling, stood conspicuously forward amid copses a couple of fields away. Its garden surrounded by a sunk fence could be seen, and the figure of a lady walking in it. Marcia stopped to look.

"What a charming place! Who lives there?"

Newbury's eyes followed hers. He hesitated a moment.

"That is the model farm."

"Mr. Betts's farm?"

"Yes. Can you manage that stile?"

Marcia tripped over it, scorning his help. But her thoughts were busy with the distant figure. Mrs. Betts, no doubt; the cause of all the trouble and talk in the neighborhood, and the occasion of Corry's outrageous letter to Lord William.

"I think I ought to tell you," she said, stopping, with a look of perplexity, "that Corry is sure to come and talk to me—about that story. I don't think I can prevent him."

"Won't you hand him on to me? It is really not a story for your ears."

He spoke gravely.

"I'm afraid Cony would call that shirking. I—I think perhaps I had better have it out with him—myself. I remember all you said to me!"

"I only want to save you." His expression was troubled, but not without a certain touch of sternness that she perceived. He changed the subject immediately, and they walked on rapidly toward the garden.

Lady William first perceived them—perceived, too, that they were hand in hand. She broke off her chat with Sir Wilfrid Bury under the limes, and rising in sudden agitation she hurried across the lawn to her husband.

The Dean and Sir Louis Ford had been discussing Woman Suffrage over their cigarettes, and Sir Louis, who was a stout opponent, had just delivered himself of the frivolous remark— in answer to some plea of the Dean's on behalf of further powers for the female sex:

"Oh, no doubt, somewhere between the Harem and the Woolsack, it will be necessary to draw the line!"—when they too caught sight of the advancing figures.

The Dean's eyebrows went up. A smile, most humorous and human, played over his round cheeks and button mouth.

"Have they drawn it? Looks like it!" he said, under his breath.

"Eh!—what?" Sir Louis, the most incorrigible of elderly gossips, eagerly put up his eyeglass. "Do you suspect anything?"

Five persons were presently gathered in the library, and Marcia was sitting with her hand in Lady William's. Everybody except Lady Coryston was in a happy agitation, and trying to conceal it. Even Lord William, who was not without his doubts and qualms, was deeply moved, and betrayed a certain moisture in his eyes, as he concluded his old world speech of welcome and blessing to his son's betrothed. Only Lady Coryston preserved an unbroken composure. She was indeed quite satisfied. She had kissed her daughter and given her consent without the smallest demur, and she had conveyed both to Newbury and his father in a few significant words that Marcia's portion would be worthy of their two families. But the day's event was already thrust aside by her burning desire to get hold of Sir Louis Ford before dinner, and to extract from him the latest and most confidential information that a member of the Opposition could bestow as to the possible date for the next general election. Marcia's affair was thoroughly nice and straightforward—just indeed what she had expected. But there would be plenty of time to talk about it after the Hoddon Grey visit was over; whereas Sir Louis was a rare bird not often to be caught.

"My dear," said Lord William in his wife's ear, "Perry must be informed of this. There must be some mention of it in our service to-night."

She assented. Newbury, however, who was standing near, caught the remark, and looked rather doubtfully at the speaker.

"You think so, father?"

"Certainly, my dear son, certainly."

Neither Marcia nor her mother heard. Newbury approached his betrothed, but perceived that there was no chance of a private word with her. For by this time other guests had been summoned to receive the great announcement, and a general flutter of laughter and congratulations was filling the room.

The Dean, who had had his turn with Marcia, and was now turning over books, looked at her keenly from time to time.

"A face," he thought, "of much character, promising developments. Will she fit herself to this medieval household? What will they make of her?"

Sir Louis, after paying his respects and expressing his good wishes to the betrothed pair, had been resolutely captured by Lady Coryston. Lord William had disappeared.

Suddenly into the talk and laughter there struck the sound of a loud and deep-toned bell. Lady William stood up with alacrity. "Dear me!—is it really chapel-time? Lady Coryston, will you come?"

Marcia's mother, her face stiffening, rose unwillingly.

"What are we supposed to do?" asked the Dean, addressing Newbury.

"We have evensong in chapel at seven," said Newbury. "My father set up the custom many years ago. It gathers us all together better than evening prayer after dinner."

His tone was simple and matter-of-fact. He turned radiantly to Marcia, and took her hand again. She followed him in some bewilderment, and he led her through the broad corridor which gave access to the chapel.

"Rather unusual, this, isn't it?" said Sir Louis Ford to Lady Coryston as they brought up the rear. His face expressed a certain restrained amusement. If there was a convinced agnostic in the kingdom it was he. But unlike the woman at his side he could always take a philosophical interest in the religious customs of his neighbors.

"Most unusual!" was the emphatic reply. But there was no help for it. Lady Coryston followed, willy-nilly.

Marcia, meanwhile, was only conscious of Newbury. As they entered the chapel together she saw his face transfigured. A mystical "recollection," shutting him away completely from the outside world, sweeping like a sunlit cloud even between himself and her, possessed it. She felt suddenly forsaken—altogether remote from him.

But he led her on, and presently they were kneeling together under a great crucifix of primitive Italian work, while through the dusk of the May evening gleamed the lamps of the chapel, and there arose on all sides of her a murmur of voices repeating the Confession. Marcia was aware of many servants and retainers; and she could see the soldierly form of Lord William kneeling in the distance, with Lady William beside him. The chapel seemed to her large and splendid. It was covered with painting and mosaic; and she felt the sharp contrast between it and the simple bareness of the house to which it was attached.

"What does all this mean?" she seemed to be asking herself. "What does it mean for *me*? Can I play my part in it?"

What had become of that early antagonism and revolt which she had expressed to "Waggin"? It had not protected her in the least from Newbury's growing ascendancy! She was indeed astonished at her own pliancy! In how short a time had she allowed Newbury's spell upon her to drive her earlier vague fears of his surroundings and traditions out of her mind!

And now it returned upon her intensified—that cold, indefinite fear, creeping through love and joy.

She turned again to look beseechingly at Newbury. But it seemed to her that she was forgotten. His eyes were on the altar—absorbed.

And presently, aghast, she heard her own name! In the midst of the General Thanksgiving, at the point where mention may be made of individual cases, the Chaplain suddenly paused to give thanks in a voice that possessed a natural and slightly disagreeable tremor, for the "happy betrothal of Edward Newbury and Marcia Coryston."

An audible stir and thrill ran through the chapel, subsiding at once into a gulf of intense silence. Marcia bowed her head with the rest; but her cheeks burned, and not only with a natural shyness. The eyes of all these kneeling figures seemed to be upon her, and she shrank under them. "I ought to have been asked," she thought, resentfully. "I ought to have been asked!"

When they left the chapel, Newbury, pale and smiling, bent over her appealingly.

"Darling!—you didn't mind?"

She quickly withdrew her hand from his.

"Don't you dine at half past eight? I really must go and dress."

And she hurried away, without waiting for him to guide her through the unknown house. Breathlessly she ran up-stairs and found her room. The sight of her maid moving about, of the lights on the dressing-table, of the roses, and her dress laid out upon the bed, brought her sudden and unspeakable relief. The color came back to her cheeks, she began to chatter to her maid about everything and nothing—laughing at any trifle, and yet feeling every now and then inclined to cry. Her maid dressed her in pale pink and told her plainly when the last hook was fastened and the last string tied that she had never looked better.

"But won't you put on these roses, miss?"

She pointed to the bunch that Lady William had gathered.

Marcia pinned them into her belt, and stood a moment looking at her reflection in the glass. Not in mere girlish vanity! Something much stronger and profounder entered in. She seemed to be measuring her resources against some hostile force—to be saying to herself:

"Which of us is to yield? Perhaps not I!"

* * * * *

Yet as soon as Marcia entered the drawing-room, rather late, to find all the party assembled, the tension of her mood dropped, thawed by the sheer kindness and good will of the people round her. Lord William was resplendent in a button-hole and new dress-clothes; Lady William had put on her best gown and some family jewels that never saw the light except on great occasions; and when Marcia entered, the friendly affectionate looks that greeted her on all sides set her blushing once more, and shamed away the hobgoblins that had been haunting her. She was taken in to dinner by Lord William and treated as a queen. The table in the long, low dining-room shone with flowers and some fine old silver which the white-haired butler had hurriedly produced from the family store. Beside Marcia's plate lay a bunch of lilies-of-the-valley which the no less ancient head gardener had gathered and tied with a true-lover's knot, in the interval between chapel and dinner. And opposite to her sat the man she was to marry, composed and gay, careful to spare his betrothed embarrassment, ready to talk politics with Sir Louis Ford and cathedral music with the Dean; yet, through it all, so radiantly and transparently happy that his father and mother, at any rate, could not look at him without melting memories of their own youth, which sometimes, and for a moment, made talk difficult.

After dinner Sir Wilfrid Bury found Lady Coryston in a secluded corner, deep in the evening papers which had just arrived. He sat down beside her.

"Well, how are you feeling?"

"If we could but revive the duel!" said Lady Coryston, looking up with eyes aflame.

"Gracious! For what and whom? Do you want to shoot your future son-in-law for taking her from you?"

"Who—Marcia? Nonsense!" said Lady Coryston, impatiently. "I was talking of this last speech of Glenwilliam's, attacking us landlords. If the duel still existed he would either never have made it or he would have been shot within twenty-four hours!"

"Hang Glenwilliam!" Sir Wilfrid's tone was brusque. "I want to talk about Marcia!"

Lady Coryston turned slowly round upon him.

"What's wrong with Marcia? I see nothing to talk about."

"Wrong! You unnatural woman! I want to know what you feel about it. Do you really like the young man? Do you think he's good enough for her?"

"Certainly I like him. A very well disposed fellow. I hope he'll manage her properly. But if you want to know what I think of his family"—she dropped her voice—"I can only say that although their virtues no doubt are legion, the atmosphere of this house is to me positively stifling. You feel it as you cross the threshold. It is an atmosphere of sheer tyranny! What on earth do they mean by bundling us into chapel like that?"

"Tyranny! *You* call it tyranny!" Sir Wilfrid's eyes danced.

"Certainly," said Lady Coryston, stiffly. "What else should I call it? One's soul is not one's own."

Sir Wilfrid settled down on the sofa beside her, and devoted himself to drawing her out. Satan rebuking sin was a spectacle of which he never tired, and the situation was the more amusing because he happened to have spent the morning in remonstrating with her—to no purpose whatever—on the manner in which she was treating her eldest son.

CHAPTER VIII

While these events were happening at Hoddon Grey, Reginald Lester was passing a solitary Sunday at Coryston, until the afternoon, at least, when visitors appeared. To be left to himself, the solitary inhabitant, save for the servants, of the great classical pile; to be able to wander about it as he liked, free to speculate on its pictures and engravings; to rummage the immense collection of china in the basement rooms which no one but himself ever looked at; to examine some new corner of the muniment-room, and to ponder the strange and gruesome collection of death-masks, made by Coryston's grandfather, and now ranged in one of the annexes of the library—gave him endless entertainment. He was a born student, in whom the antiquarian instincts would perhaps ultimately overpower the poetic and literary tastes which were now so strong in him; and on Sunday, when he put aside his catalogue, the miscellaneous possessions of an historic house represented for him a happy hunting-ground through which he was never tired of raiding.

But on Sunday, also, he generally gave some time to writing the journal of the preceding week. He had begun it in the hopes of attaining thereby a more flexible and literary style than the methods of his daily research allowed, and with various Stevensonian ambitions dinning in his head. Why should he not make himself a *writer*, like other people?

But the criticisms of books, the records of political or literary conversation, with which the parchment-bound volume had been filled for some time, had been gradually giving place to something quite different, and it had become more necessary than ever that the book should be carefully locked when done with, and put away in his most private drawer. For instance:

"What is happening, or what has probably already happened, yesterday or to-day, at Hoddon Grey? It is very easy to guess. N. has been gaining ground steadily ever since he has been able to see her away from the distracting influences of London. What is impressive and unusual in his character has room to show itself; and there are no rival forces. And yet—I doubt very much whether it would answer his purpose that she should see much of his home. She will never endure any home of her own run on the same lines; for at bottom she is a pagan, with the splendid pagan virtues, of honor, fairness, loyalty, pity, but incapable by temperament of those particular emotions on which the life of Hoddon Grey is based. Humility, to her, is a word and a quality for which she has no use; and I am sure that she has never been sorry for her 'sins,' in the religious sense, though often, it seems to me, her dear life just swings hour by hour between the two poles of impulse and remorse. She passionately wants something and must get it; and then she is consumed with fear lest in the getting it she should have injured or trampled on some one else.

"Of late she has come in here—to the library—much more frequently. I am sure she feels that I care deeply what happens to her; and I sometimes am presumptuous enough to think that she wishes me to understand and approve her.

"It has grown up inevitably—this affair; but N. little realizes how dangerous his position is. Up to a certain point the ascetic element in him and his philosophy will attract her—will draw the moth to the candle. All strong-willed characters among women are attracted by the austere, the ascetic powers in men. The history of all religious movements is there to prove it. But there are tremendous currents in our modern life making against such men as Newbury—their ideals and traditions. And to one or other of those currents it always seems to me that she is committed. She does not know it—does not dream, perhaps, whither she is being carried; but all the same there are 'murmurs and scents' from 'the infinite sea' of free knowledge and experiment which play upon her, and will never play upon Newbury.

"Coryston will make a great effort to upset the engagement—if it is an engagement; that I can see. He thinks himself justified, on the ground that she will be committing herself to an inhuman and antisocial view of life; and he will work upon her through this painful Betts case. I wonder if he will succeed. Is he really any more tolerant than his mother? And can toleration in the active-spirited be ever anything more than approximate? 'When I speak of toleration I mean not tolerated Popery,' said Milton. Lady Coryston can't tolerate her son, and Coryston can't tolerate Newbury. Yet all three must somehow live together and make a world. Doesn't that throw some light on the ideal function of women? Not voting—not direct party-fighting—but the creation of a spiritual atmosphere in which the nation may do its best, and may be insensibly urged to do its best, in fresh, spontaneous ways, like a plant flowering in a happy climate—isn't that what women might do for us?—instead of taking up with all the old-fashioned, disappointing, political machinery, that men have found out? Meanwhile Lady Coryston of course wants all the women of her sort to vote, but doesn't see how it is to be done without letting in the women of all and any sort—to vote against her.

"I have about half done my cataloguing, and have been writing some letters to Germany this morning with a view to settling on some university work there for the winter. A big book on the rise and fall of Burgundy suggests itself to me; and already I hug the thought of it. Lady Coryston has paid me well for this job, and I shall be able to do what I like for a year, and give mother and Janie some of the jam and frills of life. And who knows if I sha'n't after all be able to make my living out of what I like best? If I only could *write*! The world seems to be waiting for the historian that can write.

"But meanwhile I shall always be glad of this year with the Corystons. How much longer will this rich, leisurely, aristocratic class with all its still surviving power and privileges exist among us? It is something that obviously is in process of transmutation and decay; though in a country like England the process will be a very slow one. Personally I greatly prefer this landlord stratum to the top stratum of the trading and manufacturing world. There are buried seeds in it, often of rare and splendid kinds, which any crisis brings to life—as in the Boer war; and the mere cult of family and inheritance implies, after all, something valuable in a world that has lately grown so poor in all cults.

"Mother and daughter here show what is going on. Lady Coryston is just the full-blown *tyrannus*. She has no doubt whatever about her right to rule, and she rules for all she's worth. At the same time she knows that Demos has the last word, and she spends her time in the old see-saw between threats and cajolery. The old vicar here has told me astonishing tales of her—how she turned her own sister out-of-doors and never spoke to her afterward because she married a man who ratted to the Liberals, and the wife went with him; how her own husband dreaded her if he ever happened to differ from her politically, and a sort of armed neutrality between her and Coryston was all that could be hoped for at the best of times.

"The poor people here—or most of them—are used to her, and in a way respect her. They take her as inevitable—like the rent or the east wind; and when she sends them coal and blankets, and builds village halls for them, they think they might be worse off. On the other hand, I don't see that Coryston makes much way among them. They think his behavior to his mother unseemly; and if they were he, they would use all his advantages without winking. At the same time, there is a younger generation growing up in the village and on the farms—not so much there, however!—which is going to give Lady Coryston trouble. Coryston puzzles and excites them. But they, too, often look askance; they wonder what he, personally, is going to get out of his campaign.

"And then—Marcia? For in this book, this locked book, may I not call her by her name? Well, she is certainly no prophetess among these countryfolk. She takes up no regular duties among the poor, as the women of her family have probably always done. She is not at her ease with them; nor they with her. When she tries to make friends with them she is like a ship teased with veering winds, and glad to shrink back into harbor. And yet when something does really touch her—when something makes her *feel*—that curious indecision in her nature hardens into something irresistible. There was a half-witted girl in the village, ill-treated and enslaved by a miserly old aunt. Miss Coryston happened to hear of it from her maid, who was a relation of the girl. She went and bearded the aunt, and took the girl away bodily in her pony-cart. The scene in the cottage garden—Marcia with her arm round the poor beaten and starved creature, very pale, but keeping her head, and the old virago shrieking at her heels—must have been worth seeing. And there is an old man—a decrepit old road-mender, whose sight was injured in a shooting accident. She likes his racy talk, and she never forgets his Christmas present or his birthday, and often drops in to tea with him and his old wife. But that's because it amuses her. She goes to see them for precisely the same reasons that she would pay a call in Mayfair; and it's inspiriting to see how they guess, and how they like it. You perceive that she is shrinking all the time from the assumptions on which her mother's life is based, refusing to make them her own, and yet she doesn't know what to put in their place. Does Coryston, either?

"But the tragic figure—the tragic possibility—in all this family *galere* at the present moment, of course, is Arthur. I know, because of our old Cambridge friendship—quite against my will—a good deal about the adventure into which he has somehow slipped; and one can only feel that any day may bring the storm. His letter to me yesterday shows that he is persecuting the lady with entreaties, that she is holding him off, and that what Lady Coryston may do when she knows will greatly affect what the young lady will do. I don't believe for one moment that she will marry a penniless A. She has endless opportunities, and, I am told, many proposals—"

The journal at this point was abruptly closed and locked away. For the writer of it, who was sitting at an open window of the library, became aware of the entrance of a motor into the forecourt of the house. Arthur Coryston was sitting in it. When he perceived Lester at the window he waved to the librarian, and jumping from the car as it drew up at the front door, he came across the court to a side door, which gave access to the library staircase.

As he entered the room Lester was disagreeably struck by his aspect. It was that of a man who has slept ill and drunk unwisely. His dress was careless, his eyes haggard, and all the weaknesses of the face seemed to have leaped to view, amid the general relaxation of *tenue* and dignity. He came up to the chair at which Lester was writing, and flung himself frowning into a chair beside it.

"I hear mother and Marcia are away?"

"They have gone to Hoddon Grey for the Sunday. Didn't you know?"

"Oh yes, I knew. I suppose I knew. Mother wrote something," said the young man, impatiently. "But I have had other things to think about."

Lester glanced at him, but without speaking. Arthur rose from his seat, thrust his hands into his pockets, and began to pace the polished floor of the library. The florid, Georgian decoration of ceiling and walls, and the busts of placid gentlemen with curling wigs which stood at intervals among the glass cases, wore an air of trivial or fatuous repose beside the hunted young fellow walking up and down. Lester resolutely forbore to cross-examine him. But at last the walk came to an abrupt stop.

"Here's the last straw, Lester! Have you heard what mother

wants me to do? There's to be a big Tory meeting here in a month—mother's arranged it all—not a word to me with your leave, or by your leave!—and I'm to speak at it and blackguard Glenwilliam! I have her letter this morning. I'm not allowed a look in, I tell you! I'm not consulted in the least. I'll bet mother's had the bills printed already!"

"A reply, of course, to the Martover meeting?"

"I dare say. D—n the Martover meeting! But what *taste*!—two brothers slanging at each other—almost in the same parish. I declare women have no taste!—not a ha'porth. But I won't do it—and mother, just for once, will have to give in."

He sat down again and took the cigarette which Lester handed him—no doubt with soothing intentions. And indeed his state of excitement and agitation appeared nothing less than pitiable to the friend who remembered the self-complacent young orator, the budding legislator of early April.

"You are afraid of being misunderstood?"

"If I attack her father, as mother wishes me to attack him," said the young man, with emphasis, looking up, "Enid Glenwilliam will never speak to me again. She makes that quite plain."

"She ought to be too clever!" said Lester, with vivacity. "Can't she discriminate between the politician and the private friend?"

Arthur shook his head.

"Other people may. She doesn't. If I get up in public and call Glenwilliam a thief and a robber—and what else can I call him, with mother looking on?—there'll be an end of my chances for good and all. She's *fanatical* about her father! She's pulled me up once or twice already about him. I tell you—it's rather fine, Lester!—upon my soul, it is!"

And with a countenance suddenly softening and eyes shining, Arthur turned his still boyish looks upon his friend.

"I can quite believe it. They're a very interesting pair.... But—I confess I'm thinking of Lady Coryston. What explanation can you possibly give? Are you prepared to take her into your confidence?"

"I don't know whether I'm prepared or not. Whatever happens I'm between the devil and the deep sea. If I tell her, she'll break with me; and if I don't tell her, it won't be long before she guesses for herself!"

There was a pause, broken at last by Lester, whose blue eyes had shown him meanwhile deep in reflection. He bent forward.

"Look here, Arthur!—can't you make a last effort, and get free?"

His companion threw him a queer resentful look, but Lester persisted:

"You know what I think. You won't make each other happy. You belong to two worlds which won't and can't mix. Her friends can never be your friends nor your friends hers. You think that doesn't matter now, because you're in love. But it does matter—and it'll tell more and more every year."

"Don't I know it?" cried Arthur. "She despises us all. She looks upon us all—I mean, us people, with land and money and big houses—just as so much grist to her father's mill, so many fat cattle for him to slaughter."

"And yet you love her!"

"Of course I do! I can't make you understand, Lester! She doesn't speechify about these things—she never speechifies to me, at least. She mocks at her own side—just as much as ours.

Mrs. Humphry Ward

But it's her father she worships—and everything that he says and thinks. She adores him—she'd go to the stake for him any day. And if you want to be a friend of hers, lay a finger on him, and you'll see! Of course it's mad—I know that. But I'd rather marry her mad than any other woman sane!"

"All the same you *could* break it off," persisted Lester.

"Of course I could. I could hang—or poison—or shoot myself, I suppose, if it comes to that. It would be much the same thing. If I do have to give her up, I shall cut the whole business—Parliament—estates—everything!"

The quarter-decking began again; and Lester waited patiently on a slowly subsiding frenzy. At last he put a question.

"What are your chances?"

"With her? I don't know. She encourages me one day, and snubs me the next. But one thing I do know. If I attend that meeting, and make the sort of speech I should have made three months ago without turning a hair—and if I don't make it, mother will know the reason why!—it's all up with me."

"Why don't you apply to Coryston?"

"What—to give up the other meeting? He's very likely to climb down, isn't he?—with his damned revolutionary nonsense. He warned us all that he was coming down here to make mischief—and, by Jove, he's doing it!"

"I say, who's taking my name in vain?" said a high-pitched voice.

Lester turned to the doorway, and beheld a protruding head, with glittering greenish eyes, alive with laughter. Coryston slowly emerged, and closed the door behind him.

"Arthur, my boy, what's up now?"

Arthur paused, looked at him angrily, but was too sore and sulky to reply. Lester mildly summarized the situation. Coryston whistled. Then he deposited the butterfly-net and tin case he had been carrying, accepted a cigarette, and hoisting himself onto the corner of a heavy wooden pedestal which held the periwigged bust of an eighteenth-century Coryston, he flung an arm affectionately round the bust's neck, and sat cross-legged, smoking and pondering.

"Bar the meeting for a bit," he said at last, addressing his brother; "we'll come back to it. But meeting or no meeting, I don't see any way out for you, Arthur—upon my soul, I don't!"

"No one ever supposed you would!" cried Arthur.

"Here's your dilemma," pursued Coryston, good-humoredly. "If you engage yourself to her, mother will cut off the supplies. And if mother cuts off the supplies, Miss Glenwilliam won't have you."

"You think everybody but yourself, Corry, mercenary pigs!"

"What do *you* think? Do you see Miss Glenwilliam pursuing love in a garret—a genteel garret—on a thousand a year? For her father, perhaps!—but for nobody else! Her clothes alone would cost a third of it."

No reply, except a furious glance. Coryston began to look perturbed. He descended from his perch, and approaching the still pacing Arthur, he took his arm—an attention to which the younger brother barely submitted.

"Look here, old boy? Am I becoming a beast? Are you sure of her? Is it serious?"

"Sure of her? Good God—if I were!"

He walked to a window near, and stood looking out, so that

Mrs. Humphry Ward

his face could not be seen by his companions, his hands in his pockets.

Coryston's eyebrows went up; the eyes beneath them showed a genuine concern. Refusing a further pull at Lester's cigarettes, he took a pipe out of his pocket, lit it, and puffed away in a brown study. The figure at the window remained motionless. Lester felt the situation too delicate for an outsider's interference, and made a feint of returning to his work. Presently it seemed that Coryston made up his mind.

"Well," he said, slowly, "all right. I'll cut my meeting. I can get Atherstone to take the chair, and make some excuse. But I really don't know that it'll help you much. There's already an announcement of your meeting in the Martover paper yesterday—"

"*No*!" Arthur faced round upon his brother, his cheeks blazing.

"Perfectly true. Mother's taken time by the forelock. I have no doubt she has already written your speech."

"What on earth can I do?" He stood in helpless despair.

"Have a row!" said Coryston, laughing. "A good row and stick to it! Tell mother you won't be treated so—that you're a man, not a school-boy—that you prefer, with many thanks, to write your own speeches—*et cetera*. Play the independence card for all you're worth. It *may* get you out of the mess."

Arthur's countenance began to clear.

"I'm to make it appear a bargain—between you and me? I asked you to give up your show, and you—"

"Oh, any lies you like," said Coryston, placidly. "But as I've already warned you, it won't help you long."

"One gains a bit of time," said the young lover, in a tone

of depression.

"What's the good of it? In a year's time Glenwilliam will still be Glenwilliam—and mother mother. Of course you know you'll break her heart—and that kind of thing. Marcia made me promise to put that before you. So I do. It's perfectly true; though I don't know that I am the person to press it! But then mother and I have always disagreed—whereas *you* have been the model son."

Angry melancholy swooped once more upon Arthur.

"What the deuce have women to do with politics! Why can't they leave the rotten things to us? Life won't be worth living if they go on like this!"

"*Life*," echoed Coryston, with amused contempt. "Your life? Just try offering your billet—with all its little worries thrown in—to the next fellow you meet in the street—and see what happens!"

But the man in Arthur rebelled. He faced his brother.

"If you think that I wouldn't give up this whole show to-morrow"—he waved his hand toward the marble forecourt outside, now glistening in the sun—"for—for Enid—you never made a greater mistake in your life, Corry!"

There was a bitter and passionate accent in the voice which carried conviction. Coryston's expression changed.

"Unfortunately, it wouldn't help you with—with Enid—to give it up," he said, quietly. "Miss Glenwilliam, as I read her—I don't mean anything in the least offensive—has a very just and accurate idea of the value of money."

A sort of impatient groan was the only reply.

But Lester raised his head from his book.

"Why don't you see what Miss Coryston can do?" he asked, looking from one to the other.

"Marcia?" cried Coryston, springing up. "By the way, what are mother and Marcia after, this Sunday? Do you suppose that business is all settled by now?"

He flung out a finger vaguely in the direction of Hoddon Grey. And as he spoke all the softness which had gradually penetrated his conversation with Arthur through all his banter, disappeared. His aspect became in a moment hard and threatening.

"Don't discuss it with me, Coryston," said Lester, rather sharply. "Your sister wouldn't like it. I only mentioned her name to suggest that she might influence your mother in Arthur's case." He rose, and began to put up his papers as he spoke.

"I know that! All the same, why shouldn't we talk about her? Aren't you a friend?—her friend?—our friend?—everybody's friend?" said Coryston, peremptorily. "Look here!—if Marcia's really going to marry Newbury!"—he brought his hand down vehemently on Lester's table—"there'll be another family row. Nothing in the world will prevent my putting the Betts' case before Marcia! I have already warned her that I mean to have it out with her, and I have advised Mrs. Betts to write to her. If she can make Newbury hear reason—well and good. If she can't—or if she doesn't see the thing as she ought, herself— well!—we shall know where we are!"

"Look here, Corry," said Arthur, remonstrating, "Edward Newbury's an awfully good chap. Don't you go making mischief!"

"Rather hard on your sister, isn't it?"—the voice was Lester's— "to plunge her into such a business, at such a time!"

"If she's happy, let her make a thank-offering!" said the

inexorable Coryston. "Life won't spare her its facts—why should we? Arthur!—come and walk home with me!"

Arthur demurred, stipulated that he should not be expected to be civil to any of Coryston's Socialist lodgers—and finally let himself be carried off.

Lester was left once more to the quiet of the library.

"I have advised Mrs. Betts to write to her!"

What a shame! Why should a girl in her first love-dream be harassed with such a problem—be brought face to face with such "old, unhappy, far-off things"? He felt a fierce indignation with Coryston. And as he again sat solitary by the window, he lost himself in visualizations of what was or might be going on that summer afternoon at Hoddon Grey. He knew the old house—for Lord William had once or twice courteously invited the Coryston librarian to examine such small treasures as he himself possessed. He could see Marcia in its paneled rooms and on its old lawns—Marcia and Newbury.

Gradually his head dropped on his hands. The sun crept along the library floor in patches of orange and purple, as it struck through the lozenges of old painted glass which bordered the windows. No sound except the cooing of doves, and the note of a distant cuckoo from the river meadows.

He did his best to play the cynic with himself. He told himself that such painful longings and jealous revolts as he was conscious of are among the growing-pains of life, and must be borne, and gradually forgotten. He had his career to think of—and his mother and sister, whom he loved. Some day he too would marry and set up house and beget children, framing his life on the simple strenuous lines made necessary by the family misfortunes. It would have been easier, perhaps, to despise wealth, if he and his had never possessed it, and if his lack of it were not the first and sufficient barrier which divided him from Marcia Coryston. But his nature was sound and sane; it looked life in the face—its gifts and its denials, and those stern joys which the mere wrestle with experience brings to the fighting spirit. He had soon reconquered cheerfulness; and when Arthur returned, he submitted to be talked to for hours on that young man's tangled affairs, handling the youth with that mixture of sympathy and satire which both soothed and teased the sentimentalists who chose to confide in him.

*　*　*　*　*

Next morning Marcia and her mother returned from Hoddon Grey in excellent time. Lady Coryston never lingered over week-ends. Generally the first train on Monday morning saw her depart. In this case she was obliged to give an hour to business talk—as to settlements and so forth—with Lord William, on Monday morning. But when that was over she stepped into her motor with all possible speed.

"What a Sunday!" she said, languidly throwing herself back, with half-closed eyes, as they emerged from the park. Then remembering herself: "But you, my dear, have been happy! And of course they are excellent people—quite excellent."

Marcia sat beside her flushed and rather constrained. She had of course never expected her mother to behave like ordinary mothers on the occasion of a daughter's betrothal. She took her insignificance, the absence of any soft emotion, quite calmly. All the same she had her grievance.

"If only Edward and you—and everybody would not be in such a dreadful hurry!" she said, protesting.

"Seven weeks, my dear child, is enough for any trousseau. And what have you to wait for? It will suit me too, much best. If we put it off till the autumn I should be terribly busy—absolutely taken up—with Arthur's election. Sir Louis Ford tells me they cannot possibly stave off going to the country longer than November. And of course this time I shall have not only the usual Liberal gang—I shall have Coryston to fight!"

"I know. It's appalling!" cried Marcia. "Can't we get him to go away?" Then she looked at her mother uneasily. "I do wish, mother, you hadn't put that notice of Arthur's meeting into the *Witness* without consulting him. Why, you didn't even ask him, before you settled it all! Aren't you afraid of his cutting up rough?"

"Not in the least! Arthur always expects me to settle those things for him. As soon as Coryston had taken that outrageous step, it was imperative that Arthur should speak in his own village. We can't have people's minds in doubt as to what *he* thinks of Glenwilliam, with an election only five months off. I have written to him, of course, fully—without a word of reply! What he has been doing these last weeks I can't imagine!"

Marcia fell into a frowning silence. She knew, alack! a great deal more than she wished to know of what Arthur had been doing. Oh, she hoped Coryston had been able to talk to him—to persuade him! Edward too had promised to see him—immediately. Surely between them they would make him hear reason, before any suspicion reached their mother?

The usual pile of letters awaited Lady Coryston and Marcia on their arrival at home. But before opening hers, Lady Coryston turned to the butler.

"Is Mr. Arthur here?"

"Yes, my lady. He is out now, but he left word he would be in for luncheon."

Lady Coryston's face lit up. Marcia did not hear the question or the answer. She was absorbed in a letter which she happened to have opened first. She read it hastily, with growing astonishment. Then, still holding it, she was hurrying away to her own sitting-room when the butler intercepted her.

"There's a young lady, miss, who wants to see you. I took her to your sitting-room. She said she came from the dressmaker—something you had ordered—very particular."

"Something I had ordered?" said Marcia, mystified. "I don't know anything about it."

She ran up-stairs, still thinking of the letter in her hand.

"I won't see her!" she said to herself, vehemently, "without Edward's leave. He has a right now to say what I shall do. It is different with Coryston. He may argue with me—and with Edward—if he pleases. But Mrs. Betts herself! No—that's too much!"

Her cheeks flushed angrily. She threw open the door of her sitting-room. Some one sitting stiffly on the edge of a chair rose as she entered. To her amazement Marcia perceived a slender woman—a lady—a complete stranger to her, standing in her own private sitting-room, awaiting her arrival. A woman in rather slipshod artistic dress, with hands clasped theatrically, and tears on her cheeks.

"Who are you?" said Marcia, drawing back.

BOOK II

MARCIA

"To make you me how much so e'er I try,
You will be always you, and I be I."

CHAPTER IX

"Miss Coryston, I have done a dreadful thing," said a trembling voice. "I—I have deceived your servants—told them lies—that I might get to see you. But I implore you, let me speak to you!—don't send me away!"

Marcia Coryston looked in amazement at the shrinking, childish creature, standing suppliant before her, and repeated:

"I have not an idea who you are. Please tell me your name."

"My name—is Alice Betts," said the other, after a momentary hesitation. "Oh, perhaps you don't know anything about me. But yet—I think you must; because—because there has been so much talk!"

"Mrs. Betts?" said Marcia, slowly. Her eyes perused the other's face, which reddened deeply under the girl's scrutiny. Marcia, in her pale pink dress and hat, simple, but fresh and perfectly appointed, with her general aspect of young bloom and strength, seemed to take her place naturally against—one might almost say, as an effluence from—the background of

Mrs. Humphry Ward

bright June foliage, which could be seen through the open windows of the room; while Mrs. Betts, tumbled, powdered, and through all the juvenility of her attire—arms bare to the elbow and throat half uncovered, short skirts and shell necklace,—betraying her thirty-five years, belonged quite plainly to the used, autumnal category of her sex.

"Haven't you heard of me?" she resumed, plaintively. "I thought—Lord Coryston—"

She paused, her eyes cast down.

"Oh yes," said Marcia, mechanically. "You have seen my brother? Please sit down."

Mrs. Betts sat down, with a long sigh, still not venturing to look up. Instead she pressed her handkerchief to her eyes; beginning to speak in a broken, sobbing voice.

"If you can't help us, Miss Coryston, I—I don't know what we shall do—my poor husband and I. We heard last night—that at the chapel service—oh! my husband used to read the lessons there for years and years, and now he never goes:—but he heard from one of his men, who was there, about your engagement to Mr. Newbury—and how Mr. Perry gave it out. I am so *ashamed*, Miss Coryston, to be speaking of your private affairs!—I don't know how to excuse myself—"

She looked up humbly. She had large blue eyes in a round fair-complexioned face, and the lids fluttered as though just keeping back the tears.

"Please go on," said Marcia, coldly, quivering with excitement and annoyance. But she had been bred to self-control, and she betrayed nothing.

"And then—well then"—Mrs. Betts covered her face with her hands a moment, removing them with another long and miserable sigh—"my husband and I consulted—and we thought I might come to you and beg you, Miss Coryston, to plead for us—with Mr. Newbury and Lord William! You will be very happy, Miss Coryston—and we—we are so miserable!"

Mrs. Betts raised her eyes again, and this time the tears escaped, ran lightly over her cheek, and fell on her blue silk dress. Marcia, who had placed herself on a chair near, felt uncomfortably touched.

"I am sure nobody wishes to be unkind to you," she said, with embarrassment.

Mrs. Betts bent forward eagerly.

"Then you have heard? You know that John is to be turned out of his farm unless he will give me up?"

But a quieter manner would have served her better. The answer came stiffly:

"I cannot discuss Lord William's affairs."

"Oh dear, oh dear, what am I to do?" cried Mrs. Betts under her breath, turning her eyes from side to side like a hunted thing, and twisting a rag of a handkerchief in her small right hand. Then, suddenly, she broke into vehemence:

"You ought to listen to me!—it is cruel—heartless, if you don't listen! You are going to be happy—and rich—to have everything you can possibly wish for on this earth. How can you—how *can* you refuse—to help anybody as wretched as I am!"

The small, chubby face and slight figure had assumed a certain tragic force. The impression indeed was of some one absolutely at bay, at the bitter end of their resources, and therefore reckless as to what might be thought of them. And yet there was still the slight theatrical touch, as though the speaker observed herself, even in violence.

Marcia, troubled, intimidated, watched her in silence a few moments and then said:

"How can I possibly help you, Mrs. Betts? You shouldn't have come to me—you shouldn't, indeed. I don't know your story, and if I did I shouldn't understand it. Why didn't you ask to see my mother?"

"Lady Coryston would never look at the likes of me!" cried Mrs. Betts. "No, Miss Coryston! I know it's selfish, perhaps—but it's just because you're so young—and so—so happy—that I came to you. You don't know my story—and I can't tell it you—" The speaker covered her face a moment. "I'm not a good woman, Miss Coryston. I never pretended to be. But I've had an awfully hard time—awfully hard! You see," she went on, hurriedly, as though afraid Marcia would stop her, "you see—I was married when I was only seventeen to an old husband. My mother made me—she was dying—and she wanted to be sure I had a home. And he turned against me after a few months. It was a horrible, horrible business. I couldn't tell you what I suffered—I wouldn't for the world. He shut me up, he half starved me, he struck me, and abused me. Then"—she turned her head away and spoke in a choked, rapid voice—"there was another man—he taught me music, and—I was only a child, Miss Coryston—just eighteen. He made me believe he loved me—and I had never had kind things said to me before. It seemed like heaven—and one day—I went off with him—down to a seaside place, and there we stayed. It was wicked. I suppose I ought to have borne up against my life, but I couldn't—there! I couldn't. And so—then my husband divorced me—and for ten years I lived with my old father. The other man—deserted me. I soon found him out. I don't think he meant to be cruel to me. But his people got hold of him. They wouldn't let him marry me. So there I was left, with—with my child." Mrs. Betts threw a shrinking look at Marcia.

The girl flushed suddenly and deeply, but said nothing. Mrs. Betts resumed.

"And I just lived on somehow—with my father—who was a hard man. He hated me for what I'd done; he was always nagging and reproving me. But I couldn't earn money and be independent—though I tried once or twice. I'm not strong—and I'm not clever; and there was the child. So he just had to keep me—and it was bitter—for him and for me. Well, then, last August he was dying, and we went to Colwyn Bay for him, and took a little lodging. And one day on the sands I saw—John Betts—after fifteen years. When I was twenty—he wanted to marry me, but we'd never met since. He came up to me—and oh!—I was glad to see him! We walked along the shore, and I told him everything. Well—he was sorry for me!—and father died—and I hadn't a penny. For what father left only just paid his debts. And I had no prospects in the world, and no one to help me or my boy. So, then, Mr. Betts offered to marry me. He knew all about my divorce—he had seen it in the newspapers years ago. I didn't deceive him—not one little bit. But he knew what Lord William would think. Only it didn't seem to matter, really, to any one but him and me. I was free—and I wasn't going to bring any more disgrace on anybody."

She paused forlornly. In the strong June light, all the lost youth in the small face, its premature withering and coarsening, the traces of rouge and powder, the naturally straight hair tormented into ugly waves, came cruelly into sight. So, too, did the holes in the dirty white gloves, and some rents in the draggled but elaborate dress. Marcia could not help noticing and wondering. The wife of John Betts could not be so very poor!

Suddenly her unwelcome visitor looked up.

"Miss Coryston!—if they take John's farm away, everything that he cares for, everything that he's built up all these years, because of me, I'll kill myself! You tell Mr. Newbury that!"

The little shabby creature had in a moment dropped her shabbiness. Her slight frame stiffened as she sat; the passion in the blue eyes which sought Marcia's was sincere and threatening. Marcia, startled, could only say again in a vaguely troubled voice:

"I am sure nobody wants to harm Mr. Betts, and indeed, indeed, you oughtn't to talk to me like this, Mrs. Betts. I am very sorry for you, but I can't do anything. I would be most improper if I tried to interfere."

"Why?" cried Mrs. Betts, indignantly. "Aren't women in this world to help each other? I know that Lord Coryston has spoken to you and that he means to speak to you. Surely, surely Mr. Newbury will listen to you!—and Lord William will listen to Mr. Edward. You know what they want? Oh, it's too cruel!" She wrung her hands in despair. "They say if we'll separate, if he promises—that I shall be no more his wife—but just a friend henceforward—if we meet a few times in the year, like ordinary friends—then John may keep his farm. And they want me to go and live near a Sisterhood and work for the Sisters—and send the boy to school. Just think what that looks like to me! John and I have found each other after all these years. I have got some one to help me, at last, to make me a better woman"—sobs rose again in the speaker's throat— "some one to love me—and now I must part from him—or else his life will be ruined! You know, Miss Coryston, there's no other place in England like John's place. He's been trying experiments there for years and years with new seeds, and made soils—and all sorts of ways of growing fruit—oh, I don't understand much about it—I'm not clever—but I know he could never do the same things anywhere else—not unless you gave him another life. He'll do it—he'll go—for my sake. But it'll break his heart. And why *should* he go? What's the reason—the *justice* of it?"

Mrs. Betts rose, and with her hands on her sides and the tears on her cheeks she bent over Marcia, gasping, in a kind of frenzy. There was no acting now.

The girl of twenty-two was deeply, painfully moved. She put

out her hands gently, and drew Mrs. Betts down again to the sofa beside her.

"I'm dreadfully sorry for you! I do wish I could help you. But you know what Lord and Lady William think, what Mr. Newbury thinks about divorced people marrying again. You know—how they've set a standard all their lives—for their people here. How can they go against all they've ever preached? You must see their point of view, too. You must think of their feelings. They hate—I'm sure they hate—making any one unhappy. But if one of the chief people on the estate does this, and they think it wicked, how—"

"Ah!" cried Mrs. Betts, eagerly interrupting. "But now please, *please*, Miss Coryston, listen! This is what I want, what I beg you to say to Mr. Newbury! I can't give John up—and he'll never give me up. But I'll go away—I'll go to a little cottage John has—it was his mother's, in Charnwood Forest—far away from everybody. Nobody here will ever know! And John will come to see me, whenever he can, whenever his work will let him. He will come over in the motor—he's always running about the country—nobody would ever notice. It might be said we'd separated—so we should have separated—as far as spending our lives together goes. But I should sometimes—sometimes—have my John!—for my own—my very own—and he would sometimes have me!"

Sobs came tearing through, and, bowing her face upon the sofa, Mrs. Betts shook from head to foot.

Marcia sat silent, but strangely conscious of new horizons of feeling—of a deepening life. This was the first time she had ever come across such an experience, touched so nearly on passions and sins which had hitherto been to her as stage phantoms moving in a far distance. The girl of to-day, whatever class she belongs to, is no longer, indeed, reared in the conventional innocence of the mid-Victorian moment—a moment differing wholly from that immediately before it, no less than from those which have come after it. The manners, the plays, the talk of our generation attack such an innocence at every turn. But in place of an indirect and hearsay knowledge, here, in this humble, shabby instance, was, for the first time, the real stuff—the real, miserable thing, in flesh and blood. That was new to her.

And, in a flash of memory and association, there passed through her mind the vision of the Opera House blazing with lights—Iphigenia on the stage, wailing at her father's knees in an agony of terror and despair, and Newbury's voice:

"*This* is the death she shrinks from—"

And again, as the beautiful form, erect and calm once more, swept stately to its doom:

"And this—is the death she *accepts!*"

Newbury's face, as he spoke, was before her, quietly smiling, its handsome features alive with an exaltation which had both chilled and fascinated the girl looking at him. As she remembered it the thought arose—"*he* would accept any martyrdom for himself, in defense of what he believes and loves—and *therefore* he will inflict it inexorably on others. But that's the point! For oneself, yes—but for others who suffer and don't believe!—suffer horribly!"

A look of resolution came into the young face. She tried to rouse Mrs. Betts.

"Please don't cry so!" she said, in distress. "I see what you mean. I'll try and put it to Mr. Newbury. Nobody here, you think, need know anything about you? They'd suppose you'd separated? Mr. Betts would live here, and you would live somewhere else. That's what you mean, isn't it? That's all anybody need know?"

Mrs. Betts raised herself.

"That's it. Of course, you see, we might have pretended to accept Lord William's conditions, and then have deceived him. But my husband wouldn't do that. He simply doesn't admit that anybody else here has any right to interfere with our private affairs. But he won't tell lies to Lord William and Mr. Edward. If they won't, they won't!"

She sat up, drearily controlling herself, and began to smooth back her hair and put her hat straight. But in the middle of it she caught Marcia's hand:

"Miss Coryston! you're going to marry Mr. Newbury—because you love him. If I lose John who will ever give me a kind word—a kind look again? I thought at last—I'd found—a little love. Even bad people"—her voice broke—"may rejoice in that, mayn't they? Christ didn't forbid them that."

Her piteous look hung on her companion. The tears sprang to Marcia's eyes. Yet her temperament did not tend to easy weeping; and at the root of her mind in this very moment were feelings of repulsion and of doubt, mingled with impressions of pity. But the hours at Hoddon Grey had been hours of deep and transforming emotion; they had left her a more sensitive and responsive human being.

"I'll do what I can," she said, with slow emphasis. "I promise you that I'll speak to Mr. Newbury."

Mrs. Betts gave her effusive thanks which somehow jarred on Marcia; she was glad when they were over and Mrs. Betts rose to go. That her tearful and disheveled aspect might escape the servants Marcia took her down a side staircase of the vast house, and piloted her through some garden paths. Then the girl herself, returning, opened a gate into a wood, where an undergrowth of wild roses was just breaking into flower, and was soon pacing a mossy path out of sight and sound of the house.

She found herself in a strange confusion of mind. She still saw the small tear-stained face, the dingy finery, the tormented hair; the story she had just heard was still sounding in her ears. But what really held her was the question: "Can I move Edward? What will he say to me?"

And in the stillness of the wood all the incidents of their Sunday together came back upon her, and she stood breathless and amazed at the change which had passed over her life. Was it really she, Marcia Coryston, who had been drawn into that atmosphere of happy and impassioned religion?—drawn with a hand so gentle yet so irresistible? She had been most tenderly treated by them all, even by that pious martinet, Lord William. And yet, how was it that the general impression was that for the first time in her life she had been "dealt with," disciplined, molded, by those who had a much clearer idea than she herself had of what she was to do and where she was to go? Out of her mother's company she had been hitherto accustomed to be the center of her own young world; to find her wishes, opinions, prejudices eagerly asked for, and deferentially received. And she knew herself naturally wilful, conceited, keen to have her own way.

But at Hoddon Grey, even in the most intimate and beautiful moments of the first love scenes between herself and Newbury, she had seemed to be entering upon—moving—in a world where almost nothing was left free for her to judge; where what she thought mattered very little, because it was taken for granted that she would ultimately think as Hoddon Grey thought; would be cherished, indeed, as the latest and dearest captive of the Hoddon Grey system and the Hoddon Grey beliefs.

And she had begun already to know the exquisite, the intoxicating joys of self-surrender. Every hour had revealed to her something more of Newbury's lofty and singular character. The books and occupations amid which his home life was passed, the letters of his Oxford friends to him, and his to them; one letter in particular, from his chiefest and dearest friend, congratulating him on his engagement, which had arrived that morning—these things had been for Marcia so many steps in a new land, under new stars. The mixture in the man she was to marry, of gaiety, of an overflowing enjoyment of life, expressing itself often in an endless childish joking—with mystical sternness; the eager pursuit of beauty in art and literature, coupled with an unbending insistence on authority, on the Church's law, whether in doctrine or conduct, together with an absolute refusal to make any kind of terms with any sort of "Modernisms," so far at least as they affected the high Anglican ideal of faith and practice—in relation to these facts of Newbury's temperament and life she was still standing bewildered, half yielding and half combative. That she was loved, she knew—knew it through every vein and pulse. Newbury's delight in her, his tender worship of her, seemed to enwrap and encompass her. Now as she sat hidden amid the June trees, trembling under the stress of recollection, she felt herself enskied, exalted by such love. What could he see in her?—what was there in her—to deserve it?

And yet—and yet! Some penetrating instinct to which in this moment of solitude, of unwilling reflection, she could not help but listen, told her that the very soul of him was not hers; that the deepest foundation of his life was no human affection, but the rapture, the compelling vision of a mystical faith. And that rapture she could never share; she knew herself; it was not in her. One moment she could have cried out in despair over her own limitations and disabilities. The next she was jealous; on fire.

Jealous!—that was the real, sadly human truth; jealous, as women have always been, of the faith, or the art, or the friendship, which threatens their hold upon the lover. And there stole upon her as she sat musing, the old, old temptation—the temptation of Psyche—to test and try this man, who was to bring her into bondage, before the bonds were yet quite set. She was honestly touched by Mrs. Betts's story. To her, in her first softness of love, it seemed intolerably hard and odious that two people who clung to each other should be forcibly torn apart; two people whom no law, but only an ecclesiastical scruple condemned. Surely Edward would accept, and persuade his father to accept, the compromise which the husband and wife suggested. If Mrs. Betts withdrew from the scene, from the estate, would not this satisfy everybody? What further scandal could there be? She went on arguing it with herself, but all the time the real, deepest motive at work was not so much sympathy, as a kind of excited restlessness—curiosity. She saw herself pleading with Edward, breaking down his resistance, winning her cause, and then, instead of triumphing, flinging herself into his arms, to ask pardon for daring to fight him.

The happy tears blinded her, and fell unheeded until a mocking reaction dried them.

"Oh, what a fool!—what a fool!"

And running through the wood she came out into the sunshine at its farther end—a blaze of sun upon the lake, its swans, its stone-rimmed islands, and statuary, on the gray-white front of the pillared and porticoed house, stretching interminably. The flowers shone in the stiff beds; a rain of blossom drifted through the air. Everything glittered and sparkled. It was Corinthian, pretentious, artificial; but as Marcia hurried up the broad middle walk between the queer gods and goddesses, whom some pupil of Bernini's had manufactured in Rome for a Coryston of the eighteenth century, she was in love with the scene, which in general she disliked; in love with the summer, in love above all with the quick life of her own mind and body....

There were persons talking in her mother's sitting-room—Sir Wilfrid, Arthur, and Coryston—she perceived them through the open windows. The sight of Arthur suddenly sobered her, and diverted her thoughts. For if Newbury now held the chief place in her mind, her mother still reigned there. She—Marcia—must be on the spot to protect her mother!—in case protection were wanted, and Coryston and Sir Wilfrid had not succeeded yet in bringing that mad fellow to his senses. Ah!

but they had all a new helper and counselor now—in Edward. Let Coryston abuse him to her, if he dared! She would know how to defend him.

She hurried on.

Simultaneously, from the garden door of the library a figure emerged, a man with some books under his arm. She recognized Lester, and a rush of something which was partly shyness and partly a delicious pride came over her, to delay her steps.

They met under the wide open colonnade which carried the first story of the house. Lester came toward her smiling and flushed.

"I've just heard," he said. "I do congratulate you. It's splendid!"

She gave him her hand; and he thought as he looked at her how happiness had beautified and transformed her. All that was imperfect in the face seemed to have fallen into harmony; and her dark bloom had never been so lovely.

"Yes, I'm very happy. He'll keep me in order! At least he'll try." Her eyes danced.

"Everybody seems extremely pleased," he said, walking at her side, and not indeed knowing what to say.

"Except Coryston," replied Marcia, calmly. "I shall have a bad time with him."

"Stand up to him!" he laughed. "His bark is worse than his bite—Ah!—"

A sudden sound of vehement voices overhead—Lady Coryston's voice and Arthur's clashing—startled them both.

"Oh, I must go!" cried Marcia, frowning and paling. "Thank you—thank you so much. Good-by."

And she ran into the house. Lester remained rooted in the shadows of the colonnade for a minute or two, looking after her, with a set, abstracted face. Then the sound of the altercation overhead smote him too with alarm. He moved quickly away lest through the open windows he might catch what was said.

CHAPTER X

Marcia entered her mother's sitting-room in the midst of what seemed a babel of voices. James Coryston, indeed, who was sitting in a corner of the room while Coryston and Sir Wilfrid Bury argued across him, was not contributing to it. He was watching his mother, and she on the other side of the room was talking rapidly to her son Arthur, who could evidently hardly control himself sufficiently to listen to her.

As Marcia came in she heard Arthur say in a loud voice:

"Your attitude, mother, is perfectly unreasonable, and I will not submit to be dictated to like this!"

Marcia, staying her foot half-way across the room, looked at her youngest brother in amazement.

Was this rough-mannered, rough-voiced man, Arthur?—the tame house-brother, and docile son of their normal life? What was happening to them all?

Lady Coryston broke out:

"I repeat—you propose to me, Arthur, a bargain which is no bargain!—"

"A quid without a quo?" interrupted Coryston, who had suddenly dropped his argument with Sir Wilfrid, and had thrown himself on a sofa near his mother and Arthur.

Lady Coryston took no notice of him. She continued to address her youngest-born.

"What Coryston may do—now—after all that has passed is to me a matter of merely secondary importance. When I first saw the notice of the Martover meeting it was a shock to me—I admit it. But since then he has done so many other things—he has struck at me in so many other ways—he has so publicly and scandalously outraged family feeling, and political decency—"

"I really haven't," said Coryston, mildly. "I haven't—if this was a free country."

Lady Coryston flashed a sudden superb look at him and resumed:

"—that I really don't care what Coryston does. He has done his worst. I can't suffer any greater insult than he has already put upon me—"

Coryston shook his head, mutely protesting. He seized a pen from a table near, and began to bite and strip it with an absent face.

"But *you*, Arthur!" his mother went on with angry emphasis, "have still a character to lose or gain. As I have said, it doesn't now matter vitally to me whether Coryston is in the chair or not—I regard him as merely Glenwilliam's cat's-paw—but if *you* let this meeting at Martover pass, you will have weakened your position in this constituency, you will have disheartened your supporters, you will have played the coward—and you will have left your mother disgracefully in the lurch—though that latter point I can see doesn't move you at all!"

James and Sir Wilfrid Bury came anxiously to join the group. Sir Wilfrid approached the still standing and distressed Marcia. Drawing her hand within his arm, he patted it kindly.

"We can't persuade your mother, my dear. Suppose you try."

"Mother, you can't insist on Arthur's going through with the meeting if he doesn't wish to!" said Marcia, with animation. "Do let him give it up! It would be so easy to postpone it."

Lady Coryston turned upon her.

"Everything is easy in your eyes, no doubt, Marcia, except that he should do his duty, and spare my feelings! As a matter of fact you know perfectly well that Arthur has always allowed me to arrange these things for him."

"I don't mean, mother, to do so in future!" said Arthur, resolutely turning upon her. "You *must* leave me to manage my own life and my own affairs."

Lady Coryston's features quivered in her long bony face. As she sat near the window, on a high chair, fully illumined, in a black velvet dress, long-waisted, and with a kind of stand-up ruffle at the throat, she was amazingly Queen Bess. James, who was always conscious of the likeness, could almost have expected her to rise and say in the famous words of the Queen to Cecil—"Little man, little man, your father durst not have said 'must' to me!"

But instead she threw her son a look of furious contempt, with the words:

"You have been glad enough of my help, Arthur, in the past; you have never been able indeed to do without it. I am under no illusions as to your Parliamentary abilities—unaided."

"Mother!—" cried Marcia and James simultaneously.

Coryston shrugged his shoulders. Arthur, breaking from Sir Wilfrid's restraining hand, approached his mother. His face was inflamed with anger, his eyes bloodshot.

"You like to say these cruel things, mother. We have all put up with them long enough. My father put up with them long enough. I intend to think for myself in future. I don't think of Glenwilliam as you do. I know him—and I know his daughter."

The last words were spoken with a special emphasis. A movement of alarm—in Marcia's case, of terror—ran through all the spectators. Sir Wilfrid caught the speaker by the arm, but was impatiently shaken off.

Lady Coryston met her son's eyes with equal passion.

"An intriguer—an unscrupulous intriguer—like himself!" said Lady Coryston, with cutting emphasis.

Arthur's flush turned to pallor. Coryston, springing up, raised a warning hand. "Take care, old fellow!" Marcia and James came forward. But Arthur thrust them aside.

"Mother and I have got to settle this!" He came to lean over her, looking into her face. "I advise you to be careful, mother, of what you say!" There was a dreadful pause. Then he lifted himself and said, with folded arms, slowly, still looking hard at Lady Coryston: "I am—in love—with the lady to whom you refer in that unjustifiable manner. I wish to marry her—and I am doing my best to persuade her to marry me. *Now* you understand perhaps why I didn't wish to attack her father at this particular juncture."

"Arthur!"

Marcia threw herself upon her brother, to lead him away. Coryston, meanwhile, with lifted brows and the prominent greenish eyes beneath them starting out of his head, never ceased to observe his mother. There was trouble—and a sudden softness—in his look.

Silence reigned, for a few painful moments. The eyes of the

two combatants were on each other. The change in Lady Coryston's aspect was something quite different from what is ordinarily described as "turning pale." It represented rather the instinctive and immediate rally of the whole human personality in the presence of danger more deadly than any it has yet encountered. It was the gray rally of strength, not the pallor of fear. She laughed—as she passed her handkerchief over her lips—so Marcia thought afterward—to hide their trembling.

"I thank you for your frankness, Arthur. You will hardly expect me to wish you success in such a love affair, or to further your suit. But your confession—your astonishing confession—does at least supply some reason for your extraordinary behavior. For the present—*for the present*"—she spoke slowly—"I cease to press you to speak at this meeting which has been announced. It can at any rate be postponed. As to the other and graver matter, we will discuss it later—and in private. I must take time to think it over."

She rose. James came forward.

"May I come with you, mother?"

She frowned a little.

"Not now, James, not now. I must write some letters immediately, with regard to the meeting."

And without another look at any of her children, she walked proudly through the room. Sir Wilfrid threw the door open for her, and murmured something in her ear—no doubt an offer of consultation. But she only shook her head; and he closed the door.

Then while Arthur, his hands on his hips, walked restlessly up and down, and Coryston, lying back on the sofa, stared at the ceiling, Marcia, James, and Sir Wilfrid looked at each other in a common dismay.

Mrs. Humphry Ward

Sir Wilfrid spoke first:

"Are we really, Arthur, to take the statement you have just made seriously?"

Arthur turned impatiently.

"Do I look like joking?"

"I wish you did," said Sir Wilfrid, dryly. "It would be a comfort to us."

"Luckily mother doesn't believe a word of it!"

The voice was Coryston's, directed apparently at the Adam decoration of the ceiling.

Arthur stood still.

"What do you mean?"

"No offense. I dare say she believed *you*. But the notion strikes her as too grotesque to be bothered about."

"She may be right there," said Arthur, gloomily, resuming his walk.

"Whether she is or not, she'll take good care, my boy, that nothing comes of it," was Coryston's murmured comment. But the words were lost in his mustache. He turned to look at James, who was standing at the open window gazing into the garden. Something in his brother's meditative back seemed to annoy him. He aimed at it with a crumpled envelope he held in his hand, and hit it. James turned with a start.

"Look here, James—this isn't Hegel—and it isn't Lotze—and it isn't Bergson—it's life. Haven't you got a remark to contribute?"

James's blue eyes showed no resentment.

"I'm very sorry for you all," he said, quietly, "especially for mother."

"Why?"

"Because she's the oldest. We've got the future. She hasn't."

The color rushed to Marcia's face. She looked gratefully at her brother. Sir Wilfrid's gray head nodded agreement.

"Hm!" said Coryston, "I don't see that. At least, of course it has a certain truth. But it doesn't present itself to me as a ground for sparing the older generation. In fact"—he sprang to his feet—"present company—present family excepted—we're being ruined—stick stock ruined—by the elder generation! They're in our way everywhere! Why don't they withdraw— and let *us* take the stage? We know more than they. We're further evolved—we're better informed. And they will insist on pitting their years against our brains all over the field. I tell you the world can't get on like this. Something will have to be done. We're choked up with the older generation."

"Yes, for those who have no reverence—and no pity!" said Marcia.

The low intensity of her voice brought the looks of all three brothers upon her in some evident surprise. None of them had yet ceased to regard their sister as a child, with opinions not worth speculating about. Coryston flushed, involuntarily.

"My withers are unwrung," he said, not without bravado. "You don't understand, my dear. Do I want to do the elder generation any damage? Not at all! But it is time the elder generation withdrew to the chimney-corner and gave us our rights! You think that ungrateful—disrespectful? Good heavens! What do we *care* about the people, our contemporaries, with whom we are always fighting and scuffling in what we are pleased to call *action*? The people who matter to us are the people who rest us—and calm us—and bind up our wounds. If instead of finding a woman to argue and wrestle with I had found just a mother here, knitting by the fire"—he threw out a hand toward Lady Coryston's empty chair—"with time to smile and think and jest—with no ax to grind—and no opinions to push—do you think I shouldn't have been at her feet—her slave, her adorer? Besides, the older generation have ground their axes, and pushed their opinions, long enough—they have had thirty years of it! We should be the dancers now, and they the wall-flowers. And they won't play the game!"

"Don't pretend that you and your mother could ever have played any game—together—Corry," said Sir Wilfrid, sharply.

Coryston looked at him queerly, good-humoredly.

"One might argue till doomsday—I agree—as to which of us said 'won't play' first. But there it is. It's our turn. And you elders won't give it us. Now mother's going to try a little tyranny on Arthur—having made a mess of me. What's the sense of it? It's *we* who have the youth—*we* who have the power—*we* who know more than our elders simply because we were born thirty years later! Let the old submit, and we'll cushion the world for them, and play them out of it with march-music! But they *will* fight us—and they can't win!"

His hands on his sides, Coryston stood confronting them all, his eyes glittering.

"What stuff you do talk, Coryston!" said Arthur, half angrily, half contemptuously. "What good does it do to anybody?" And he resumed his restless walk.

"All flung, too, at a man of peace like me," said the white-haired Sir Wilfrid, with his quiet smile. "It takes all sorts, my dear Corry, to play the game of a generation—old and young. However, the situation is too acute for moralizing. Arthur, are you open to any sort of advice from an old friend?"

"Yes," said Arthur, unwillingly, "if I weren't so jolly sure what it would be."

"Don't be so sure. Come and take me a turn in the lime avenue before lunch."

The two disappeared. James followed them. Marcia, full of disquiet, was going off to find Lady Coryston when Coryston stopped her.

"I say, Marcia—it's true—isn't it? You're engaged to Newbury?"

She turned proudly, confronting him.

"I am."

"I'm not going to congratulate you!" he said, vehemently. "I've got a deal to say to you. Will you allow me to say it?"

"Whenever you like," said Marcia, indifferently.

Coryston perched himself on the edge of a table beside her, looking down upon her, his hands thrust into his pockets.

"How much do you know of this Betts business?" he asked her, abruptly.

"A good deal—considering you sent Mrs. Betts to see me this morning!"

"Oh, she came, did she? Well, do you see any common sense, any justice, any Christianity in forcing that woman to leave her husband—in flinging her out to the wolves again, just as she has got into shelter?"

"In Edward's view, Mr. Betts is not her husband," said Marcia, defiantly. "You seem to forget that fact."

"'Edward's view'?" repeated Coryston, impatiently. "My dear, what's Edward got to do with it? He's not the law of the land. Let him follow his own law if he likes. But to tear up other people's lives by the roots, in the name of some private particular species of law that you believe in and they don't, is really too much—at this time of day. You ought to stop it, Marcia!—and you must!"

"Who's tyrannizing now?" said Marcia. "Haven't other people as good a right to live their beliefs as you?"

"Yes, so long as they don't destroy other people in the process. Even I am not anarchist enough for that."

"Well," said Marcia, coolly, "the Newburys are making it disagreeable for Mr. and Mrs. Betts because they disapprove of them. And what else are you doing with mamma?"

She threw a triumphant look at her brother.

"Stuff and nonsense!" cried Coryston, jumping up. "The weakest 'score' I ever heard. Don't you know the difference between the things that are vital and the things that are superficial—between fighting opinions, and *destroying a life*, between tilting and boxing, however roughly—and *murdering*?"

He looked at her fiercely.

"Who talks of murdering!" The tone was scornful.

"I do! If the Newburys drive those two apart they will have a murder of souls on their conscience. And if you talked to that woman this morning you know it as well as I!"

Marcia faltered a little.

"They could still meet as friends."

"Yes, under the eyes of holy women!—spying lest any impropriety occur! That's the proposal, I understand. Of all the vile and cold-blooded suggestions!—"

And restraining himself with the utmost difficulty, as one might hang on to the curb of a bolting horse, Coryston stamped up and down the room, till speech was once more possible. Then he came to an abrupt pause before his sister.

"Are you really in love with this man, Marcia?"

So challenged, Marcia did not deign to answer. She merely looked up at Coryston, motionless, faintly smiling. He took his answer, dazzled at the same time by her emerging and developing beauty.

"Well, if you do love him," he said, slowly, "and he loves you, *make* him have pity! Those two, also, love each other. That woman is a poor common little thing. She was a poor common little actress with no talent, before her first husband married her—she's a common little actress now, even when she feels most deeply. You probably saw it, and it repelled you. *You* can afford, you see, to keep a fine taste, and fastidious feelings! But if you tear her from that man, you kill all that's good in her—you ruin all her miserable chances. That man's raising her. Bit by bit he'll stamp his own character into hers—because she loves him. And Betts himself, a great, silent, hard man, who has once in his life done a splendid thing!—forgotten himself head over ears for a woman—and is now doing his level best to make a good job of her—you Christians are going to reward him first by breaking his heart, and tearing his life-work to pieces!—God!—I wish your Master were here to tell you what He'd think of it!"

"You're not His only interpreter!" cried Marcia, breathing quickly. "It's in His name that Edward and his father are acting. You daren't say—you daren't *think*—that it's for mere authority's sake—mere domination's sake!"

Coryston eyed her in silence a little.

"No use in arguing this thing on its merits," he said, curtly, at last. "You don't know enough about it, and Newbury and I shouldn't have a single premise in common. But I just warn you and him—it's a ticklish game playing with a pair of human lives like these. They are sensitive, excitable people—I don't threaten—I only say—*take care!*"

"'Game,' 'play'—what silly words to use about such men as Edward and his father, in such a matter!" said Marcia as she rose, breathing contempt. "I shall talk to Edward—I promised Mrs. Betts. But I suppose, Corry, it's no good saying, to begin with, that when you talk of tyranny, you seem to *me* at any rate, the best tyrant of the lot."

The girl stood with her head thrown back, challenging her brother, her whole slender form poised for battle.

Coryston shook his head.

"Nonsense! I play the gadfly—to all the tyrants." "*A tyrant*," repeated his sister, steadily. "And an unkind wretch into the bargain! I was engaged—yesterday—and have you said one nice, brotherly word to me?"

Her lips trembled. Coryston turned away.

"You are giving yourself to the forces of reaction," he said, between his teeth, "the forces that are everywhere fighting liberty—whether in the individual—or the State. Only, unfortunately "—he turned with a smile, the sudden gaiety of which fairly startled his sister—"as far as matrimony is concerned, I seem to be doing precisely the same thing myself."

"Corry! what on earth do you mean?"

"Ah! wouldn't you like to know? Perhaps you will some day," said Coryston, with a provoking look. "Where's my hat?" He looked round him for the battered article that served him for head-gear. "Well, good-by, Marcia. If you can pull this thing off with your young man, I'm your servant and his. I'd even grovel to Lord William. The letter I wrote him was a pretty stiff document, I admit. If not—"

"Well, if not?"

"War!" was the short reply, as her brother made for the door.

Then suddenly he came back to say:

"Keep an eye on mother. As far as Arthur's concerned—she's dangerous. She hasn't the smallest intention of letting him marry that girl. And here too it'll be a case of meddling with forces you don't understand. Keep me informed."

"Yes—if you promise to help him—and her—to break it off," said Marcia, firmly.

Coryston slowly shook his head; and went.

Meanwhile Lady Coryston, having shaken off all companions, had betaken herself for greater privacy to a solitary walk. She desired to see neither children nor friends nor servants till she had made up her mind what she was going to do. As generally happened with her in the bad moments of life, the revelation of what threatened her had steeled and nerved her to a surprising degree. Her stately indoor dress had been exchanged for a short tweed gown, and, as she walked briskly along, her white hair framed in the drawn hood of black silk which she wore habitually on country walks, she had still a wonderful air of youth, and indeed she had never felt herself more vigorous, more alert. Occasionally a strange sense of subterranean peril made itself felt in the upper regions of the mind, caused by something she never stopped to analyze. It was not without kinship with the feeling of the gambler who has been lucky too long, and knows that the next stroke may—probably will— end it, and bring down the poised ruin. But it made no difference whatever to the gradual forging of her plan and the clearness of her resolve.

So now she understood all that during the two preceding months had increasingly perplexed her. Arthur had been laid hands on by the temptress just before his maiden speech in Parliament, and had done no good ever since. At the time when his mother had inflicted a social stigma as public as she could make it on a Minister who in her eyes deserved impeachment, by refusing to go through even the ordinary conventions of allowing him to arm her down to dinner and take his seat beside her at a large London party, Arthur was courting the daughter of the criminal; and the daughter was no doubt looking forward with glee to the moment of her equally public triumph over his mother. Lady Coryston remembered the large mocking eyes of Enid Glenwilliam, as seen amid the shadows of a dark drawing-room, about a fortnight later than the dinner-party, when with a consistency which seemed to her natural, and also from a wish to spare the girl's feelings, she had declined to be introduced, at the suggestion of another blundering hostess, to Glenwilliam's daughter. And all the time—all the time—the handsome, repellent creature was holding Arthur's life and Arthur's career in the hollow of her hand!

Well, she would not hold them so for long. Lady Coryston said to herself that she perfectly understood what Miss Glenwilliam was after. The circumstances of Coryston's disinheritance were now well known to many people; the prospects of the younger son were understood. The Glenwilliams were poor; the prospects of the party doubtful; the girl ambitious. To lay hands on the Coryston estates and the position which a Coryston marriage could give the daughter of the Yorkshire check-weigher—the temptation had only to be stated to be realized. And, no doubt, in addition, there would be the sweetness—for such persons as the Glenwilliams—of a planned and successful revenge.

Well, the scheme was simple; but the remedy was simple also. The Martover meeting was still rather more than three weeks off. But she understood from Page that after it the Chancellor and his daughter were to spend the week-end at the cottage on the hill, belonging to that odious person, Dr. Atherstone. A note sent on their arrival would prepare the way for an interview, and an interview that could not be refused. No time was to be lost, unless Arthur's political prospects were to be completely and irretrievably ruined. The mere whisper of such a courtship, in the embittered state of politics, would be quite enough to lose him his seat—to destroy that slender balance of votes on the right side, which the country districts supplied, to neutralize the sour radicalism of the small towns in his division.

She reached a rising ground in the park, where was a seat under a fine oak, commanding a view. The green slopes below her ran westward to a wide sky steeped toward the horizon in all conceivable shades of lilac and pearl, with here and there in the upper heaven lakes of blue and towering thunder-clouds brooding over them, prophesying storm. She looked out over her domain, in which, up to a short time before, her writ, so to speak, had run, like that of a king. And now all sense of confidence, of security, was gone. There on the hillside was the white patch of Knatchett—the old farmhouse, where Coryston had settled himself. It showed to her disturbed mind like the patch of leaven which, scarcely visible at first, will grow and grow "till the whole is leavened." A leaven of struggle and revolt. And only her woman's strength to fight it.

Suddenly—a tremor of great weakness came upon her. Arthur, her dearest! It had been comparatively easy to fight Coryston. When had she not fought him? But Arthur! She thought of all the happy times she had had with him—electioneering for him, preparing his speeches, watching his first steps in the House of Commons. The years before her, her coming old age, seemed all at once to have passed into a gray eclipse; and some difficult tears forced their way. Had she, after all, mismanaged her life? Were prophecies to which she had always refused to listen—she seemed to hear them in her dead husband's voice!—coming true? She fell into a great and lonely anguish of mind; while the westerly light burned on the broidery of white hawthorns spread over the green spaces below, and on the loops and turns of the little brimming trout-stream that ran so merrily through the park.

But she never wavered for one moment as to her determination to see Enid Glenwilliam after the Martover meeting; nor did the question of Arthur's personal happiness enter for one moment into her calculations.

CHAPTER XI

The breakfast gong had just sounded at Hoddon Grey. The hour was a quarter to nine. Prayers in the chapel were over, and Lord and Lady Newbury, at either end of the table, spectacles on nose, were opening and reading their letters.

"Where is Edward?" said Lady William, looking round.

"My dear!" Lord William's tone was mildly reproachful.

"Of course—I forgot for a moment!" And on Lady William's delicately withered cheek there appeared a slight flush. For it was their wedding-day, and never yet, since his earliest childhood, had their only son, their only child, failed, either personally or by deputy, to present his mother with a bunch of June roses on the morning of this June anniversary. While he was in India the custom was remitted to the old head gardener, who always received, however, from the absent son the appropriate letter or message to be attached to the flowers. And one of the most vivid memories Lady William retained of her son's boyhood showed her the half-open door of an inn bedroom at Domodossola, and Edward's handsome face—the face of a lad of eleven—looking in, eyes shining, white teeth grinning, as he held aloft in triumph the great bunch of carnations and roses for which the little fellow had scoured the sleepy town in the early hours. They had taken him abroad for the first time, during a break between his preparatory school and Eton, when he was convalescing from a dangerous attack of measles; and Lady William could never forget the charm of

Mrs. Humphry Ward

the boy's companionship, his eager docility and sweetness, his delight in the Catholic churches and services, his ready friendships with the country-folk, with the coachman who drove them, and the *sagrestani* who led them through dim chapels and gleaming monuments.

But when indeed had he not been their delight and treasure from his youth up till now? And though in the interest of a long letter from her Bishop to whom she was devoted, Lady William had momentarily forgotten the date, this wedding-day was, in truth, touched, for both parents, with a special consecration and tenderness, since it was the first since Edward's own betrothal. And there beside Lady William's plate lay a large jeweler's case, worn and old-fashioned, whereof the appearance was intimately connected both with the old facts and the new.

Meanwhile, a rainy morning, in which, however, there was a hidden sunlight, threw a mild illumination into the Hoddon Grey dining-room, upon the sparely provided breakfast-table, the somewhat austere line of family portraits on the gray wall, the Chippendale chairs shining with the hand-polish of generations, the Empire clock of black and ormolu on the chimney-piece and on the little tan spitz, sitting up with wagging tail and asking eyes, on Lady William's left. Neither she nor her husband ever took more than—or anything else than—an egg with their coffee and toast. They secretly despised people who ate heavy breakfasts, and the extra allowance made for Edward's young appetite, or for guests, was never more than frugal. Sir Wilfrid Bury, who was a hearty eater, was accustomed to say of the Hoddon Grey fare that it deprived the Hoddon Grey fasts—which were kept according to the strict laws of the Church—of any merit whatever. It left you nothing to give up.

Nevertheless, this little morning scene at Hoddon Grey possessed, for the sensitive eye, a peculiar charm. The spaces of the somewhat empty room matched the bareness of the white linen, the few flowers standing separately here and there upon it, and the few pieces of old silver. The absence of any loose abundance of food or gear, the frugal refined note, were of course symbolic of the life lived in the house. The Newburys were rich. Their beautifully housed, and beautifully kept estate, with its nobly adorned churches, its public halls and institutions, proclaimed the fact; but in their own private sphere it was ignored as much as possible.

"Here he is!" exclaimed Lady William, turning to the door with something of a flutter. "Oh, Edward, they are lovely!"

Her son laid the dewy bunch beside her plate and then kissed his mother affectionately.

"Many happy returns!—and you, father! Hullo—mother, you've got a secret—you're blushing! What's up?"

And still holding Lady William by the arm, he looked smilingly from her to the jeweler's case on the table.

"They must be reset, dear; but they're fine."

Lady William opened the case, and pushed it toward him. It contained a necklace and pendant, two bracelets, and a stomacher brooch of diamonds and sapphire—magnificent stones in a heavy gold setting, whereof the Early Victorianism cried aloud. The set had been much admired in the great exhibition of 1851, where indeed it had been bought by Lady William's father as a present to his wife. Secretly Lady William still thought it superb; but she was quite aware that no young woman would wear it.

Edward looked at it with amusement.

"The stones are gorgeous. When Cartier's had a go at it, it'll be something like! I can remember your wearing it, mother, at Court, when I was a small child. And you're going to give it to Marcia?" He kissed her again.

"Take it, dear, and ask her how she'd like them set," said his mother, happily, putting the box into his hand; after which he was allowed to sit down to his breakfast.

Lord William meanwhile had taken no notice of the little incident of the jewels. He was deep in a letter which seemed to have distracted his attention entirely from his son and to be causing him distress. When he had finished it he pushed it away and sat gazing before him as though still held by the recollection of it.

"I never knew a more sad, a more difficult case," he said, presently, speaking, it seemed, to himself.

Edward turned with a start.

"Another letter, father?"

Lord William pushed it over to him.

Newbury read it, and as he did so, in his younger face there appeared the same expression as in his father's; a kind of grave sadness, in which there was no trace of indecision, though much of trouble. Lady William asked no question, though in the course of her little pecking meal, she threw some anxious glances at her husband and son. They preserved a strict silence at table on the subject of the letter; but as soon as breakfast was over, Lord William made a sign to his son, and they went out into the garden together, walking away from the house.

"You know we can't do this, Edward!" said Lord William, with energy, as soon as they were in solitude.

Edward's eyes assented.

His father resumed, impetuously: "How can I go on in close relations with a man—my right hand in the estate—almost more than my agent—associated with all the church institutions and charities—a communicant—secretary of the communicant's guild!—our friend and helper in all our religious business—who has been the head and front of the campaign against immorality in this village—responsible, with us, for many decisions that must have seemed harsh to poor things in trouble—who yet now proposes, himself, to maintain what we can only regard—what everybody on this estate has been taught to regard—as an immoral connection with a married woman! Of course I understand his plea. The thing is not to be done openly. The so-called wife is to move away; nothing more is to be seen of her here; but the supposed marriage is to continue, and they will meet as often as his business here makes it possible. Meanwhile his powers and duties on this estate are to be as before. I say the proposal is monstrous! It would falsify our whole life here,—and make it one ugly hypocrisy!"

There was silence a little. Then Newbury asked:

"You of course made it plain once more—in your letter yesterday—that there would be no harshness—that as far as money went—"

"I told him he could have *whatever* was necessary! We wished to force no man's conscience; but we could not do violence to our own. If they decided to remain together—then he and we must part; but we would make it perfectly easy for them to go elsewhere—in England or the colonies. If they separate, and she will accept the arrangements we propose for her—then he remains here, our trusted friend and right hand as before."

"It is, of course, the wrench of giving up the farm—"

Lord William raised his hands in protesting distress.

"Perfectly true, of course, that he's given the best years of his life to it!—that he's got all sorts of experiments on hand—that he can never build up exactly the same sort of thing elsewhere—that the farm is the apple of his eye. It's absolutely true—every word of it! But then, why did he take this desperate step!—without consulting any of his friends! It's no responsibility of ours!"

The blanched and delicate face of the old man showed the grief, the wound to personal affection he did not venture to let himself express, mingled with a rocklike steadiness of will.

"You have heard from the Cloan Sisters?"

"Last night. Nothing could be kinder. There is a little house close by the Sisterhood where she and the boy could live. They would give her work, and watch over her, like the angels they are,—and the boy could go to a day school. But they won't hear of it—they won't listen to it for a moment; and now— you see—they've put their own alternative plan before us, in this letter. He said to me, yesterday, that she was not religious by temperament—that she wouldn't understand the Sisters— nor they her—that she would be certain to rebel against their rules and regulations—and then all the old temptations would return. 'I have taken her life upon me,' he said, 'and I can't give her up. She is mine, and mine she will remain.' It was terribly touching. I could only say that I was no judge of his conscience, and never pretended to be; but that he could only remain here on our terms."

"The letter is curiously excitable—hardly legible even—very unlike Betts," said Newbury, turning it over thoughtfully.

"That's another complication. He's not himself. That attack of illness has somehow weakened him. I can't reason with him as I used to do."

The father and son walked on in anxious cogitation, till Newbury observed a footman coming with a note.

"From Coryston Place, sir. Waiting an answer."

Newbury read it first with eagerness, then with a clouded brow.

"Ask the servant to tell Miss Coryston I shall be with them for luncheon."

When the footman was out of earshot, Newbury turned to his father, his face showing the quick feeling behind.

"Did you know that Mr. and Mrs. Betts are trying to get at Marcia?"

"No! I thought Coryston might be endeavoring to influence her. That fellow's absolutely reckless! But what can she have to do with the Bettses themselves? Really, the questions that young women concern themselves with to-day!" cried Lord William, not without vehemence. "Marcia must surely trust you and your judgment in such a matter."

Newbury flushed.

"I'm certain—she will," he said, rather slowly, his eyes on the ground. "But Mrs. Betts has been to see her."

"A great impertinence! A most improper proceeding!" said Lord William, hotly. "Is that what her note says? My dear Edward, you must go over and beg Marcia to let this matter *alone*! It is not for her to be troubled with at all. She must really leave it to us."

The wandlike old man straightened his white head a trifle haughtily.

*   *   *   *   *

A couple of hours later Newbury set out to walk to Coryston. The day was sultry, and June in all its power ruled the countryside. The hawthorns were fading; the gorse was over; but the grass and the young wheat were rushing up, the wild roses threw their garlands on every hedge, and the Coryston trout-stream, beside which Newbury walked, brimming as it was, on its chalk bed, would soon be almost masked from sight by the lush growths which overhung its narrow stream, twisting silverly through the meadows.

The sensitive mind and conscience of a man, alive, through the long discipline of religion, to many kinds of obligation, were, at this moment, far from happy, even with this flaming June about him, and the beloved brought nearer by every step. The thought of Marcia, the recollection of her face, the expectation of her kiss, thrilled indeed in his veins. He was not yet thirty, and the forces of his life were still rising. He had never felt his manhood so vigorous, nor his hopes so high. Nevertheless he was haunted—pursued—by the thought of those two miserable persons, over whom he and his father held, it seemed, a power they had certainly never sought, and hated to exercise. Yet how disobey the Church!—and how ignore the plain words of her Lord—"*He that marrieth her that is put away committeth adultery*"?

"Marriage is for Christians indissoluble. It bears the sacramental stamp. It is the image, the outward and visible sign of that most awful and most sacred union between Christ and the soul. To break the church's law concerning it, and to help others to break it, is—for Christians—to *sin*. To acquiesce in it, to be a partner to the dissolution of marriage for such reasons as Mrs. Betts had to furnish, was to injure not only the Christian church, but the human society, and, in the case of people with a high social trust, to betray that trust."

These were the ideas, the ideas of his family, and his church, which held him inexorably. He saw no escape from them. Yet he suffered from the enforcement of them, suffered truly and sincerely, even in the dawn of his own young happiness. What could he do to persuade the two offenders to the only right course!—or if that were impossible, to help them to take up life again where he and his would not be responsible for what they did or accomplices in their wrong-doing?

Presently, to shorten his road, he left the park, and took to a lane outside it. And here he suddenly perceived that he was on the borders of the experimental farm, that great glory of the estate, famous in the annals of English country life before John Betts had ever seen it, but doubly famous during the twenty years that he had been in charge of it. There was the thirty-acre field like one vast chessboard, made up of small green plots; where wheat was being constantly tempted and tried with new soils and new foods; and farmers from both the old and new worlds would come eagerly to watch and learn. There were the sheds where wheat was grown, not in open ground, but in pots under shelter; there was the long range of buildings devoted to cattle, and all the problems of food; there was the new chemical laboratory which his father had built for John Betts; and there in the distance was the pretty dwelling-house which now sheltered the woman from whose presence on the estate all the trouble had arisen.

A trouble which had been greatly aggravated by Coryston's presence on the scene. Newbury, for all that his heart was full of Marcia, was none the less sorely indignant with her brother, eager to have it out with him, and to fling back his charges in his face.

Suddenly, a form appeared behind a gate flanked by high hedges.

Newbury recognized John Betts. A tall, broad-shouldered man, with slightly grizzled hair, a countenance tanned and seamed by long exposure, and pale-blue spectacled eyes, opened the gate and stepped into the road.

"I saw you coming, Mr. Edward, and thought I should like a word with you."

"By all means," said Newbury, offering his hand. But Betts took no notice of it. They moved on together—a striking pair: the younger man, with his high, narrow brow and strong though slender build, bearing himself with the unconscious air of authority, given by the military life, and in this case also, no doubt, by the influence of birth and tradition; as fine a

Mrs. Humphry Ward

specimen of the English ruling class at its moral and physical best, as any student of our social life would be likely to discover; and beside him a figure round whom the earth-life in its primitive strength seemed to be still clinging, though the great brain of the man had long since made him its master and catechist, and not, like the ordinary man of the fields, farmer or laborer, its slave. He, too, was typical of his class, of that large modern class of the new countryman, armed by science and a precise knowledge, which has been developed from the primitive artists of the world—plowman, reaper, herdsman; who understood nothing and discovered everything. A strong, taciturn, slightly slouching fellow; vouched for by the quiet blue eyes, and their honest look; at this moment, however, clouded by a frown of distress. And between the two men there lay the memory of years of kindly intercourse—friendship, loyalty, just dealing.

"Your father will have got a letter from me this morning, Mr. Edward," began Betts, abruptly.

"He did. I left him writing to you." The young man's voice was singularly gentle, even deferential.

"You read it, I presume?"

Newbury made a sign of assent.

"Is there any hope for us, Mr. Edward?"

Betts turned to look into his companion's face. A slight tremor in the normally firm lips betrayed the agitation behind the question.

Newbury's troubled eyes answered him.

"You don't know what it costs us—not to be able to meet you—in that way!"

"You think the arrangement we now propose—would still

compromise you?"

"How could we?" pleaded the younger man, with very evident pain. "We should be aiding and abetting—what we believe to be wrong—conniving at it indeed; while we led people—deliberately—to believe what was false."

"Then it is still your ultimatum—that we must separate?"

"If you remain here, in our service—our representative. But if you would only allow us to make the liberal provision we would like to make for you—elsewhere!"

Betts was silent a little; then he broke out, looking round him.

"I have been twenty years at the head of that farm. I have worked for it night and day. It's been my life. Other men have worked for their wives and children. I've worked for the farm. There are experiments going on there—you know it, Mr. Edward—that have been going on for years. They're working out now—coming to something—I've earned that reward. How can I begin anywhere else? Besides, I'm flagging. I'm not the man I was. The best of me has gone into that farm." He raised his arm to point. "And now, you're going to drive me from it."

"Oh, Betts—why did you—why *did* you!" cried Newbury, in a sudden rush of grief. The other turned.

"Because—a woman came—and clung to me! Mr. Edward, when you were a boy I saw you once take up a wounded leveret in the fields—a tiny thing. You made yourself kill it for mercy's sake—and then you sat down and cried over it—for the thought of all it had suffered. Well, my wife—she *is* my wife too!—is to me like that wounded thing. Only I've given her *life*!—and he that takes her from me will kill her."

"And the actual words of our Blessed Lord, Betts, matter nothing to you?" Newbury spoke with a sudden yet controlled passion. "I have heard you quote them often. You seemed to believe and feel with us. You signed a petition we all sent to the Bishop only last year."

"That seems so long ago, Mr. Edward,—so long ago. I've been through a lot since—a lot—" repeated Betts, absently, as though his mind had suddenly escaped from the conversation into some dream of its own. Then he came to a stop.

"Well, good morning to you, sir—good morning. There's something doing in the laboratory I must be looking after."

"Let me come and talk to you to-night, Betts! We have some notion of a Canadian opening that might attract you. You know the great Government farm near Ottawa? Why not allow my father to write to the Director—"

Betts interrupted.

"Come when you like, Mr. Edward. Thank you kindly. But—it's no good—no good."

The voice dropped.

With a slight gesture of farewell, Betts walked away.

Newbury went on his road, a prey to very great disturbance of mind. The patience—humbleness even—of Betts's manner struck a pang to the young man's heart. The farm director was generally a man of bluff, outspoken address, quick-tempered, and not at all accustomed to mince his words. What Newbury perceived was a man only half persuaded by his own position; determined to cling to it, yet unable to justify it, because, in truth, the ideas put up against him by Newbury and his father were the ideas on which a large section of his own life had been based. It is not for nothing that a man is for years a devout communicant, and in touch thereby with all the circle of beliefs on which Catholicism, whether of the Roman or Anglican sort, depends.

The white towers of Coryston appeared among the trees. His steps quickened. Would she come to meet him?

Then his mind filled with repugnance. *Must* he discuss this melancholy business again with her—with Marcia? How could he? It was not right!—not seemly! He thought with horror of the interview between her and Mrs. Betts—his stainless Marcia, and that little besmirched woman, of whose life between the dissolution of her first marriage, and her meeting with Betts, the Newburys knew more than they wished to know, more, they believed, than Betts himself knew.

And the whole June day protested with him—its beauty, the clean radiance of the woods, the limpid flashing of the stream....

He hurried on. Ah, there she was!—a fluttering vision through the new-leafed trees.

The wood was deep—spectators none. She came to his arms, and lightly clasped her own round his neck, hiding her face....

When they moved on together, hand in hand, Marcia, instinctively putting off what must be painful, spoke first of the domestic scene of the day before—of Arthur and her mother—and the revelation sprung upon them all.

"You remember how *terrified* I was—lest mother should know? And she's taken it so calmly!"

She told the story. Lady Coryston, it seemed, had canceled all the arrangements for the Coryston meeting, and spoke no more of it. She was cool and distant, indeed, toward Arthur, but only those who knew her well would perhaps have noticed it. And he, on his side, having gained his point, had been showing himself particularly amiable; had gone off that morning to pay political visits in the division; and was doing his duty in the afternoon by captaining the village cricket team in their Whitsuntide match. But next week, of course, he would be in London again for the reassembling of Parliament, and hanging about the Glenwilliams' house, as before.

"They're not engaged?"

"Oh dear, no! Coryston doesn't believe *she* means it seriously at all. He also thinks that mother is plotting something."

"When can I see Coryston?" Newbury turned to her with a rather forced smile. "You know, darling, he'll have to get used to me as a brother!"

"He says he wants to see you—to—to have it out with you," said Marcia, awkwardly. Then with a sudden movement, she clasped both her hands round Newbury's arm.

"Edward!—do—*do* make us all happy!"

He looked down on the liquid eyes, the fresh young face raised appealingly to his.

"How can I make you happy?" He lifted one hand and kissed it. "You darling!—what can I do?"

But as he spoke he knew what she meant and dreaded the coming moment. That she should ask anything in these magical days that he could not at once lay at her feet!—she, who had promised him herself!

"*Please*—let Mr. Betts stay—please, Edward! Oh, I was so sorry for her yesterday!"

"We are all so sorry for her," he said, after a pause. "My father and mother will do all they can."

"Then you *will* let him stay?" Her white brow dropped caressingly against him.

"Of course!—if he will only accept my father's conditions," he said, unwillingly, hating to see her bright look darkening.

She straightened herself.

"If they separate, you mean?"

"I'm afraid that's what they ought to do."

"But it would break their hearts."

He threw her a sudden flashing look, as though a sword gleamed.

"It would make amends."

"For what they have done? But they don't feel like that!" she pleaded, her color rising. "They think themselves properly married, and that no one has a right to interfere with them. And when the law says so too, Edward?—Won't everybody think it *very* hard?"

"Yes, we shall be blamed," he said, quietly. "But don't you see, dearest, that, if they stay, we seem to condone the marriage, to say that it doesn't matter,—what they have done?—when in truth it seems to us a black offense—"

"Against what—or whom?" she asked, wondering.

The answer came unflinchingly:

"Against our Lord—and His Church."

The revolt within showed itself in her shining eyes.

"Ought we to set up these standards for other people? And they don't ask to stay *here*!—at least she doesn't. That's what Mrs. Betts came to say to me—"

Marcia threw herself into an eager recapitulation of Mrs.

Betts's arguments. Her innocence, her ignorance, her power of feeling, and her instinctive claim to have her own way and get what she wanted,—were all perceptible in her pleading. Newbury listened with discomfort and distress—not yielding, however, by the fraction of an inch, as she soon discovered. When she came to an abrupt pause, the wounded pride of a foreseen rebuff dawning in her face, Newbury broke out:

"Darling, I *can't* discuss it with you! Won't you trust me— Won't you believe that neither father nor I would cause these poor things one moment's pain—if we could help it?"

Marcia drew away from him. He divined the hurt in her as she began twisting and untwisting a ribbon from her belt, while her lip trembled.

"I can't understand," she said, frowning—"I can't!"

"I know you can't. But won't you trust me? Dearest, you're going to trust me with your whole life? Won't you?"

He took her in his arms, bending his handsome head to hers, pleading with her in murmured words and caresses. And again she was conquered, she gave way; not without a galling consciousness of being refused, but thrilled all the same by the very fact that her lover could refuse her, in these first moments of their love. It brought home to her once more that touch of inaccessible strength, of mysterious command in Newbury, which from the beginning had both teased and won her.

But it was on her conscience at least to repeat to him what Coryston had said. She released herself to do it.

"Coryston said, Edward, I was to tell you to 'take care.' He has seen Mr. and Mrs. Betts, and he says they are very excitable people—and very much in love. He can't tell what might happen."

Newbury's face stiffened.

"I think I know them as well as Coryston. We will take every care, dearest. And as for thinking of it—why, it's hardly ever out of my mind—except when I'm with you! It hangs over me from morn till night."

Then at last she let the subject be dismissed; and they loitered home through the woods, drawing into their young veins the scents and hues of the June day. They were at that stage in love, when love has everything to learn, and learns it through ways as old and sweet as life. Each lover is discovering the other, and over the process, Nature, with her own ends in view, throws the eternal glamour.

Yet before they reached the house the "sweet bells" in Marcia's consciousness were once more jangling. There could be nothing but pleasure, indeed, in confessing how each was first attracted to the other; in clearing up the little misunderstandings of courtship; in planning for the future—the honeymoon—their London house—the rooms at Hoddon Grey that were to be refurnished for them. Lady William's jewels emerged from Newbury's pocket, and Marcia blazed with them, there and then, under the trees. They laughed together at the ugly setting, and planned a new one. But then a mention by Newbury of the Oxford friend who was to be his "best man" set him talking of the group of men who had been till now the leading influence in his life—friends made at Oxford, and belonging all of them to that younger High Church party of which he seemed to be the leader. Of two of them especially he talked with eager affection; one, an overworked High Churchman, with a parish in South London; another who belonged to a "Community," the Community of the Ascension, and was soon to go out to a mission-station in a very lonely and plague-stricken part of India.

And gradually, as he talked, Marcia fell silent. The persons he was speaking of, and the ideas they represented, were quite strange to her; although, as a matter of mere information, she knew of course that such people and such institutions existed. She was touched at first, then chilled, and if the truth be told—bored. It was with such topics, as with the Hoddon Grey view of the Betts case. Something in her could not understand.

She guided him deftly back to music, to the opera, to the night of Iphigenia. No jarring there! Each mind kindled the other, in a common delight. Presently they swung along, hand in hand, laughing, quoting, reminding each other of this fine thing, and that. Newbury was a considerable musician; Marcia was accustomed to be thought so. There was a new and singular joy in feeling herself but a novice and ignoramus beside him.

"How much you know!"—and then, shyly—"You must teach me!" With the inevitable male retort—"Teach you!—when you look at me like that!"

It was a golden hour. Yet when Marcia went to take off her hat before luncheon, and stood absently before the glass in a flush of happiness, it was as though suddenly a door opened behind her, and two sad and ghostly figures entered the room of life, pricking her with sharp remorse for having forgotten them.

And when she rejoined Newbury down-stairs, it seemed to her, from his silent and subdued manner, that something of the same kind had happened also to him.

*　　*　　*　　*　　*

"You haven't tackled Coryston yet?" said Sir Wilfrid, as he and Newbury walked back toward Hoddon Grey in the late afternoon, leaving Marcia and Lady Coryston in the clutches of a dressmaker, who had filled the drawing-room with a gleaming show of "English silks," that being Lady Coryston's special and peremptory command for the *trousseau*.

"No. He hasn't even vouchsafed me a letter."

Newbury laughed; but Sir Wilfrid perceived the hurt feeling which mingled with the laugh.

"Absurd fellow!" said Sir Wilfrid. "His proceedings here amuse me a good deal—but they naturally annoy his mother. You have heard of the business with the Baptists?"

Newbury had seen some account of it in the local paper.

"Well now they've got their land—through Coryston. There always was a square piece in the very middle of the village—an *enclave* belonging to an old maid, the daughter of a man who was a former butler of the Corystons, generations ago. She had migrated to Edinburgh, but Coryston has found her, got at her, and made her sell it—finding, I believe, the greater part of the money. It won't be long before he'll be laying the foundation-stone of the new Bethel—under his mother's nose."

"A truly kind and filial thing to do!" said the young High Churchman, flushing.

Sir Wilfrid eyed him slyly.

"Moral—don't keep a conscience—political or ecclesiastical. There's nothing but mischief comes of it. And, for Heaven's sake, don't be a posthumous villain!"

"What's that?"

"A man who makes an unjust will, and leaves everything to his wife," said Sir Wilfrid, calmly. "It's played the deuce in this family, and will go on doing it."

Whereupon the late Lord Coryston's executor produced an outline of the family history—up to date—for the benefit of Lady Coryston's future son-in-law. Newbury, who was always singularly ignorant of the town gossip on such matters, received it with amazement. Nothing could be more unlike the strictly traditional ways which governed his own family in matters of money and inheritance.

"So Arthur inherits everything!"

"Hm—does he?" said Sir Wilfrid.

"But I thought—"

"Wait and see, my dear fellow, wait and see. He will only marry Miss Glenwilliam over his mother's body—and if he does marry her he may whistle for the estates."

"Then James will have them?" said Newbury, smiling.

"Why not Marcia? She has as good a chance as anybody."

"I hope not!" Newbury's tone showed a genuine discomfort.

"What is Lady Coryston doing?"

"About the Glenwilliam affair? Ah!—what isn't she doing?" said Sir Wilfrid, significantly. "All the same, she lies low." As he spoke, his eyes fell upon the hillside and on the white cottage of the Atherstones emerging from the wood. He pointed.

"They will be there on Sunday fortnight—after the Martover meeting."

"Who? The Glenwilliams?"

Sir Wilfrid nodded.

"And I am of opinion that something will happen. When two highly inflammable bodies approach each other, something generally does happen."

CHAPTER XII

The weeks that followed offered no particular A event, but were none the less important to this history. Coryston was called off to an election in the north, where he made a series of speeches which perhaps in the end annoyed the Labor candidate he was supporting as much as the Tory he was attacking. For, generally reckoned a Socialist by friends and opponents alike, he preached openly, on this occasion, that Socialism was absurd, and none but fools would upset kings and cabinets, to be governed by committees.

And on one of his spare evenings he wrote a letter to Edward Newbury, loftily accepting him as a brother-in-law—on conditions.

"I see no reason," he wrote, "why you and I should not be good friends—if only I can induce you to take the line of common humanity in this pitiful case, which, as you know, has set our whole neighborhood aflame. Your *opinions* on divorce don't matter, of course, to me—nor mine to you. But there are cruelties of which all men are judges. And if you must—because of your opinions—commit yourself to one of them—why then, whether you marry Marcia or no, you and I can't be friends. It would be mere hypocrisy to suppose it. And I tell you quite frankly that I shall do my best to influence Marcia. There seem to me to be one or two ways out of the business, that would at any rate relieve you of any active connivance with what you hold to be immorality. I have dealt with them in my letter to your father. But if you stand on your present fiat—"Separate—or go—" well, then you and I'll come to blows—Marcia or no Marcia. And I warn you that Marcia is at bottom a humanist—in the new sense—like me."

To which Newbury promptly replied:

"My dear Coryston—I am quite prepared to discuss the Betts case with you, whenever you return, and we can meet. But we cannot discuss it to any useful purpose, unless you are prepared to allow me, before we begin, the same freedom of opinion that you claim for yourself. It is no good ruling out opinion— or rather conviction—and supposing that we can agree, apart from conviction, on what is cruelty in this case, and what isn't. The omitted point is vital. I find it difficult to write about Marcia—perhaps because my heart and mind are so full of her. All I can say is that the happiness she has brought me by consenting to be my wife must necessarily affect all I think and feel. And to begin with, it makes me very keen to understand and be friends with those she loves. She is very much attached to you—though much troubled often, as of course you know, by the line you have taken down here.... Let me know when you return—that I may come over to Knatchett. We can be brothers, can't we?—even though we look at life so differently."

But to this Coryston, who had gone on to a Labor Congress in Scotland, made no reply.

The June days passed on, bringing the "high midsummer pomps." Every day Newbury and Marcia met, and the Betts case was scarcely mentioned between them after Newbury had been able to tell her that Lord William in London had got from some Canadian magnates who happened to be there, a cordial and even enthusiastic promise of employment for John Betts, in connection with a Government experiment in Alberta. An opening was ready; the Newburys guaranteed all expenses; and at last Betts himself seemed to be reconciled to the prospect of emigration, being now, as always, determined to stick to his marriage. Nobody wished to hurry him; he was considering the whole proposal; and in a week or two Newbury quite hoped that matters might be arranged.

Meanwhile, though the pride of the Newburys concealed the fact as much as possible, not only from Marcia but from each other, the dilemma on the horns of which John and Alice Betts had found themselves impaled, was being eagerly, even passionately discussed through the whole district. The supporters of the Newburys were many, for there were scores of persons on the Newbury estates who heartily sympathized with their point of view; but on the whole the defenders of the Betts marriage were more. The affair got into the newspapers, and a lecturer representing the "Rational Marriage Union" appeared from London, and addressed large and attentive audiences in the little towns. After one of these lectures, Newbury returning home at night from Coryston was pelted with stones and clods by men posted behind a hedge. He was only slightly hurt, and when Marcia tried to speak of it, his smile of frank contempt put the matter by. She could only be thankful that Coryston was still away.

For Lady Coryston, meanwhile, the Betts case scarcely existed. When it did come up, she would say impatiently that in her opinion such private matters were best left to the people concerned to settle; and it was evident that to her the High Anglican view of divorce was, like the inconvenient piety of Hoddon Grey, a thing of superfluity. But Marcia knew very well that her mother had no mind to give to such a trifle—or to anything, indeed—her own marriage not excepted—but Arthur's disclosure, and Arthur's intentions. What her mother's plans were she could not discover. They lingered on at Coryston when, with the wedding so close in view, it would have been natural that they should return at once to London for shopping; and Marcia observed that her mother seemed to be more closely absorbed in politics than ever, while less attentive, perhaps, than usual to the affairs of the estate and the village. A poster announcing the Martover meeting was lying about in her sitting-room, and from a fragment of conversation overheard between her mother and Mr. Page, the agent, it seemed that Lady Coryston had been making elaborate inquiries as to those queer people, the Atherstones, with whom the Glenwilliams were to stay for the meeting. Was her mother afraid that Arthur would do something silly and public when they came down! Not the least likely! He had plenty of opportunities in London, with no local opinion, and no mother to worry him. Yet when Parliament reassembled, and Arthur, with an offhand good-by to his mother, went back to his duties, Marcia in vain suggested to Lady Coryston that they also should return to St. James's Square, partly to keep an eye on the backslider, partly with a view to "fittings," Lady Coryston curtly replied, that Marcia might have a motor whenever she pleased, to take her up to town, but that she herself meant for another fortnight to stay at Coryston. Marcia, much puzzled, could only write to James to beg him to play watch-dog; well aware, however, that if Arthur chose to press the pace, James could do nothing whatever to stop him.

On the day before the Glenwilliam meeting Lady Coryston, who had gone out westward through the park, was returning by motor from the direction of Martover, and reached her own big and prosperous village of Coryston Major about seven o'clock. She had been holding conference with a number of persons in the old borough of Martover, persons who might be trusted to turn a Radical meeting into a howling inferno, if the smallest chink of opportunity were given them; and she was conscious of a good afternoon's work. As she sat majestically erect in the corner of the motor, her brain was alive with plans. A passion of political—and personal—hatred charged every vein. She was tired, but she would not admit it. On the contrary, not a day passed that she did not say to herself that she was in the prime of life, that the best of her work as a party woman was still to do, and that even if Arthur did fail her— incredible defection!—she, alone, would fight to the end, and leave her mark, so far as a voteless woman of great possessions might, upon the country and its fortunes.

Yet the thought of Arthur was very bitter to her, and the expectation of the scene which—within forty-eight hours—she was deliberately preparing for herself. She meant to win her battle,—did not for one moment admit the possibility of losing it. But that her son would make her suffer for it she foresaw, and though she would not allow them to come into the open, there were dim fears and misgivings in the corners of her mind which made life disagreeable.

It was a fine summer evening, bright but cool. The streets of Coryston were full of people, and Lady Coryston distributed a suzerain's greetings as she passed along. Presently, at a spot ahead of her, she perceived a large crowd, and the motor slowed down.

"What's the matter, Patterson?" she asked of her chauffeur.

"Layin' a stone—or somethin'—my lady," said the chauffeur in a puzzled voice.

"Laying a stone?" she repeated, wondering. Then, as the crowd parted before the motor, she caught sight of a piece of orchard ground which only that morning had been still hidden behind the high moss-grown palings which had screened it for a generation. Now the palings had been removed sufficiently to allow a broad passage through, and the crowd outside was but an overflow from the crowd within. Lady Coryston perceived a platform with several black-coated persons in white ties, a small elderly lady, and half a dozen chairs upon it. At one end of the platform a large notice-board had apparently just been reared, for a couple of men were still at work on its supports. The board exhibited the words—"Site of the new Baptist Chapel for Coryston Major. All contributions to the building fund thankfully received."

There was no stone to be seen, grass and trees indeed were still untouched, but a public meeting was clearly proceeding, and in the chair, behind a small table, was a slight, fair-haired man, gesticulating with vigor.

Lady Coryston recognized her eldest son.

Mrs. Humphry Ward

"Drive on, Patterson!" she said, furiously.

"I can't, my lady—they're too thick."

By this time the motor had reached the center of the gathering which filled the road, and the persons composing it had recognized Lady Coryston. A movement ran through the crowd; faces turned toward the motor, and then toward the platform; from the mother—back to the son. The faces seemed to have but one smile, conscious, sly, a little alarmed. And as the motor finally stopped—the chauffeur having no stomach for manslaughter—in front of the breach in the railings, the persons on the platform saw it, and understood what was the matter with the audience.

Coryston paused in his speech. There was a breathless moment. Then, stepping in front of the table, to the edge of the platform, he raised his voice:

"We scarcely expected, my friends, to see my mother, Lady Coryston, among us this evening. Lady Coryston has as good a right to her opinion as any of us have to ours. She has disapproved of this enterprise till now. She did not perhaps think there were so many Baptists—big and little Baptists—in Coryston—" he swept his hand round the audience with its fringe of babies. "May we not hope that her presence to-night means that she has changed her mind—that she will not only support us—but that she will even send a check to the Building Fund! Three cheers for Lady Coryston!"

He pointed to the notice-board, his fair hair blown wildly back from his boyish brow, and queer thin lips; and raising his hand, he started the first "Hip!—hip—"

"Go on, Patterson," cried Lady Coryston again, knocking sharply at the front windows of the open landaulette. The crowd cheered and laughed, in good-humored triumph; the chauffeur hooted violently, and those nearest the motor fled with shrieks and jeers; Lady Coryston sat in pale endurance. At last the way was clear, and the motor shot forward. Coryston stepped back to the table and resumed his speech as though nothing had happened.

"Infamous! Outrageous!"

The words formed themselves on Lady Coryston's angry lips. So the plot in which she had always refused to believe had actually been carried through! That woman on the platform was no doubt the butler's daughter, the miserly spinster who had guarded her Naboth's vineyard against all purchasers for twenty years. Coryston had squared her, and in a few months the Baptist Chapel his mother had staved off till now, would be flaunting it in the village.

And this was Coryston's doing. What taste—what feeling! A mother!—to be so treated! By the time she reached her own sitting-room, Lady Coryston was very near a womanish weeping. She sat silently there awhile, in the falling dusk, forcing back her self-control, making herself think of the next day, the arrival of the Glenwilliams, and how she would need all her strength and a clear head to go through with what she meant to do—more important, that, than this trumpery business in the village!

A sound of footsteps roused her from her thoughts, and she perceived Marcia outside, coming back through the trees to the house. Marcia was singing in a low voice as she came. She had taken off her hat, which swung in her left hand, and her dark curls blew about her charming face. The evening light seemed to halo and caress her; and her mother thought—"she has just parted from Edward!" A kind of jealousy of her daughter for one strange moment possessed her—jealousy of youth and love and opening life. She felt herself thwarted and forgotten; her sons were all against her, and her daughter had no need of her. The memory of her own courting days came back upon her, a rare experience!—and she was conscious of a dull longing for the husband who had humored her every wish—save one; had been proud of her cleverness, and indolently glad of her activity. Yet when she thought of him, it was to see him as he lay on his death-bed, during those long last hours of obstinate silence, when his soul gave no sign to hers, before the end.

Marcia's state and Marcia's feelings, meanwhile, were by no means so simple as her mother imagined. She was absorbed, indeed, by the interest and excitement of her engagement. She could never forget Newbury; his influence mingled with every action and thought of her day; and it was much more than an influence of sex and passion. They had hardly indeed been engaged a few days, before Marcia had instinctively come to look upon their love as a kind of huge and fascinating adventure. Where would it lead?—how would it work out? She was conscious always of the same conflicting impulses of submission and revolt; the same alternations of trust and resentment. In order not to be crushed by the strength of his character, she had brought up against him from the very beginning the weapons of her young beauty, carrying out what she had dimly conceived, even on the first day of their betrothal. The wonder of that perpetual contrast, between the natural sweetness of his temperament and the sternness with which he controlled and disciplined his life, never ceased to affect her. His fierce judgment of opinions—his bitter judgment, often, of men—repelled and angered her. She rose in revolt, protesting; only to be made to feel that in such bitterness, or such fierceness, there was nothing personal whatever. He was but a soldier under orders, mysterious orders; moved by forces she only faintly perceived. Once or twice, during the fortnight, it was as though a breath of something infinitely icy and remote blew across their relation; nor was it till, some years afterward, she read Madame Perrier's life of her brother, Blaise Pascal, that she understood in some small degree what it had meant.

And just as some great physical and mental demand may bring out undreamt-of powers in a man or woman, so with the moral and spiritual demand made by such a personality as Newbury. Marcia rose in stature as she tried to meet it. She was braced, exalted. Her usual egotisms and arrogancies fell away ashamed. She breathed a diviner air, and life ran, hour by hour, with a wonderful intensity, though always haunted by a sense of danger she could not explain. Newbury's claim upon her indeed was soon revealed as the claim of lover, master, friend, in one; his love infused something testing and breathless into every hour of every day they were together.

On the actual day of the Martover meeting Marcia was left alone at Coryston. Newbury had gone—reluctantly for once— to a diocesan meeting on the farther side of the county. Lady Coryston, whose restlessness was evident, had driven to inspect a new farm some miles off, and was to take informal dinner on her way back with her agent, Mr. Page, and his wife—a house in which she might reckon on the latest gossip about the Chancellor's visit, and the great meeting for which special trains were being run from town, and strangers were pouring into the district.

Marcia spent the day in writing letters of thanks for wedding presents, and sheets of instructions to Waggin, who had been commandeered long before this, and was now hard at work in town on the preparations for the wedding; sorely hampered the while by Lady Coryston's absence from the scene. Then, after giving some last thoughts to her actual wedding-dress, the bride-elect wandered into the rose-garden and strolled about aimlessly gathering, till her hands were full of blooms, her thoughts meanwhile running like a mill-race over the immediate past and the immediate future. This one day's separation from Newbury had had a curious effect. She had missed him sharply; yet at the same time she had been conscious of a sort of relief from strain, a slackening of the mental and moral muscles, which had been strangely welcome.

Presently she saw Lester coming from the house, holding up a note.

"I came to bring you this. It seems to want an answer." He approached her, his eyes betraying the pleasure awakened by the sight of her among the roses, in her delicate white dress, under the evening sky. He had scarcely seen her of late, and in her happiness and preoccupation she seemed at last to have practically forgotten his presence in the house.

She opened the note, and as she read it Lester was dismayed to see a look of consternation blotting the brightness from her face.

"I must have the small motor—at once! Can you order it for me?"

"Certainly. You want it directly?"

"Directly. Please hurry them!" And dropping the roses, without a thought, on the ground, and gathering up her white skirts, she ran toward one of the side doors of the facade which led to her room. Lester lifted the fragrant mass of flowers she had left scattered on the grass, and carried them in. What could be the matter?

He saw to the motor's coming round, and when a few minutes later he had placed her in it, cloaked and veiled, he asked her anxiously if he could not do anything to help her, and what he should say to Lady Coryston on her return.

"I have left a note for my mother. Please tell Sir Wilfrid I sha'n't be here for dinner. No—thank you!—thank you! I must go myself!" Then, to the chauffeur—"Redcross Farm!— as quick as you can!"

Lester was left wondering. Some new development of the Betts trouble? After a few minutes' thought he went toward the smoking-room in search of Sir Wilfrid Bury.

Meanwhile Marcia was speeding through the summer country, where the hay harvest was beginning and the fields were still full of folk. The day had been thunderously fine, with threats of change. Broad streaks of light and shadow lay on the shorn grass; children were tumbling in the swaths, and a cheerful murmur of voices rose on the evening air. But Marcia could only think of the note she still held in her hand.

"Can you come and see me? to-night—at once. Don't bring anybody. I am alarmed about my husband. Mr. Edward is away till to-morrow.—ALICE BETTS."

This sudden appeal to her had produced in Marcia a profound intensity of feeling. She thought of Coryston's "Take care!"— and trembled. Edward would not be home till the following day. She must act alone—help alone. The thought braced her will. Her mother would be no use—but she wished she had thought of asking Sir Wilfrid to come with her....

The car turned into the field lane leading to the farm. The wind had strengthened, and during all the latter part of her drive heavy clouds had been rising from the west, and massing themselves round the declining sun. The quality of the light had changed, and the air had grown colder.

"Looks like a storm, miss," said the young chauffeur, a lad just promoted to driving, and the son of the Coryston head gardener. As he spoke, a man came out of a range of buildings on the farther side of a field and paused to look at the motor. He was carrying something in his arms—Marcia thought, a lamb. The sight of the lady in the car seemed to excite his astonishment, but after a moment or two's observation he turned abruptly round the corner of the building behind him and disappeared.

"That's the place, miss, where they try all the new foods," the chauffeur continued, eagerly,—"and that's Mr. Betts. He's just wonderful with the beasts."

"You know the farm, Jackson?"

"Oh, father's great friends with Mr. Betts," said the youth, proudly. "And I've often come over with him of a Sunday. Mr. Betts is a very nice gentleman. He'll show you everything."

At which point, however, with a conscious look, and a blush, the young man fell silent. Marcia wondered how much he knew. Probably not much less than she did, considering the agitation in the neighborhood.

They motored slowly toward the farm-house, an old building with modern additions and a small garden round it, standing rather nakedly on the edge of the famous checkered field, a patchwork quilt of green, yellow, and brown, which Marcia had often passed on her drives without understanding in the least what it meant. About a stone's-throw from the front door rose a substantial one-storied building, and, seeing Miss Coryston glance at it curiously, Jackson was again eager to explain:

"That's the laboratory, miss—His lordship built that six years ago. And last year there was a big meeting here. Father and I come over to the speeches—and they gave Mr. Betts a gold medal—and there was an American gentleman who spoke— and he said as how this place of Mr. Betts—next to that place, Harpenden way—Rothamsted, I think they call it—was most 'ighly thought of in the States—and Mr. Betts had done fine. And that's the cattle-station over there, miss, where they fattens 'em, and weighs 'em. And down there's the drainage field where they gathers all the water that's been through the crops, when they've manured 'em—and the mangel field— and—"

"Mind that gate, Jackson," said Marcia. The youth silenced, looked to his steering, and brought the motor up safely to the door of the farm.

A rather draggled maid-servant answered Marcia's ring, examined her furtively, and showed her into the little drawing-room. Marcia stood at the window, looking out. She saw the motor disappearing toward the garage which she understood was to be found somewhere on the premises. The storm was drawing nearer; the rising grounds to the west were in black shadow—but on the fields and scattered buildings in front, wild gleams were striking now here, now there. How trim everything was!—how solid and prosperous. The great cattle-shed on the one hand—the sheep-station on the other, with its pens and hurdles—the fine stone-built laboratory—the fields stretching to the distance.

She turned to the room in which she stood. Nothing trim or solid there! A foundation indeed of simple things, the chairs and tables of a bachelor's room, over which a tawdry taste had gone rioting. Draperies of "art" muslin; photographs in profusion—of ladies in very low dresses and affected poses, with names and affectionate messages written across the corners;—a multitude of dingy knick-knacks; above the mantelpiece a large colored photograph of Mrs. Betts herself as Ariel; clothes lying about; muddy shoes; the remains of a meal: Marcia looked at the medley with quick repulsion, the wave of feeling dropping.

The door opened. A small figure in a black dress entered softly, closed the door behind her, and stood looking at Miss Coryston. Marcia was at first bewildered. She had only seen Mrs. Betts once before, in her outdoor things, and the impression left had been of a red-eyed, disheveled, excitable woman, dressed in shabby finery, the sort of person who would naturally possess such a sitting-room as that in which they stood. And here was a woman austerely simple in dress and calm in manner! The black gown, without an ornament of any kind, showed the still lovely curves of the slight body, and the whiteness of the arms and hands. The face was quiet, of a dead pallor; the hair gathered loosely together and held in place by a couple of combs, was predominantly gray, and there had been no effort this time to disguise the bareness of the temples, or the fresh signs of age graven round eyes and lips.

For the first time the quick sense of the girl perceived that Mrs. Betts was or had been a beautiful woman. By what dramatic instinct did she thus present herself for this interview? A wretched actress on the boards, did she yet possess some subtle perception which came into play at this crisis of her own personal life?

"It was very kind of you to come, Miss Coryston." She pushed forward a chair. "Won't you sit down? I'm ashamed of this room. I apologize for it." She looked round it with a gesture of weary disgust, and then at Marcia, who stood in flushed agitation, the heavy cloak she had worn in the motor falling back from her shoulders and her white dress, the blue motor veil framing the brilliance of her eyes and cheeks.

"I musn't sit down, thank you—I can't stay long," said the girl, hurriedly. "Will you tell me why you sent for me? I came at once. But my mother, when she comes home, will wonder where I am."

Without answering immediately, Mrs. Betts moved to the window, and looked out into the darkening landscape, and the trees already bending to the gusts which precede the storm.

"Did you see my husband as you came?" she asked, turning slightly.

"Yes. He was carrying something. He saw me, but I don't think he knew who I was."

"He never came home last night at all," said Mrs. Betts, looking away again out of the window. "He wandered about the fields and the sheds all night. I looked out just as it was getting light, and saw him walking about among the wheat plots, sometimes stopping to look, and sometimes making a note in his pocket-book, as he does when he's going his rounds. And at four o'clock, when I looked again, he was coming out of the cattle-shed, with something in his hand, which he took into the laboratory. I saw him unlock the door of the laboratory and I bent out of my window, and tried to call him. But he never looked my way, and he stayed there till the sun was up. Then I saw him again outside, and I went out and brought him in. But he wouldn't take any rest even then. He went into the office and began to write. I took him some tea, and then—"

The speaker's white face quivered for the first time. She came to Marcia and laid both hands on the girl's arm.

"He told me he was losing his memory and his mind. He thought he had never quite got over his illness before he went to Colwyn Bay—and now it was this trouble which had done for him. He had told Mr. Edward he would go to Canada—but he knew he never should. They wouldn't want a man so broken up. He could never begin any new work—his life was all in this place. So then—"

The tears began quietly to overflow the large blue eyes looking into Marcia's. Mrs. Betts took no notice of them. They fell on the bosom of her dress; and presently Marcia timidly put up her own handkerchief, and wiped them away, unheeded.

"So then I told him I had better go. I had brought him nothing but trouble, and I wasn't worth it. He was angry with me for saying it. I should never leave him—never—he said—but I must go away then because he had letters to write. And I was just going, when he came after me, and—and—he took me in his arms and carried me up-stairs and laid me on the bed and covered me up warmly. Then he stayed a little while at the foot of the bed looking at me, and saying queer things to himself—and at last he went down-stairs.... All day he has been out and about the farm. He has never spoken to me. The men say he's so strange—they don't like to leave him alone—but he drives them away when they go to speak to him. And when he didn't come in all day, I sat down and wrote to you—"

She paused, mechanically running her little hand up and down the front of Marcia's cloak.

"I don't know anybody here. John's lots of friends—but they're not my friends—and even when they're sorry for us—they know—what I've done—and they don't want to have much to do with me. You said you'd speak for us to Mr. Edward—and I know you did—Mr. Edward told John so. You've been kinder to me than any one else here. So I just wanted to tell *you*—what I'm going to do. I'm going away— I'm going right away. John won't know, nobody'll know where I'm gone. But I want you to tell Mr. Newbury—and get him and Lord William to be kind to John—as they used to be. He'll get over it—by and by!"

Then, straightening herself, she drew herself away.

"I'm not going to the Sisterhood!" she said, defiantly. "I'd sooner die! You may tell Mr. Newbury I'll live my own life— and I've got my boy. John won't find me—I'll take care of that. But if I'm not fit for decent people to touch—there's plenty like me. I'll not cringe to anybody—I'll go where I'm welcome. So now you understand, don't you—what I wanted to ask you?"

"No indeed I don't," cried Marcia, in distress. "And you won't—you sha'n't do anything so mad! Please—please, be patient!—I'll go again to Mr. Newbury. I shall see him to-morrow!"

Mrs. Betts shook her head. "No use—no use. It's the only thing to do for me to take myself off. And no one can stop it. If you were to tell John now, just what I've said, it wouldn't make any difference. He couldn't stop me. I'm going!—that's settled. But *he* sha'n't go. He's got to take up his work here again. And Mr. Edward must persuade him—and look after him—and watch him. What's their religion good for, if it can't do that? Oh, how I *hate* their religion!"

Her eyes lit up with passion; whatever touch of acting there might have been in her monologue till now, this rang fiercely true:

"Haven't I good reason?" Her hands clenched at the words. "It's that which has come between us, as well as the farm. Since he's been back here, it's the old ideas that have got hold of him again. He thinks he's in mortal sin—he thinks he's damned—and yet he won't—he can't give me up. My poor old John!—We were so happy those few weeks!—why couldn't they leave us alone!—That hard old man, Lord William!—and Mr. Edward—who's got you—and everything he wants besides in the world! There—now I suppose you'll turn against me too!"

She stood superbly at bay, her little body drawn up against the wall, her head thrown back. To her own dismay, Marcia found herself sobbing—against her will.

"I'm not against you. Indeed—indeed—I'm not against you! You'll see. I'll go again to Mr. Newbury—I promise you! He's not hard—he's not cruel—he's not!..."

"Hush!" said Mrs. Berts, suddenly, springing forward—"there he is!" And trembling all over, she pointed to the figure of her husband, standing just outside the window and looking in upon them. Thunder had been rumbling round the house during the whole of this scene, and now the rain had begun. It beat on the bare grizzled head of John Betts, and upon his weather-beaten cheeks and short beard.

His expression sent a shudder through Marcia. He seemed to be looking at them—and yet not conscious of them; his tired eyes met hers, and made no sign. With a slight puzzled gesture he turned away, back into the pelting rain, his shoulders bent, his step faltering and slow.

"Oh! go after him!" said Marcia, imploringly. "Don't trouble about me! I'll find the motor. Go! Take my cloak!" She would have wrapped it round Mrs. Betts and pushed her to the door. But the woman stopped her.

"No good. He wouldn't listen to me. I'll get one of the men to bring him in. And the servant'll go for your motor." She went out of the room to give the order, and came back. Then as she saw Marcia under the storm light, standing in the middle of the room, and struggling with her tears, she suddenly fell on her knees beside the girl, embracing her dress, with stifled sobs and inarticulate words of thanks.

"Make them do something for John. It doesn't matter about me. Let them comfort John. Then I'll forgive them."

CHAPTER XIII

Marion Atherstone sat sewing in the cottage garden. Uncertain weather had left the grass wet, and she had carried her work-table into the shelter of a small summer-house, whence the whole plain, drawn in purple and blue on the pale grounding of its chalk soil, could be seen—east, west, and north. Serried ranks, line above line, of purplish cloud girded the horizon, each circle of the great amphitheater rising from its shadowy foundations into pearly white and shining gray, while the topmost series of all soared in snowy majesty upon a sea of blue, above the far-spread woods and fields. From these hills, the Dane in his high clearings had looked out upon the unbroken forests below, and John Hampden had ridden down with his yeomen to find death at Chalgrove Field.

Marion was an Englishwoman to the core; and not ill-read. From this post of hers, she knew a hundred landmarks, churches, towns, hills, which spoke significantly of Englishmen and their doings. But one white patch, in particular, on an upland not three miles from the base of the hills, drew back her eyes and thoughts perpetually.

The patch was Knatchett, and she was thinking of Lord Coryston. She had not seen him for a fortnight; though a stout packet of his letters lay within, in a drawer reserved to things she valued; but she was much afraid that, as usual, he had been the center of stormy scenes in the north, and had come back embittered in spirit. And now, since he had returned, there had been this defiance of Lady Coryston, and this planting of

Mrs. Humphry Ward

the Baptist flag under the very tower of the old church of Coryston Major. Marion Atherstone shook her head over it, in spite of the humorous account of the defeat of Lady Coryston which her father had given to the Chancellor, at their little dinner of the night before; and those deep laughs which had shaken the ample girth of Glenwilliam.

... Ah!—the blind was going up. Marion had her eyes on a particular window in the little house to her right. It was the window of Enid Glenwilliam's room. Though the church clock below had struck eleven, and the bell for morning service had ceased to ring, Miss Glenwilliam was not yet out of bed. Marion had stayed at home from church that she might enjoy her friend's society, and the friend had only just been called. Well, it was Enid's way; and after all, who could wonder? The excitement of that huge meeting of the night before was still tingling even in Marion's quiet Conservative veins. She had not been carried away by Glenwilliam's eloquence at all; she had thought him a wonderful, tawdry, false man of genius, not unlikely to bring himself and England to ruin. All the same, he must be an exhausting man for a daughter to live with; and a daughter who adored him. She did not grudge Enid her rest.

Ah, there was the little gate opening! Somehow she had expected the opener—though he had disappeared abruptly from the meeting the night before, and had given no promise that he would come.

Coryston walked up the garden path, looking about him suspiciously. At sight of Marion he took off his cap; she gave him her hand, and he sat down beside her.

"Nobody else about? What a blessing!"

She looked at him with mild reproach.

"My father and the Chancellor are gone for a walk. Enid is not yet down."

"Why? She is perfectly well. If she were a workman's wife and had to get up at six o'clock, get his breakfast and wash the children, it would do her a world of good."

"How do you know? You are always judging people, and it helps nothing."

"Yes, it does. One must form opinions—or burst. I can tell you, I judged Glenwilliam last night, as I sat listening to him."

"Father thought it hardly one of his best speeches," said Marion, cautiously.

"Sheer wallowing claptrap, wasn't it! I was ashamed of him, and sick of Liberalism, as I sat there. I'll go and join the Primrose League."

Marion lifted her blue eyes and laughed—with her finger on her lip.

"Hush! She might hear." She pointed to the half-open window on the first floor.

"And a good thing too," growled Coryston. "She adores him—and makes him worse. Why can't he *work* at these things—or why can't his secretaries prime him decently! He makes blunders that would disgrace an undergraduate—and doesn't care a rap—so long as a hall-full of fools cheer him."

"You usen't to talk like this!"

"No—because I had illusions," was the sharp reply. "Glenwilliam was one of them. Land!—what does he know about land?—what does a miner—who won't learn!—know about farming? Why, that man—that fellow, John Betts"—he pointed to the Hoddon Grey woods on the edge of the plain— "whom the Newburys are driving out of his job, because he picked a woman out of the dirt—just like these Christians!— John Betts knows more about land in his little finger than

Glenwilliam's whole body! Yet, if you saw them together, you'd see Glenwilliam patronizing and browbeating him, and Betts not allowed a look in. I'm sick of it! I'm off to Canada with Betts."

Marion looked up.

"I thought it was to be the Primrose League."

"You like catching me out," said Coryston, grimly. "But I assure you I'm pretty downhearted."

"You expect too much," said Marion, softly, distressed as she spoke, to notice his frayed collar and cuffs, and the tear in his coat pocket. "And," she added, firmly, "you should make Mrs. Potifer mend your coat."

"She's another disillusion. She's idle and dirty. And Potifer never does a stroke of work if he can help it. Moral—don't bother your head about martyrs. There's generally some excellent reason for martyrizing them."

He broke off—looking at her with a clouded brow.

"Marion!"

She turned with a start, the color flooding her plain, pleasant face.

"Yes, Lord Coryston!"

"If you're so critical of my clothes, why don't you come and look after them and me?"

She gasped—then recovered herself.

"I've never been asked," she said, quietly.

"Asked! Haven't you been scolding and advising me for weeks?

Is there a detail of my private or public life that you don't meddle with—as it pleases you? Half a dozen times a day when I'm with you, you make me feel myself a fool or a brute. And then I go home and write you abject letters—and apologize—and explain. Do you think I'd do it for any other woman in the world? Do you dare to say you don't know what it means?"

He brought his threatening face closer to hers, his blue eyes one fiery accusation. Marion resumed her work, her lip twitching.

"I didn't know I was both a busybody—and a Pharisee!"

"Hypocrite!" he said, with energy. His hand leaped out and captured hers. But she withdrew it.

"My dear friend—if you wish to resume this conversation—it must be at another time. I haven't been able to tell you before, I didn't know it myself till late last night, when Enid told me. Your mother—Lady Coryston—will be here in half an hour—to see Enid."

He stared.

"My mother! So *that's* what she's been up to!"

"She seems to have asked Enid some days ago for an interview. My father's taken Mr. Glenwilliam out of the way, and I shall disappear shortly."

"And what the deuce is going to happen?"

Marion replied that she had no idea. Enid had certainly been seeing a great deal of Arthur Coryston; London, her father reported, was full of talk; and Miss Atherstone thought that from his manner the Chancellor knew very well what was going on.

"And can't stick it?" cried Coryston, his eyes shining.

"Glenwilliam has his faults, but I don't believe he'll want Arthur for a son-in-law—even with the estates. And of course he has no chance of getting both Arthur and the estates."

"Because of your mother?"

Coryston nodded. "So there's another strong man—a real big 'un!—dependent, like Arthur and me—on the whim of a woman. It'll do Glenwilliam nothing but good. He belongs to a class that's too fond of beating its wives. Well, well—so my mother's coming!" He glanced round the little house and garden. "Look here!" He bent forward peremptorily. "You'll see that Miss Glenwilliam treats her decently?"

Marion's expression showed a certain bewilderment.

"I wouldn't trust that girl!" Coryston went on, with vehemence. "She's got something cruel in her eyes."

"Cruel! Why, Lady Coryston's coming—"

"To trample on her? Of course. I know that. But any fool can see that the game will be Miss Glenwilliam's. She'll have my mother in a cleft stick. I'm not sure I oughtn't to be somewhere about. Well, well. I'll march. When shall we 'resume the conversation,' as you put it?"

He looked at her, smiling. Marion colored again, and her nervous movement upset the work-basket; balls of cotton and wool rolled upon the grass.

"Oh!" She bent to pick them up.

"Don't touch them!" cried Coryston. She obeyed instantly, while, on hands and knees, he gathered them up and placed them in her hand.

"Would you like to upset them again? Do, if you like. I'll pick them up." His eyes mocked her tenderly, and before she could reply he had seized her disengaged hand and kissed it. Then he stood up.

"Now I'm going. Good-by."

"How much mischief will you get into to-day?" she asked, in a rather stifled voice.

"It's Sunday—so there isn't so much chance as usual. First item." He checked them on his fingers. "Go to Redcross Farm, see Betts, and—if necessary—have a jolly row with Edward Newbury—or his papa. Second, Blow up Price—my domestic blacksmith—you know!—the socialist apostle I rescued from my mother's clutches and set up at Patchett, forge and all—blow him up sky-high, for evicting a widow woman in a cottage left him by his brother, with every circumstance of barbarity. There's a parable called, I believe, 'The Unjust Servant,' which I intend to rub into him. Item, No. 3, Pitch into the gentleman who turned out the man who voted for Arthur—the Radical miller—Martover gent—who's coming to see me at three this afternoon, to ask what the deuce I mean by spreading reports about him. Shall have a ripping time with him!"

"Why, he's one of the Baptists who were on the platform with you yesterday." Marion pointed to the local paper lying on the grass.

"Don't care. Don't like Baptists, except when they're downtrodden." A vicious kick given to a stone on the lawn emphasized the remark. "Well, good-by. Shall look in at Coryston this afternoon to see if there's anything left of my mother."

And off he went whistling. As he did so, the head and profile of a young lady richly adorned with red-gold hair might have been seen in the upper window. The owner of it was looking after Coryston.

"Why didn't you make him stay?" said Enid Glenwilliam, composedly, as she came out upon the lawn and took a seat on the grass in front of the summer-house.

"On the contrary, I sent him away."

"By telling him whom we were expecting? Was it news to him?"

"Entirely. He hoped you would treat Lady Coryston kindly." Then, with a sudden movement, Marion looked up from her mending, and her eyes—challenging, a little stern,—struck full on her companion.

Enid laughed, and, settling herself into the garden chair, she straightened and smoothed the folds of her dress, which was of a pale-blue crape and suited her tall fairness and brilliance to perfection.

"That's good! I shouldn't have minded his staying at all."

"You promised to see Lady Coryston alone—and she has a right to it," said Marion, with emphasis.

"Has she? I wonder if she has a right to anything?" said Enid Glenwilliam, absently, and lifting a stalk of grass, she began to chew it in silence while her gaze wandered over the view.

"Have you at all made up your mind, Enid, what you are going to say?"

"How can I, till I know what *she's* going to say?" laughed Miss Glenwilliam, teasingly.

"But of course you know perfectly well."

"Is it so plain that no Conservative mother could endure me? But I admit it's not very likely Lady Coryston could. She is the living, distilled essence of Conservative mothers. The question is, mightn't she have to put up with me?"

"I do not believe you care for Arthur Coryston," said Marion, with slow decision, "and if you don't care for him you ought not to marry him."

"Oh, but you forget a lot of things!" was the cool reply. "You simplify a deal too much."

"Are you any nearer caring for him—really—than you were six weeks ago?"

"He's a very—nice—dear fellow." The girl's face softened. "And it would be even sweeter to dish the pack of fortune-hunting mothers who are after him, now, than it was six weeks ago."

"Enid!"

"Can't help it, dear. I'm made like that. I see all the ugly shabby little sides of it—the 'scores' I should make, the snubs I should have to put up with, the tricks Lady Coryston would certainly play on us. How I should love fighting her! In six months Arthur would be my father's private secretary."

"You would despise him if he were!"

"Yes, I suppose I should. But it would be I who would write his speeches for him then—and they'd make Lady Coryston sit up! Ah! didn't you hear something?"

A distant humming on the hill leading to the house became audible.

Marion Atherstone rose.

"It sounds like a motor. You'll have the garden quite to yourselves. I'll see that nobody interrupts you."

Enid nodded. But before Marion had gone half across the lawn she came quickly back again.

"Remember, Enid," her voice pleaded, "his mother's devoted to him. Don't make a quarrel between them—unless you must." Enid smiled, and lightly kissed the face bending over her.

"Did Lord Coryston tell you to say that?"

Marion departed, silenced.

Enid Glenwilliam waited. While the humming noise drew nearer she lifted the local paper from the ground and looked eagerly at the account of the Martover meeting. The paper was a Radical paper, and it had blossomed into its biggest head-lines for the Chancellor. "Chancellor goes for the Landlords," "Crushing attack," "Tories writhe under it," "Frantic applause."

She put it down, half contemptuous, half pleased. She had grown accustomed to the mouthings of party politics, and could not do without them. But her brain was not taken in by them. "Father was not so good as usual last night," she said to herself. "But nobody else would have been half so good!" she added, with a fierce protectiveness.

And in that spirit she rose to meet the stately lady in black, whom the Atherstones' maid-servant was showing across the garden.

"Miss Glenwilliam, I believe?"

Lady Coryston paused and put up her eyeglass. Enid Glenwilliam advanced, holding out her hand.

"How do you do, Lady Coryston?"

The tone was gay, even amused. Lady Coryston realized at

once she was being scanned by a very sharp pair of eyes, and that their owner was, or seemed to be, in no sort of embarrassment. The first advantage, indeed, had been gained by the younger woman. Lady Coryston had approached her with the formality of a stranger. Enid Glenwilliam's easy greetings suggested that they had already met in many drawing-rooms.

Miss Glenwilliam offered a seat.

"Are you afraid of the grass? We could easily go indoors."

"Thank you. This does very well. It was very kind of you to say you would see me."

"I was delighted—of course."

There was a moment's pause. The two women observed each other. Lady Coryston had taken Marion's chair, and sat erect upon it. Her face, with its large and still handsome features, its prominent eyes and determined mouth, was well framed in a black hat, of which the lace strings were tied under her chin. Her flowing dress and scarf of some thin black material, delicately embroidered with jet, were arranged, as usual, with a view to the only effect she ever cared to make—the effect of the great lady, in command—clearly—of all possible resources, while far too well bred to indulge in display or ostentation.

Enid Glenwilliam's blood had quickened, in spite of her apparent ease. She had taken up an ostrich-feather fan—a traditional weapon of the sex—and waved it slowly to and fro, while she waited for her visitor to speak.

"Miss Glenwilliam," began Lady Coryston, "you must no doubt have thought it a strange step that I should ask you for this conversation?"

The tone of this sentence was slightly interrogative, and the girl on the grass nodded gravely.

"But I confess it seemed to me the best and most straightforward thing to do. I am accustomed to go to the point, when a matter has become serious; and I hate shilly-shallying. You, we all know, are very clever, and have much experience of the world. You will, I am sure, prefer that I should be frank."

"Certainly," smiled Enid, "if I only knew what the matter was!"

Lady Coryston's tone became a trifle colder.

"That I should have thought was obvious. You have been seeing a great deal of my son, Miss Glenwilliam; your—your friendship with him has been very conspicuous of late; and I have it from himself that he is in love with you, and either has asked you, or will ask you, to marry him."

"He has asked me several times," said the girl, quietly. Then, suddenly, she laughed. "I came away with my father this week-end, that I might, if possible, prevent his asking me again."

"Then you have refused him?" The voice was indiscreetly eager.

"So far."

"So far? May I ask—does that mean that you yourself are still undecided?"

"I have as yet said nothing final to him."

Lady Coryston paused a few seconds, to consider the look presented to her, and then said, with emphasis:

"If that is so, it is fortunate that we are able to have this talk— at this moment. For I wish, before you take any final decision, to lay before you what the view of my son's family must inevitably be of such a marriage."

"The view of Lord Coryston and yourself?" said Miss Glenwilliam, in her most girlish voice.

"My son Coryston and I have at present no interests in common," was Lady Coryston's slightly tart reply. "That, I should have thought, considering his public utterances, and the part which I have always taken in politics, was sufficiently evident."

Her companion, without speaking, bent over the sticks of the fan, which her long fingers were engaged in straightening.

"No! When I speak of the family," resumed Lady Coryston, "I must for the present, unfortunately, look upon myself as the only sure guardian of its traditions; but that I intend to be—while I live. And I can only regard a marriage between my son and yourself as undesirable—not only for my son—but first and foremost, Miss Glenwilliam, for yourself."

"And why?"

Laying down the fan upon her knee, the young lady now applied her nimble fingers to smoothing the white and curling tips of the feathers.

The color rushed into Lady Coryston's lightly wrinkled cheeks.

"Because it rarely or never answers that persons from such different worlds, holding such different opinions, and with such different antecedents, should marry," she said, firmly. "Because I could not welcome you as a daughter—and because a marriage with you would disastrously affect the prospects of my son."

"I wonder what you mean by 'such different worlds,'" said Miss Glenwilliam, with what seemed an innocent astonishment. "Arthur and I always go to the same dances."

Lady Coryston's flush deepened angrily. She had some

difficulty in keeping her voice in order.

"I think you understand what I mean. I don't wish to be the least rude."

"Of course not. But—is it my birth, or my poverty, that you most dislike?"

"Poverty has nothing to do with it—nothing at all. I have never considered money in connection with Arthur's marriage, and never shall."

"Because you have so much of it?" Lifting her broad, white brow from the fan on her knee, Enid turned the astonishing eyes beneath it on the lady in black sitting beside her. And for the first time the lady in black was conscious of the malice lurking in the soft voice of the speaker.

"That, perhaps, would be your way of explaining it. In any case, I repeat, money has nothing to do with the present case. But, Miss Glenwilliam, my son belongs to a family that has fought for its convictions."

At this the younger lady shot a satiric glance at the elder, which for the moment interrupted a carefully prepared sentence.

Enid was thinking of a casual remark of her father's made that morning at breakfast: "Oh yes, the Corystons are an old family. They were Whigs as long as there were any bones to pick on that side. Then Pitt bought the first Lord Coryston— in his earliest batch of peers—with the title and a fat post— something to do with the navy. That was the foundation of their money—then came the Welsh coal—et cetera."

But she kept her recollections to herself. Lady Coryston went on:

"We have stood for generations for certain principles. We are proud of them. My husband died in them. I have devoted my life to them. They are the principles of the Conservative party. Our eldest son, as of course you know, departed from them. My dear husband did not flinch; and instead of leaving the estates to Coryston, he left them to me—as trustee for the political faith he believed in; that faith of which your father has been—excuse my frankness, it is really best for us both—and is now—the principal enemy! I then had to decide, when I was left a widow, to whom the estates were to go on my death. Painful as it was, I decided that my trust did not allow me to leave them to Coryston. I made Arthur my heir three months ago."

"How very interesting!" said the listener, behind the fan. Lady Coryston could not see her face.

"But it is only fair to him and to you," Arthur's mother continued, with increased deliberation, "that I should say frankly, now that this crisis has arisen, that if you and Arthur marry, it is impossible that Arthur should inherit his father's estates. A fresh disposition of them will have to be made."

Enid Glenwilliam dropped the fan and looked up. Her color had gone.

"Because—Lady Coryston—I am my father's daughter?"

"Because you would bring into our family principles wholly at variance with our traditions—and I should be false to my trust if I allowed it." The conscious dignity of pose and voice fitted the solemnity of these final words.

There was a slight pause.

"Then—if Arthur married me—he would be a pauper?" said the girl, bending forward.

"He has a thousand a year."

"That's very disturbing! I shall have to consider everything again."

Lady Coryston moved nervously.

"I don't understand you."

"What I *couldn't* have done, Lady Coryston—would have been to come into Arthur's family as in any way dependent on his mother!"

The girl's eyes shone. Lady Coryston had also paled.

"I couldn't of course expect that you would have any friendly feeling toward me," she said, after a moment.

"No—you couldn't—you couldn't indeed!"

Enid Glenwilliam sprang up, entered the summer-house, and stood over her visitor, lightly leaning forward, her hands supporting her on a rustic table that stood between them, her breath fluttering.

"Yes—perhaps now I could marry him—perhaps now I could!" she repeated. "So long as I wasn't your dependent—so long as we had a free life of our own—and knew exactly where we stood, with nothing to fear or to hope—the situation might be faced. We might hope, too—father and I—to bring *our* ideas and *our* principles to bear upon Arthur. I believe he would adopt them. He has never had any ideas of his own. You have made him take yours! But of course it seems inconceivable to you that we should set any store by *our* principles. You think all I want is money. Well, I am like anybody else. I know the value of money. I like money and luxury, and pretty things. I have been sorely tempted to let Arthur marry me as he has once or twice proposed, at the nearest registry office, and present you next day with the *fait accompli*—to take or leave. I believe you would have surrendered to the *fait accompli*—yes, I believe you would!

Arthur was convinced that, after sulking a little, you would forgive him. Well, but then—I looked forward—to the months—or years—in which I should be courting—flattering—propitiating you—giving up my own ideas, perhaps, to take yours—turning my back on my father—on my old friends—on my party—for *money*! Oh yes, I should be quite capable of it. At least, I dare say I should. And I just funked it! I had the grace—the conscience—to funk it. I apologize for the slang—I can't express it any other way. And now you come and say: 'Engage yourself to him—and I'll disinherit him *at once*. That makes the thing look clean and square!—that tempts the devil in one, or the angel—I don't know which. I like Arthur. I should get a great many social advantages by marrying him, whatever you may do or say; and a thousand a year to me looks a great deal more than it does to you. But then, you see, my father began life as a pit-boy—Yes, I think it might be done!"

The speaker raised herself to her full height, and stood with her hands behind her, gazing at Lady Coryston.

In the eyes of that poor lady the Chancellor's daughter had suddenly assumed the aspect of some glittering, avenging fate. At last Lady Coryston understood something of the power, the spell, there was in this girl for whom her son had deserted her; at last she perceived, despairingly perceived, her strange beauty. The long thin mouth, now breathing scorn, the short chin, and prominent cheekbones denied Enid Glenwilliam any conventional right indeed to that great word. But the loveliness of the eyes and hair, of the dark brows, sustaining the broad and delicate forehead, the pale rose and white of the skin, the setting of the head, her wonderful tallness and slenderness, these, instinct as the whole woman was, at the moment, with a passion of defiance, made of her a dazzling and formidable creature. Lady Coryston beheld her father in her; she seemed to feel the touch, the terror of Glenwilliam.

Bewilderment and unaccustomed weakness overtook Lady Coryston. It was some moments before, under the girl's

Mrs. Humphry Ward

threatening eyes, she could speak at all. Then she said, with difficulty:

"You may marry my son, Miss Glenwilliam—but you do not love him! That is perfectly plain. You are prepared none the less, apparently, to wreck his happiness and mine, in order—"

"I don't love him? Ah! that's another story altogether! Do I love him? I don't know. Honestly, I don't know. I don't believe I am as capable of falling in love as other girls are—or say they are. I like him, and get on with him—and I might marry him; I might—have—married him," she repeated, slowly, "partly to have the sweetness, Lady Coryston, of punishing you for the slight you offered my father!—and partly for other things. But you see—now I come to think of it—there is some one else to be considered—"

The girl dropped into a chair, and looked across the table at her visitor, with a sudden change of mood and voice.

"You say you won't have it, Lady Coryston. Well, that doesn't decide it for me—and it wouldn't decide it for Arthur. But there's some one else won't have it."

A pause. Miss Glenwilliam took up the fan again and played with it—considering.

"My father came to my room last night," she said, at last, "in order to speak to me about it. 'Enid,' he said, 'don't marry that man! He's a good enough fellow—but he'll drive a wedge into our life. We can't find a use for him—you and I. He'll divide us, my girl—and it isn't worth it—you don't love him!' And we had a long talk—and at last I told him—I wouldn't—I *wouldn't*! So you see, Lady Coryston, if I don't marry your son, it's not because you object—but because my father—whom you insulted—doesn't wish me to enter your family—doesn't approve of a marriage with your son—and has persuaded me against it."

Lady Coryston stared into the face of the speaker, and quailed before the flash of something primitive and savage in the eyes that met her own. Under the sting of it, however, she found a first natural and moving word, as she slowly rose from her seat.

"You love your father, Miss Glenwilliam. You might remember that I, too, love my son—and there was never a rough word between us till he knew you."

She wavered a little, gathering up her dress. And the girl perceived that she had grown deadly white, and was suddenly ashamed of her own vehemence. She too rose.

"I'm sorry, Lady Coryston. I've been a brute. But when I think of my father, and those who hate him, I see red. I had no business to say some of the things I have said. But it's no good apologizing. Let me, however, just say this: Please be careful, Lady Coryston, about your son. He's in love with me—and I'm very, *very* sorry for him. Let me write to him first—before you speak to him. I'll write—as kindly as I can. But I warn you—it'll hurt him—and he may visit it on you—for all I can say. When will he be at Coryston?"

"To-night."

"I will send a letter over to-morrow morning. Is your car waiting?"

They moved across the lawn together, not speaking a word. Lady Coryston entered the car. Enid Glenwilliam made her a low bow, almost a curtsey, which the elder lady acknowledged; and the car started.

Enid came back to the summer-house, sat down by the table, and buried her face in her hands.

After a little while a hurried step was heard approaching the summer-house. She looked up and saw her father. The Chancellor's burly form filled up the door of the little house.

Mrs. Humphry Ward

His dark, gipsy face looked down with amusement upon his daughter.

"Well, Enid, how did you get through? Did she trample on you—did she scratch and spit? I wager she got as good as she gave? Why, what's the matter, my girl? Are you upset?"

Enid got up, struggling for composure.

"I—I behaved like a perfect fiend."

"Did you?" The Chancellor's laughter filled the summer-house. "The old harridan! At last somebody has told her the truth. The idea of her breaking in upon you here!—to threaten you, I suppose, with all sorts of pains and penalties, if you married her precious son. You gave her what for. Why, Enid, what's the matter—don't be a fool, my dear! You don't regret him?"

"No." He put his arm tenderly round her, and she leaned against him. Suddenly she drew herself up and kissed him.

"I shall never marry, father. It's you and I, isn't it, against the world?"

"Half the world," said Glenwilliam, laughing. "There's a jolly big half on our side, my dear, and lots of good fellows in it for you to marry." He looked at her with proud affection.

She shook her head, slipped her hand in his, and they walked back to the house together.

CHAPTER XIV

The state of mind in which Lady Coryston drove home from the Atherstones' cottage would have seemed to most people unreasonable. She had obtained—apparently—everything for which she had set out, and yet there she was, smarting and bruised through all her being, like one who has suffered intolerable humiliation and defeat. A woman of her type and class is so well sheltered as a rule from the roughnesses of life, so accustomed to the deference of their neighbors, that to be handled as Enid Glenwilliam had handled her victim, destroys for the time nerve and self-respect. Lady Coryston felt as if she had been physically as well as morally beaten, and could not get over it. She sat, white and shaken, in the darkness of a closed motor, the prey to strange terrors. She would not see Arthur that night! He was only to return late, and she would not risk it. She must have a night's rest, indeed, before grappling with him. She was not herself, and the violence of that extraordinary girl had upset her. Conscious of a very rapid pulse, she remembered for a moment, unwillingly, certain warnings that her doctor had given her before she left town— "You are overtaxing yourself, Lady Coryston—and you badly want a rest." Pure nonsense! She came of a long-lived stock, persons of sound hearts and lungs, who never coddled themselves. All the same, she shrank physically, instinctively, from the thought of any further emotion or excitement that day—till she had had a good night. She now remembered that she had had practically no sleep the preceding night. Indeed, ever since the angry scene with Arthur a fortnight before, she had been conscious of bodily and mental strain.

Mrs. Humphry Ward

Which perhaps accounted for the feeling of irritation with which she perceived the figure of her daughter standing on the steps of Coryston House beside Sir Wilfrid Bury. Marcia had come to her that morning with some tiresome story about the Newburys and the divorced woman Mrs. Betts. How could she think of such things, when her mind was full of Arthur? Girls really should be more considerate.

The car drew up at the steps, and Marcia and Sir Wilfrid awaited it. Even preoccupied as she was, Lady Coryston could not help noticing that Marcia was subdued and silent. She asked her mother no questions, and after helping Lady Coryston to alight, she went quickly into the house. It vaguely crossed the mother's mind that her daughter was depressed or annoyed—perhaps with her? But she could not stop to think about it.

Sir Wilfrid, however, followed Lady Coryston into the drawing-room.

"What have you been doing?" he asked her, smiling, taking the liberty of an old friend and co-executor. "I think I guess!"

She looked at him somberly.

"She won't marry him! But not a word to Arthur, please—not a word!—till I give you leave. I have gone through—a great deal."

Her look of weakness and exhaustion did indeed strike him painfully. He put out his hand and pressed hers.

"Well, so far, so good," he said, gravely. "It must be a great relief to your mind." Then in another and a lower tone he added, "Poor old boy!"

Lady Coryston made no reply except to say that she must get ready for luncheon. She left the room just as Sir Wilfrid perceived a rider on a bay horse approaching through the park, and recognized Edward Newbury.

"Handsome fellow!" he thought, as he watched him from the window; "and sits his horse uncommonly well. Why doesn't that girl fly to meet him? They used to in my days."

But Newbury dismounted with only a footman to receive him, and Marcia did not appear till the gong had rung for luncheon.

Sir Wilfrid's social powers were severely taxed to keep that meal going. Lady Coryston sat almost entirely silent and ate nothing. Marcia too ate little and talked less. Newbury indeed had arrived in radiant spirits, bringing a flamboyant account of Marcia's trousseau which he had extracted from a weekly paper, and prepared to tease her thereon. But he could scarcely get the smallest rise out of her, and presently he, too, fell silent, throwing uneasy glances at her from time to time. Her black hair and eyes were more than usually striking, by contrast with a very simple and unadorned white dress; but for beauty, her face required animation; it could be all but plain in moments of languor or abstraction; and Sir Wilfrid marveled that a girl's secret instinct did not save her from presenting herself so unattractively to her lover.

Newbury, it appeared, had spent the preceding night in what Sir Wilfrid obstinately called a "monkery"—*alias* the house of an Anglican brotherhood or Community—the Community of the Ascension, of which Newbury's great friend, Father Brierly, was Superior. In requital for Newbury's teasing of Marcia, Sir Wilfrid would have liked to tease Newbury a little on the subject of the "monkery." But Newbury most dexterously evaded him. He would laugh, but not at the hosts he had just quitted; and through all his bantering good temper there could be felt the throb of some deep feeling which was not allowed to express itself. "Damned queer eyes!" was Bury's inward comment, as he happened once to observe Newbury's face during a pause of silence. "Half in a dream all the time— even when the fellow's looking at his sweetheart."

After luncheon Marcia made a sign, and she and Newbury slipped away. They wandered out beyond the lake into a big wood, where great pools of pink willow-herb, in its open spaces, caught the light as it struck through the gray trunks of the beeches. Newbury found a seat for Marcia on a fallen trunk, and threw himself beside her. The world seemed to have been all washed by the thunder-storm of the night before; the odors of grass, earth, and fern were steaming out into the summer air. The wood was alive with the hum of innumerable insects, which had become audible and dominant with the gradual silencing of the birds. In the half-cut hay-fields the machines stood at rest; rarely, an interlaced couple could be dimly seen for a moment on some distant footpath of the park; sometimes a partridge called or a jay screamed; otherwise a Sabbath stillness—as it seemed to Marcia, a Sabbath dreariness—held the scene.

Newbury put up his arms, drew her down to him, and kissed her passionately. She yielded; but it was more yielding than response; and again he was conscious of misgiving as at luncheon.

"Darling!—is there anything wrong—anything that troubles you?" he said, anxiously. "Do you think I've forgotten you for one moment, while I've been away?"

"Yes; while you were asleep." She smiled shyly, while her fingers caressed his.

"Wrong—quite wrong! I dreamed of you both nights. And oh, dearest, I thought of you last night."

"Where—when?" Her voice was low—a little embarrassed.

"In chapel—the chapel at Blackmount—at Benediction."

She looked puzzled.

"What is Benediction?"

"A most beautiful service, though of late origin—which, like fools, we have let the Romans monopolize. The Bishops bar it, but in private chapels like our own, or Blackmount, they can't interfere. To me, yesterday evening"—his voice fell—"it was like the gate of heaven. I longed to have you there."

She made no reply. Her brow knitted a little. He went on:

"Of course a great deal of what is done at places like Blackmount is not recognized—yet. To some of the services—to Benediction for instance—the public is not admitted. But the brothers keep every rule—of the strictest observance. I was present last night at the recitation of the Night Office—most touching—most solemn! And—my darling!"—he pressed her hand while his face lit up—"I want to ask you—though I hardly dare. Would you give me—would you give me the greatest joy you could give me, before our marriage? Father Brierly—my old friend—would give us both Communion, on the morning of our wedding—in the little chapel of the Brotherhood, in Red Street, Soho—just us two alone. Would it be too much for you, too tiring?" His voice was tenderness itself. "I would come for you at half past seven—nobody but your mother would know. And then afterward—afterward!—we will go through with the great ceremony—and the crowds—and the bridesmaids. Your mother tells me it's to be Henry the Seventh's chapel—isn't it? But first, we shall have received our Lord, we two alone, into our hearts—to feed upon Him, forever!"

There was silence. He had spoken with an imploring gentleness and humility, yet nevertheless with a tender confidence which did not escape the listener. And again a sudden terror seized on Marcia—as though behind the lover, she perceived something priestly, directive, compelling—something that threatened her very self. She drew herself back.

"Edward!—ought you—to take things for granted about me—like this?"

His face, with its "illuminated," exalted look, scarcely changed.

"I don't take anything for granted, dearest. I only put it before you. I talked it over with Brierly—he sent you a message—"

"But I don't know him!" cried Marcia. "And I don't know that I want to know him. I'm not sure I think as you do, Edward. You assume that I do—but indeed—indeed—my mind is often in confusion—great confusion—I don't know what to think—about many things."

"The Church decides for us, darling—that is the great comfort—the great strength."

"But what Church? Everybody chooses his own, it seems to me! And you know that that Roman priest who was at Hoddon Grey the other day thinks you just as much in the wrong as—well, as he'd think me!—*me*, even!" She gave a little tremulous laugh. Then, with a quick movement she sat erect. Her great, dark eyes fixed him eagerly. "And Edward, I've got something so different, so very different to talk to you about! I've been so unhappy—all night, all to-day. I've been pining for you to come—and then afraid what you'd say—"

She broke off, her lips parting eagerly, her look searching his.

And this time, as she watched him, she saw his features stiffen, as though a suspicion, a foreboding ran through him. She hurried on.

"I went over to see Mrs. Betts, yesterday, Edward. She sent for me. And I found her half mad—in despair! I just persuaded her to wait till I'd seen you. But perhaps you've seen her—to-day?" She hung on his answer.

"Indeed, no." The chill, the alteration in his tone were evident. "I left Blackmount this morning, after matins, motored home, just saw my father and mother for a moment—heard nothing—and rode on here as fast as I could. What is there fresh, dearest? I thought that painful business was settled. And I confess I feel very indignant with Mrs. Betts for dragging you—insisting upon dragging you—into it!"

"How could she help it? She's no friends, Edward! People are very sorry for him—but they fight shy of her. I dare say it's right—I dare say she's deserved it—I don't want to know. But oh it's so miserable—so pitiable! She's *going!*—she's made up her mind to that—she's going. That's what she wanted to tell me—and asked that I should tell you."

"She could do nothing better for herself, or him," said Newbury, firmly.

"But she's not going, in the way you proposed! Oh no. She's going to slip away—to hide! He's not to know where she is—and she implores you to keep him here—to comfort him—and watch over him."

"Which of course we should do."

The quiet, determined voice sent a shiver through Marcia. She caught Newbury's hand in hers, and held it close.

"Yes, but Edward!—listen!—it would kill them both. His mind seems to be giving way. I got a letter from her again this morning, inclosing one from their doctor. And she—she says if she does go, if decent people turn her out, she'll just go back to people like herself—who'll be kind to her. Nothing will induce her to go to the Cloan Sisters."

"She must, of course, be the judge of that," said Newbury, coldly.

"But you can't allow it!—you *can't!*—the poor, poor things!" cried Marcia. "I saw him too, Edward—I shall never forget it!" And with a growing excitement she gave a full account of her visit to the farm, of her conversation with Mrs. Betts, of that gray, grief-stricken face at the window.

"He's fifty-two. How can he start again? He's just torn between his work—and her. And if she goes away and hides from him, it'll be the last straw. He believes he saved her from a bad life—and now he'll think that he's only made things worse. And he's ill—his brain's had a shake. Edward—dear Edward!—let them stay!—for my sake, let them stay!"

All her soul was in her eyes. She had never been more winning—more lovely. She placed her hands on his shoulders as he sat beside her, and leaned her soft cheek against his.

"Do you mean—let them stay on at the Farm?" he asked, after a pause, putting his arms round her.

"Couldn't they? They could live so quietly. She would hardly ever leave the house—and so long as he does his work—his scientific work—need anything else trouble you? Need you have any other relations with them at all? Wouldn't everybody understand—wouldn't everybody know you'd done it for pity?"

Again a pause. Then he said, with evident difficulty: "Dear Marcia—do you ever think of my father in this?"

"Oh, mayn't I go!—and *beg* Lord William—"

"Ah, but wait a minute. I was going to say—My father's an old man. This has hit him hard. It's aged him a good deal. He trusted Betts implicitly, as he would himself. And now—in addition—you want him to do something that he feels to be wrong."

"But Edward, they *are* married! Isn't it a tyranny"—she brought the word out bravely—"when it causes so much suffering!—to insist on more than the law does?"

"For us there is but one law—the law of Christ!" And then, as a flash of something like anger passed through his face, he added, with an accent of stern conviction: "For us they are *not* married—and we should be conniving at an offense and a scandal, if we accepted them as married persons. Oh, dear Marcia, why do you make me say these things? I *can't* discuss them with you!" he repeated, in a most real distress.

She raised herself, and moved a little further from him. A passionate hopelessness—not without resentment—was rising in her.

"Then you won't try to persuade your father—even for my sake, Edward?"

He made no reply. She saw his lip tremble, but she knew it was only because he could not bear to put into words the refusal behind.

The silence continued. Marcia, raising her head, looked away into the green vistas of the wood, while the tears gathered slowly in her eyes. He watched her, in a trouble no less deep. At last she said—in a low, lingering voice:

"And I—I couldn't marry—and be happy—with the thought always—of what had happened to them—and how—you couldn't give me—what I asked. I have been thinking it out for hours and hours. I'm afraid, Edward—we—we've made a great mistake!"

She drew her hand away, and looked at him, very pale and trembling, yet with something new—and resolute—in her aspect.

"Marcia!" It was a sound of dismay.

"Oh! it was my fault!"—and she clasped her hands in a gesture at once childish and piteous—"I somehow knew from the beginning that you thought me different from what I am. It was quite natural. You're much older than I, and of course—of course—you thought that if—if I loved you—I'd be guided by you—and think as you wish. But Edward, you see I've had to live by myself—and think for myself—more than other girls—because mother was always busy with other things—that didn't concern me—that I didn't care about—and I was left alone—and had to puzzle out a lot of things that I never talked about. I'm obstinate—I'm proud. I must believe for myself—and not because some one else does. I don't know where I shall come out. And that's the strange thing! Before we were engaged, I didn't know I had a mind!" She smiled at him pitifully through her tears. "And ever since we've been engaged—this few weeks—I've been doing nothing but think and think—and all the time it's been carrying me away from you. And now this trouble. I *couldn't*"—she clenched her hand with a passionate gesture—"I *couldn't* do what you're doing. It would kill me. You seem to be obeying something outside—which you're quite sure of. But if *I* drove those two people to despair, because I thought something was wrong that they thought right, I should never have any happiness in my heart—my *own heart*—again. Love seems to me everything!—being kind—not giving pain. And for you there's something greater—what the Church says—what the Bible says. And I could never see that. I could never agree. I could never submit. And we should be miserable. You'd think I was wicked—and I—well!"—she panted a little, trying for her words—"there are ugly—violent—feelings in me sometimes. I couldn't hate *you*—but—Edward—just now—I felt I could hate—what you believe!"

The sudden change in his look smote her to the heart. She held out her hands, imploring.

"Forgive me! Oh, do forgive me!"

During her outburst he had risen, and was now leaning against a young tree beside her, looking down upon her—white and motionless. He had made no effort to take her hands, and they dropped upon her knee.

"This is terrible!" he said, as though to himself, and half-consciously—"terrible!"

"But indeed—indeed—it's best." Her voice, which was little more than a whisper, was broken by a sob. She buried her face in the hands he had left untaken.

The minutes seemed endless till he spoke again; and then it was with a composure which seemed to her like the momentary quiet that may come—the sudden furling of the winds—in the very midst of tempest. She divined the tempest, in this man of profound and concentrated feeling; but she had not dared to watch it.

"Marcia—is it really true? Couldn't I make you happy? Couldn't I lead you to look at things as I do? As you say, I am older, I have had more time to think and learn. If you love me, wouldn't it be right, that—I should influence you?"

"It might be," she said, sadly. "But it wouldn't happen. I know more of myself—now. This has made me know myself—as I never did. I should wound and distress you. And to struggle with you would make me hard—and bad."

Another silence. But for both it was one of those silences when the mind, as it were, reaps at one stroke a whole harvest of ideas and images which, all unconsciously to itself, were standing ready to be reaped; the silences, more active far than speech, which determine life.

At the end of it, he came to sit beside her.

"Then we must give it up—we must give it up. I bless you for the happiness you gave me—this little while. I pray God to bless you—now and forever."

Sobbing, she lifted her face to him, and he kissed her for the last time. She slipped off her engagement ring and gave it to him. He looked at it with a sad smile, pressed his lips to it, and then stooping down, he took a stick lying by the log, and scooped out a deep hole in the mossy, fibrous earth. Into it he dropped the ring, covering it again with all the leafy "rubble

Mrs. Humphry Ward

and wreck" of the wood. He covered his eyes for a moment, and rose.

"Let me take you home. I will write to Lady Coryston to-night."

They walked silently through the wood, and to the house. Never, in her whole life, had Marcia felt so unhappy. And yet, already, she recognized what she had done as both inevitable and past recall.

They parted, just with a lingering look into each other's eyes, and a piteous murmur from her: "I'm sorry!—oh, I'm *sorry*!"

At the moment when Marcia and Newbury were crossing the formal garden on the west front of the house, one of two persons in Lady Coryston's sitting-room observed them.

These persons were—strange to say—Lady Coryston and her eldest son. Lady Coryston, after luncheon, had felt so seriously unwell that she had retired to her sitting-room, with strict injunctions that she must be left alone. Sir Wilfrid and Lester started on a Sunday walk; Marcia and Newbury had disappeared.

The house, through all its innumerable rooms and corridors, sank into deep silence. Lady Coryston was lying on her sofa, with closed eyes. All the incidents of her conversation with Enid Glenwilliam were running perpetually through her mind—the girl's gestures and tones—above all the words of her final warning.

After all it was not she—his mother—who had done it. Without her it would have happened all the same. She found herself constantly putting up this plea, as though in recurrent gusts of fear. Fear of whom?—of Arthur? What absurdity! Her proud spirit rebelled.

And yet she knew that she was listening—listening in

dread—for a footstep in the house. That again was absurd. Arthur was staying with friends on the further side of the country, and was to leave them after dinner by motor. He could not be home till close on midnight; and there would be no chance of her seeing him—unless she sent for him—till the following morning, after the arrival of the letter. *Then*—she must face him.

But still the footstep haunted her imagination, and the remembrance of him as he had stood, light and buoyant, on the floor of the House of Commons, making his maiden speech. In April—and this was July. Had that infatuation begun even then, which had robbed her of her dearest—her Benjamin?

She fell into a restless sleep after a while, and woke suddenly, in alarm. There was somebody approaching her room—evidently on tiptoe. Some one knocking—very gently. She sat up, trembling. "Come in!"

The door opened—and there was Coryston.

She fell back on her cushions, astonished and annoyed.

"I said I was not to be disturbed, Coryston."

He paused on the threshold.

"Am I disturbing you? Wouldn't you like me to read to you— or something?"

His tone was so gentle that she was disarmed—though still annoyed.

"Come in. I may perhaps point out that it's a long time since you've come to see me like this, Coryston."

"Yes. Never mind. What shall I read?"

She pointed to a number of the *Quarterly* that was lying open, and to an article on "The later years of Disraeli."

Coryston winced. He knew the man who had written it, and detested him. But he sat down beside her, and began immediately to read. To both of them his reading was a defense against conversation, and yet to both of them, after a little while, it was pleasant.

Presently indeed he saw that it had soothed her and that in spite of her efforts to keep awake she had fallen fitfully asleep again. He let the book drop, and sat still, studying his mother's strong, lined face in its setting of gray hair. There was something in her temporary quiescence and helplessness that touched him; and it was clear to him that in these last few months she had aged considerably. As he watched, a melancholy softness—as of one who sees deeper than usual into the human spectacle—invaded and transformed his whole expression; his thin body relaxed; his hands dropped at his side. The dead quiet of the house also oppressed him—like a voice—an omen.

He knew that she had seen Enid Glenwilliam that morning. A little note from Marion Atherstone that afternoon spoke anxiety and sympathy. "Enid confesses she was violent. I am afraid it was a painful scene." And now there was Arthur to be faced—who would never believe, of course, but that his mother had done it.

A movement in the garden outside diverted his attention. He looked up and saw two figures—Marcia and Newbury. A sight which roused in him afresh—on the instant—all his fiercest animosities. That fellow!—and his creed! That old hide-bound inquisitor, his father!

Well!—he peered at them—has she got anything whatever out of young Tartuffe? Not she! He knew the breed. He rose discreetly, so as not to wake Lady Coryston, and standing by the window, he watched them across the garden, and saw their parting. Something in their demeanor struck him. "Not demonstrative anyway," he said to himself, with a queer satisfaction.

He sat down again, and tossing the *Quarterly* away, he took up a volume of Browning. But he scarcely read a line. His mind was really possessed by the Betts' story, and by the measures that might be taken—Marcia or no Marcia!—to rouse the country-side against the Newburys, and force them to bow to public opinion in the matter of this tragedy. He himself had seen the two people concerned, again, that morning—a miserable sight! Neither of them had said anything further to him of their plans. Only Mrs. Betts had talked incoherently of "waiting to hear from Miss Coryston." Poor soul!—she might wait.

Twenty minutes passed, and then he too heard a footfall in the passage outside, and the swish of a dress. Marcia!

He opened the door.

"Don't come in. Mother's asleep."

Marcia stared at him in amazement. Then she stepped past him, and stood on the threshold surveying her mother. Her pathetic look conveyed the instinctive appeal of the young girl turning in the crisis of her life to her natural friend, her natural comforter. And it remained unanswered. She turned and beckoned to Coryston.

"Come with me—a moment." They went noiselessly down the staircase leading from Lady Coryston's wing, into a room which had been their schoolroom as children, on the ground floor. Marcia laid a hand on her brother's arm.

"Coryston—I was coming to speak to mother. I have broken off my engagement."

"Thank the Lord!" cried Coryston, taken wholly aback.

"Thank the Lord!"

He would have kissed her in his relief and enthusiasm. But Marcia stepped back from him. Her pale face showed a passionate resentment.

"Don't speak about him, Corry! Don't say another word about him. You never understood him, and I'm not going to discuss him with you. I couldn't bear it. What's wrong with mother?"

"She's knocked over—by that girl, Enid Glenwilliam. She saw her this morning."

He described the situation. Marcia showed but a languid interest.

"Poor mother!" she said, absently. "Then I won't bother her with my affairs—till to-morrow. Don't tell her anything, Corry. Good-by."

"I say, Marcia—old woman—don't be so fierce with me. You took me by surprise—" he muttered, uncomfortably.

"Oh, it doesn't matter. Nobody in this world—seems to be able to understand anybody else—or make allowances for anybody else. Good-by."

Coryston had long since departed. Lady Coryston had gone to bed, seeing no one, and pleading headache. Marcia, too, had deserted Sir Wilfrid and Lester after dinner, leaving Sir Wilfrid to the liveliest and dismalest misgivings as to what might have been happening further to the Coryston family on this most inexplicable and embarrassing day.

Marcia was sitting in her room by the open window. She had been writing a long letter to Newbury, pouring out her soul to him. All that she had been too young and immature to say to him face to face, she had tried to say to him in these closely written and blotted pages. To write them had brought relief, but also exhaustion of mind and body.

The summer night was sultry and very still. Above a bank of purple cloud, she looked into depths of fathomless azure, star-sprinkled, with a light in the southeast prophesying moonrise. Dark shapes of woods—the distant sound of the little trout-stream, where it ran over a weir—a few notes of birds—were the only sounds; otherwise the soul was alone with itself. Once indeed she heard a sudden burst of voices far overhead, and a girl's merry laugh. One of the young servants no doubt—on the top floor. How remote!—and yet how near.

And far away over those trees was Newbury, smarting under the blow she had given him—suffering—suffering. That poor woman, too, weeping out her last night, perhaps, beside her husband. What could she do for her—how could she help her? Marcia sat there hour after hour, now lost in her own grief, now in that of others; realizing through pain, through agonized sympathy, the energy of a fuller life.

She went to bed, and to sleep—for a few hours—toward morning. She was roused by her maid, who came in with a white face of horror.

"Oh, miss!"

"What is the matter?"

Marcia sat up in bed. Was her mother ill?—dead?

The girl stammered out her ghastly news. Briggs the head gardener had just brought it. The head foreman at Redcross Farm going his rounds in the early hours, had perceived a light burning in the laboratory. The door was locked, but on forcing his way in, he had come suddenly on a spectacle of horror. John Betts was sitting—dead—in his chair, with a bullet wound in the temple; Mrs. Betts was on a stool beside him, leaning against his knee. She must have found him dead, have taken up the revolver, as it had dropped from his hand, and after an interval, long or short, have deliberately unfastened her dress—The bullet had passed through her heart, and death had been a matter of seconds. On the table was lying a scrap of paper on which were the words in John Betts's handwriting: "Mad—forgive." And beside it a little twisted note, addressed to "Miss Marcia Coryston." The foreman had given it to Briggs. Her maid placed it in Marcia's hands.

She tried to read it, but failed. The girl beside her saw her slip back, fainting, on her pillows.

CHAPTER XV

It was the old housekeeper at Coryston, one Mrs. Drew, who had been the presiding spirit of the house in all its domestic aspects for some thirty years, who came at the summons of Marcia's frightened maid, and helped the girl to revive her mistress, without alarming Lady Coryston. And before the news could reach her mother in other ways, Marcia herself went in to tell her what she must know.

Lady Coryston had had a bad night, and was sitting up in bed gazing straight before her, her gaunt hands lying listlessly on a pile of letters she had not yet opened. When Marcia came in, a white ghost, still shivering under nervous shock, her mother looked at her in sudden dismay. She sprang forward in bed.

"What!—Marcia!—have you seen Arthur?"

Marcia shook her head.

"It's not Arthur, mother!"

And standing rigid beside her mother's bed, she told her news, so far as those piteous deaths at Redcross Farm were concerned. Of her own position, and of the scene which had passed between herself and Newbury the preceding day, she said not a word.

On the facts presented to her, Lady Coryston was first bewildered, then irritated. Why on earth should Marcia take

Mrs. Humphry Ward

this morbid and extravagant interest in the affairs of such people? They were not even tenants of the Coryston estates! It was monstrous that she should have taken them up at all, and most audacious and unbecoming that she should have tried to intercede for them with the Newburys, as she understood, from her daughter's hardly coherent story, had been the case. And now, she supposed, as Marcia had actually been so foolish, so headstrong, as to go herself—without permission either from her mother or her betrothed—to see these two people at the farm, the very day before this horrible thing happened, she might have to appear at the inquest. Most improper and annoying!

However, she scarcely expressed her disapproval aloud with her usual trenchancy. In the first place, Marcia's tremulous state made it difficult. In the next, she was herself so far from normal that she could not, after the first few minutes, keep her attention fixed upon the matter at all. She began abruptly to question Marcia as to whether she had seen Arthur the night before—or that morning?

"I had gone up-stairs before he arrived last night—and this morning he's not yet down," said the girl, perfunctorily, as though she only answered the question with her lips, without attaching any real meaning to it. Then her mother's aspect, which on her entrance she had scarcely noticed, struck her with a sudden and added distress.

"You don't look well, mother. Don't come down to-day."

"I shall certainly come down by luncheon-time," said Lady Coryston, sharply. "Tell Arthur that I wish to have some conversation with him before he goes back to London. And as for you, Marcia, the best thing you can do is to go and rest for a time, and then to explain all you have been doing to Edward. I must say I think you will have a great deal to explain. And I shall scold Bellows and Mrs. Drew for letting you hear such a horrible thing at all—without coming to me first."

"Mother!" cried Marcia, in a kind of despair. "Aren't you—aren't you sorry for those two people?—and don't you understand that I—I hoped I might have helped them?"

At last she began to weep. The tears ran down her cheeks. Lady Coryston frowned.

"Certainly, I'm sorry. But—the fact is, Marcia—I can't stand any extra strain this morning. We'll talk about it again when you're more composed. Now go and lie down."

She closed her eyes, looking so gray and old that Marcia, seized with a new compunction, could only obey her at once. But on the threshold she was called back.

"If any messenger arrives with a letter for Arthur—tell them down-stairs to let me know."

"Yes, mother."

As soon, however, as she had closed the door Marcia's tired mind immediately dismissed the subject of Arthur, even of her mother. The tumult of anguish returned upon her in which she had stood ever since she had come back from her faint to the bitter consciousness of a world—an awful world—where people can die of misery for lack of pity, for lack of help, and yet within a stone's-throw of those who yearned to give them both.

She went back to her room, finished her dressing mechanically, wrote a short letter, blotting it with tears, and then went tottering down-stairs. In the central hall, a vast pillared space, crowded with statuary and flowers, where the men of the house were accustomed to smoke and read the newspapers after breakfast, she perceived Reginald Lester sitting alone.

He sprang up at sight of her, came to her, took her hands, looked into her face, and then stooped and kissed her fingers, respectfully, ardently; with such an action as a brother might have used to a much younger sister.

She showed no surprise. She simply lifted her eyes to him, like a miserable child—saying under her breath:

"You know—I saw them—the night before last?"

"I know. It has been a fearful shock. Is there anything I can do for you?" For he saw she had a letter in her hand.

"Please tell them to send this letter. And then—come back. I'll go to the library."

She went blindly along the passages to the library, hearing and flying from the voices of Sir Wilfrid and Arthur in the dining-room as she passed. When Lester returned, he saw her standing by his desk, lost in an abstraction of grief. But she roused herself at sight of him, and asked for any further news there might be. Lester, who had been suffering from a sprained wrist, had that morning seen the same doctor who had been called in on the discovery of the tragedy.

"It must all have happened within an hour. His sister, who had come to stay with them, says that John Betts had seemed rather brighter in the evening, and his wife rather less in terror. She spoke very warmly to her sister-in-law of your having come to see her, and said she had promised you to wait a little before she took any step. Then he went out to the laboratory, and there, it is supposed, he was overcome by a fit of acute depression—the revolver was in his drawer—he scrawled the two words that were found—and you know the rest. Two people on the farm heard the shot—but it was taken as fired by the night watcher in a field beyond, which was full of young pheasants. About midnight Mrs. Betts went out to bring him in—her sister-in-law having gone up to bed. She never came back again—no one heard a sound—and they were not discovered till the morning. How long she was alone with him before she killed herself cannot even be guessed."

Marcia's trembling fingers fumbled at the bosom of her dress. She drew out a crumpled paper, and pushed it toward him. He read:

"Good-by, dear Miss Coryston. He sits so still—not much injured. I have often seen him look so. My John—my John—I can't stay behind. Will you please do something for my boy? John—John—if only we hadn't met again—"

It ended incoherently in blots and smudges.

"You poor child!" said Lester, involuntarily, as he looked up from the letter. It was a word of sudden compassion wrested from him by the sight of Marcia's intolerable pain. He brought forward one of the deep library chairs, and made her sit in it, and as he bent over her his sympathy drew from her piteous little cries and stifled moans which he met with answering words of comfort. All consciousness of sex dropped away; the sharp-chinned face, the blue, black-fringed eyes, behind their spectacles, the noble brow under its pile of strong grizzled hair:—she saw them all as an embodied tenderness—courage and help made visible—a courage and help on which she gradually laid hold. She could not stop to ask herself how it was that, in this moment of shock and misery, she fell so naturally into this attitude of trust toward one with whom she had never yet set up any relation but that of a passing friendship. She only knew that there was comfort in his voice, his look, in his understanding of her suffering, in the reticence with which he handled it. She had lived beside him in the same house for months without ever really knowing him. Now suddenly—here was a friend—on whom to lean.

But she could not speak to him of Newbury, though it was the thought of Newbury that was burning her heart. She did mention Coryston, only to say with energy: "I don't want to see him yet—not *yet*!" Lester could only guess at her meaning, and would not have probed her for the world.

But after a little she braced herself, gave him a grateful,

shrinking look, and, rising, she went in search of Sir Wilfrid and Arthur.

Only Sir Wilfrid was in the hall when she reentered it. He had just dismissed a local reporter who had got wind of Miss Coryston's visit to the farm, and had rushed over to Coryston, in the hope of seeing her.

"My dear child!" He hurried to meet her. "You look a perfect wreck! How *abominable* that you should be mixed up with this thing!"

"I couldn't help it," she said, vaguely, turning away at once from the discussion of it. "Where is Arthur? Mother wanted me to give him a message."

Sir Wilfrid looked uneasy.

"He was here till just now. But he is in a curious state of mind. He thinks of nothing but one thing—and one person. He arrived late last night, and it is my belief that he hardly went to bed. And he is just hanging on the arrival of a letter—"

"From Enid Glenwilliam?"

"Evidently. I tried to get him to realize this horrible affair—the part the Newburys had played in it—the effect on you—since that poor creature appealed to you. But no—not a bit of it! He seems to have neither eyes nor ears—But here he is!"

Sir Wilfrid and Marcia stepped apart. Arthur came into the hall from the library entrance. Marcia saw that he was much flushed, and that his face wore a hard, determined look, curiously at variance with its young features and receding chin.

"Hullo, Marcia! Beastly business, this you've been getting into. Think, my dear, you'd have done much better to keep out of it—especially as you and Newbury didn't agree. I've just seen Coryston in the park—he confessed he'd set you on—and that you and Newbury had quarreled over it. *He's* perfectly mad about it, of course. That you might expect. I say—mother is late!"

He looked round the hall imperiously.

Marcia, supporting herself on a chair, met his eyes, and made no reply. Yet she dimly remembered that her mother had asked her to give him some message.

"Arthur, remember that your sister's had a great shock!" said Sir Wilfrid, sternly.

"I know that! Sorry for you, Marcia—awfully—but I expect you'll have to appear at the inquest—don't see how you can get out of it. You should have thought twice about going there—when Newbury didn't want you to. And what's this they say about a letter?"

His tone had the peremptory ring natural to many young men of his stamp, in dealing with their inferiors, or—until love has tamed them—with women; but it came strangely from the good-tempered and easy-going Arthur.

Marcia's hand closed instinctively on the bosom of her dress, where the letter was.

"Mrs. Betts wrote me a letter," she said, slowly.

"You'd better let me see it. Sir Wilfrid and I can advise you."

He held out an authoritative hand. Marcia made no movement, and the hand dropped.

"Oh, well, if you're going to take no one's advice but your own, I suppose you must gang your own gait!" said her brother, impatiently. "But if you're a sensible girl you'll make it up with Newbury and let him keep you out of it as much as possible. Betts was always a cranky fellow. I'm sorry for the little woman, though."

And walking away to a distant window at the far end of the hall, whence all the front approaches to the house could be seen, he stood drumming on the glass and fixedly looking out. Sir Wilfrid, with an angry ejaculation, approached Marcia.

"My dear, your brother isn't himself!—else he could never have spoken so unkindly. Will you show me that letter? It will, of course, have to go to the police."

She held it out to him obediently.

Sir Wilfrid read it. He blew his nose, and walked away for a minute. When he returned, it was to say, with lips that twitched a little in his smooth-shaven actor's face:

"Most touching! If one could only have known! But dear Marcia, I hope it's not true—I hope to God, it's not true!— that you've quarreled with Newbury?"

Marcia was standing with her head thrown back against the high marble mantelpiece. The lids drooped over her eyes.

"I don't know," she said, in a faint voice. "I don't know. Oh no, not *quarreled*—"

Sir Wilfrid looked at her with a fatherly concern; took her limp hand and pressed it.

"Stand by him, dear, stand by him! He'll suffer enough from this—without losing you."

Marcia did not answer. Lester had returned to the hall, and he and Bury then got from her, as gently as possible, a full account of her two interviews with Mrs. Betts. Lester wrote it down, and Marcia signed it. The object of the two men was to make the police authorities acquainted with such testimony as Marcia had to give, while sparing her if possible an appearance at the inquest. While Lester was writing, Sir Wilfrid threw occasional scathing glances toward the distant Arthur, who seemed to be alternately pacing up and down and reading the newspapers. But the young man showed no signs whatever of doing or suggesting anything further to help his sister.

Sir Wilfrid perceived at once how Marcia's narrative might be turned against the Newburys, round whom the hostile feeling of a whole neighborhood was probably at that moment rising into fury. Was there ever a more odious, a more untoward situation!

But he could not be certain that Marcia understood it so. He failed, indeed, altogether, to decipher her mind toward Newbury; or to get at the truth of what had happened between them. She sat, very pale, and piteously composed; answering the questions they put to her, and sometimes, though rarely, unable to control a sob, which seemed to force its way unconsciously. At the end of their cross-examination, when Sir Wilfrid was ready to start for Martover, the police headquarters for the district, she rose, and said she would go back to her room.

"Do, do, dear child!" Bury threw a fatherly arm round her, and went with her to the foot of the stairs. "Go and rest—sleep if you can."

As Marcia moved away there was a sudden sound at the end of the hall. Arthur had run hurriedly toward the door leading to the outer vestibule. He opened it and disappeared. Through the high-arched windows to the left, a boy on a bicycle could be seen descending the long central avenue leading to the fore-court.

It was just noon. The great clock set in the center of the eastern facade had chimed the hour, and as its strokes died away on the midsummer air Marcia was conscious, as her mother had been the preceding afternoon, of an abnormal stillness round her. She was in her sitting-room, trying to write a letter to Mrs. Betts's sister about the boy mentioned in his mother's last words. He was not at the farm, thank God!—that she knew. His stepfather had sent him at Easter to a good preparatory school.

It seemed to help her to be doing this last poor service to the dead woman. And yet in truth she scarcely knew what she was writing. Her mind was torn between two contending imaginations—the thought of Mrs. Betts, sitting beside her dead husband, and waiting for the moment of her own death; and the thought of Newbury. Alternately she saw the laboratory at night—the shelves of labeled bottles and jars—the tables and chemical apparatus—the electric light burning—and in the chair the dead man, with the bowed figure against his knee:—and then—Newbury—in his sitting-room, amid the books and portraits of his college years—the crucifix over the mantelpiece—the beautiful drawings of Einsiedeln—of Assisi.

Her heart cried out to him. It had cried out to him in her letter. The thought of the agony he must be suffering tortured her. Did he blame himself? Did he remember how she had implored him to "take care"? Or was it all still plain to him that he had done right? She found herself praying with all her strength that he might still feel he could have done no other, and that what had happened, because of his action, had been God's will, and not merely man's mistake. She longed—sometimes—to throw her arms round him, and comfort him. Yet there was no passion in her longing. All that young rising of the blood seemed to have been killed in her. But she would never draw back from what she had offered him—never. She would go to him, and stand by him—as Sir Wilfrid had said—if he wanted her.

The gong rang for luncheon. Marcia rose unwillingly; but she was still more unwilling to make her feelings the talk of the household. As she neared the dining-room she saw her mother approaching from the opposite side of the house. Lady Coryston walked feebly, and her appearance shocked her daughter.

"Mother!—do let me send for Bryan!" she pleaded, as they met—blaming herself sharply the while for her own absorption and inaction during the morning hours. "You don't look a bit fit to be up."

Lady Coryston replied in a tone which forbade discussion that she was quite well, and had no need whatever of Dr. Bryan's attendance. Then she turned to the butler, and inquired if Mr. Arthur was in the house.

"His motor came round, my lady, about twelve o'clock. I have not seen him since."

The lunch passed almost in complete silence between the two ladies. Lady Coryston was informed that Sir Wilfrid and Lester had gone to Martover in connection with Marcia's share in the events at Redcross Farm. "They hope I needn't appear," said Marcia, dully.

"I should rather think not!"

Lady Coryston's indignant tone seemed to assume that English legal institutions were made merely to suit the convenience of the Coryston family. Marcia had enough of Coryston in her to perceive it. But she said nothing.

As they entered the drawing-room after luncheon she remembered—with a start.

"Mother—I forgot!—I'm so sorry—I dare say it was nothing. But I think a letter came for Arthur just before twelve—a letter he was expecting. At least I saw a messenger-boy come down the avenue. Arthur ran out to meet him. Then I went up-stairs, and I haven't seen him since."

Lady Coryston had turned whiter than before. She groped for a chair near and seated herself, before she recovered sufficient self-possession to question her daughter as to the precise moment of the messenger's appearance, the direction from which he arrived, and so forth.

But Marcia knew no more, and could tell no more. Nor could she summon up any curiosity about her brother, possessed and absorbed as her mind was by other thoughts and images. But in a vague, anxious way she felt for her mother; and if Lady Coryston had spoken Marcia would have responded.

And Lady Coryston would have liked to speak, first of all to scold Marcia for forgetting her message, and then to confide in her—insignificant as the daughter's part in the mother's real life and thoughts had always been. But she felt physically incapable of bearing the emotion which might spring out upon her from such a conversation. It was as though she possessed— and knew she possessed—a certain measured strength; just enough—and no more—to enable her to go through a conversation which *must* be faced. She had better not waste it beforehand. Sometimes it occurred to her that her feeling toward this coming interview was wholly morbid and unnatural. How many worse things had she faced in her time!

But reasoning on it did not help her—only silence and endurance. After resting a little in the drawing-room she went up to her sitting-room again, refusing Marcia's company.

"Won't you let me come and make you comfortable?—if you're going to rest, you'll want a shawl and some pillows," said the girl, as she stood at the foot of the staircase, wistfully looking after her.

But Lady Coryston shook her head.

"Thank you—I don't want anything."

* * * * *

So—for Marcia—there was nothing to be done with these weary hours—but wait and think and weep! She went back to her own sitting-room, and lingeringly put Newbury's letters together, in a packet, which she sealed; in case—well, in case—nothing came of her letter of the morning. They had been engaged not quite a month. Although they had met almost every day, yet there were many letters from him; letters of which she felt anew the power and beauty as she reread them. Yet from that power and beauty, the natural expression of his character, she stood further off now than when she had first known him. The mystery indeed in which her nascent love had wrapped him had dropped away. She knew him better, she respected him infinitely; and all the time—strangely, inexplicably—love had been, not growing, but withering.

Meanwhile, into all her thoughts about herself and Newbury there rushed at recurrent intervals the memory, the overwhelming memory, of her last sight of John and Alice Betts. That gray face in the summer dusk, beyond the window, haunted her; and the memory of those arms which had clung about her waist.

Was there a beyond?—where were they?—those poor ghosts! All the riddles of the eternal Sphinx leaped upon Marcia—riddles at last made real. Twenty-four hours ago, two brains, two hearts, alive, furiously alive, with human sorrow and human revolt. And now? Had that infinitely pitiful Christ in whom Newbury believed, received the two tormented souls?—were they comforted—purged—absolved? Had they simply ceased to be—to feel—to suffer? Or did some stern doom await them—still—after all the suffering here? A shudder ran through the girl, evoking by reaction the memory of immortal words—"*Her sins which are many are forgiven; for she loved much.*" She fed herself on the divine saying; repressing with all her strength the skeptical, pessimistic impulses that were perhaps natural to her temperament, forcing herself, as it were, for their sakes, to hope and to believe.

Again, as the afternoon wore away, she was weighed down by the surrounding silence. No one in the main pile of building but her mother and herself. Not a sound, but the striking of the great gilt clock outside. From her own room she could see the side windows of her mother's sitting-room; and once she thought she perceived the stately figure passing across them. But otherwise Lady Coryston made no sign; and her daughter dared not go to her without permission.

Why did no letter come for her, no reply? She sat at her open windows for a time, watching the front approaches, and looking out into a drizzling rain which veiled the afternoon. When it ceased she went out—restlessly—to the East Wood— the wood where they had broken it off. She lay down with her face against the log—a prone white figure, among the fern. The buried ring—almost within reach of her hand—seemed to call to her like a living thing. No!—let it rest.

If it was God's will that she should go back to Edward, she would make him a good wife. But her fear, her shrinking, was all there still. She prayed; but she did not know for what.

Meanwhile at Redcross Farm, the Coroner was holding his inquiry. The facts were simple, the public sympathy and horror profound. Newbury and Lord William had given their evidence amid a deep and, in many quarters, hostile silence. The old man, parchment-pale, but of an unshaken dignity, gave a full account of the efforts—many and vain—that had been made both by himself and his son to find Betts congenial work in another sphere and to persuade him to accept it.

"We had nothing to do with his conscience, or with his private affairs—in themselves. All we asked was that we should not be called on to recognize a marriage which in our eyes was not a marriage. Everything that we could have done consistently with that position, my son and I may honestly say we have done."

Sir Wilfrid Bury was called, to verify Marcia's written statement, and Mrs. Betts's letter was handed to the Coroner, who broke down in reading it. Coryston, who was sitting on the opposite side of the room, watched the countenances of the two Newburys while it was being read, with a frowning attention.

When the evidence was over, and the jury had retired, Edward Newbury took his father to the carriage which was waiting. The old man, so thin and straight, from his small head and narrow shoulders to his childishly small feet, leaned upon his son's arm, and apparently saw nothing around him. A mostly silent throng lined the lane leading to the farm. Half-way stood the man who had come down to lecture on "Rational Marriage," surrounded by a group of Martover Socialists. From them rose a few hisses and groans as the Newburys passed. But other groups represented the Church Confraternities and clubs of the Newbury estate. Among them heads were quietly bared as the old man went by, or hands were silently held out. Even a stranger would have realized that the scene represented the meeting of two opposing currents of thought and life.

Newbury placed his father in the carriage, which drove off. He then went back himself to wait for the verdict.

As he approached the door of the laboratory in which the inquiry had been held, Coryston emerged.

Newbury flushed and stopped him. Coryston received it as though it had been the challenge of an enemy. He stepped back, straightening himself fiercely. Newbury began:

"Will you take a message from me to your sister?"

A man opened the door in front a little way.

"Mr. Edward, the jury are coming back."

The two men went in; Coryston listened with a sarcastic mouth to the conventional verdict of "unsound mind" which drapes impartially so many forms of human ill. And again he found himself in the lane with Newbury beside him.

"One more lie," he said, violently, "to a jury's credit!"

Newbury looked up. It was astonishing what a mask he could make of his face, normally so charged—over-charged—with expression.

"What else could it have been? But this is no time or place for us to discuss our differences, Coryston—"

"Why not!" cried Coryston, who had turned a dead white. "'Our differences,' as you call them, have led to *that*!" He turned and flung out a thin arm toward the annex to the laboratory, where the bodies were lying. "It is time, I think, that reasonable men should come to some understanding about 'differences' that can slay and madden a pair of poor hunted souls, as these have been slain!"

"'Hunted?' What do you mean?" said Newbury, sternly, while his dark eyes took fire.

"Hunted by the Christian conscience!—that it might lie comfortable o' nights," was the scornful reply.

Newbury said nothing for a few moments. They emerged on the main road, crossed it, and entered the Hoddon Grey park. Here they were alone, out of sight of the crowd returning from the inquest to the neighboring village. As they stepped into one of the green rides of the park they perceived a motorcar descending the private road which crossed it a hundred yards away. A man was driving it at a furious pace, and Coryston clearly recognized his brother Arthur. He was driving toward Coryston. Up to the moment when the news of the farm tragedy had reached him that morning, Coryston's mind had been very full of what seemed to him the impending storm between his mother and Arthur. Since then he had never thought of it, and the sight of his brother rushing past, making for Coryston, no doubt, from some unknown point, excited but a moment's recollection, lost at once in the emotion which held him.

Newbury struck in, however, before he could express it further; in the same dry and carefully governed voice as before.

"You are Marcia's brother, Coryston. Yesterday morning she and I were still engaged to be married. Yesterday afternoon we broke it off—although—since then—I have received two letters from her—"

He paused a moment, but soon resumed, with fresh composure.

"Those letters I shall answer to-night. By that time—perhaps —I shall know better—what my future life will be."

"Perhaps!" Coryston repeated, roughly. "But I have no claim to know, nor do I want to know!"

Newbury gave him a look of wonder.

"I thought you were out for justice—and freedom of cons-cience?" he said, slowly. "Is the Christian conscience—alone—excepted? Freedom for every one else—but none for us?"

"Precisely! Because your freedom means other men's slavery!" Coryston panted out the words. "You can't have your freedom! It's too costly in human life. Everywhere Europe has found that out. The freedom you Catholics—Anglican or Roman—want, is anti-social. We sha'n't give it you!"

"You will have to give it us," said Newbury, calmly, "because in putting us down—which of course you could do with ease—you would destroy all that you yourselves value in civilization. It would be the same with us, if we had the upper hand, as you have now. Neither of us can destroy the other. We stand face to face—we shall stand face to face—while the world lasts."

Coryston broke into passionate contradiction. Society, he was confident, would, in the long run, put down Catholicism, of all sorts, by law.

"Life is hard enough, the devil knows! We can't afford—we simply can't afford—to let you make it harder by these damned traditions! I appeal to those two dead people! They did what *you* thought wrong, and your conscience judged and sentenced them. But who made you a judge and divider over them? Who asked you to be the dispenser for them of blessing and cursing?"

Newbury stood still.

"No good, Coryston, your raving like this! There is one question that cuts the knot—that decides where you stand— and where I stand. You don't believe there has ever been any living word from God to man—any lifting of the eternal veil. We do! We say the heavens *have* opened—a God *has* walked this earth! Everything else follows from that."

"Including the deaths of John Betts and his wife!" said Coryston, with bitter contempt. "A God suffers and bleeds, for that! No!—for us, if there is a God, He speaks in love—in love only—in love supremely—such love as those two poor things had for each other!"

After which they walked along in silence for some time. Each had said the last word of his own creed.

Presently they reached a footpath from which the house at Hoddon Grey could be reached. Newbury paused.

"Here, Coryston, we part—and we may never meet again."

He raised his heavy eyes to his companion. All passion had died from his face, which in its pale sorrow was more beautiful than Coryston had ever seen it.

"Do you think," he said, with deliberate gentleness, "that I feel nothing—that life can ever be the same for me again—after this? It has been to me a sign-post in the dark—written in letters of flame—and blood. It tells me where to go—and I obey."

He paused, looking, as it seemed, through Coryston, at things beyond. And Coryston was aware of a strange and sudden awe in himself which silenced him.

But Newbury recalled his thoughts. He spoke next in his ordinary tone.

"Please, tell—Marcia—that all arrangements have been made for Mr. Betts's boy, with the relatives' consent. She need have no anxiety about him. And all I have to say to her for her letter—her blessed letter—I will say to-night."

He walked away, and was soon lost to sight among the trees.

CHAPTER XVI

Coryston walked back to Knatchett at a furious pace, jumped on his bicycle, and went off to find Marion Atherstone—the only person with whom he could trust himself at the moment. He more than suspected that Marcia in a fit of sentimental folly would relent toward Newbury in distress—and even his rashness shrank from the possibility of a quarrel which might separate him from his sister for good. But liberate his soul he must; and he thirsted for a listener with whom to curse bigots up and down. In Marion's mild company, strangely enough, the most vigorous cursing, whether of men or institutions, had always in the end calming results. To Marion, however, led by a sure instinct, he went.

Meanwhile the motor which passed Newbury and Coryston in the park had sped to its goal. It had already carried Arthur Coryston over half the county. That morning he had been told at the Atherstones' cottage, on his breathless arrival there, just before luncheon, that while the Chancellor had returned to town, Miss Glenwilliam had motored to a friend's house, some twenty miles north, and was not going back to London till the evening. Arthur Coryston at once pursued her. Sorely against her will, he had forced the lady to an interview, and in the blind rage of his utter defeat and discomfiture, he left her again in hot quest of that explanation with his mother which Enid Glenwilliam had honestly—and vainly—tried to prevent.

Lady Coryston meanwhile was bewildered by his absence.

During the lonely hours when Marcia, from a distance, had once caught sight of her crossing an open window in her sitting-room, she had not been able to settle to any occupation, still less to rest. She tried to write out the Agenda of an important Primrose League meeting over which she was to preside; to put together some notes of her speech. In vain. A strange heaviness weighed upon her. The only stimulus that worked—and that only for a time—was a fierce attack on Glenwilliam in one of the morning papers. She read it hungrily; but it brought on acute headache, which reduced her to idleness and closed eyes.

After a while she roused herself to pull down a blind against a teasing invasion of sun, and in doing so she perceived a slim, white figure hurrying away from the house, through the bright-colored mazes of the Italian garden. Marcia! She remembered vaguely that Marcia had come to her that morning in trouble about what? She could not remember. It had seemed to her of importance.

At last, about half an hour after she had seen Marcia disappear in the shrubbery paths leading to the East Wood, Lady Coryston, startled by a sound from the fore-court, sat suddenly erect on her sofa. A motor?

She rose, and going to a little mirror on the wall, she straightened the lace coiffure she habitually wore. In doing so she was struck—dismayed even—by her own aspect.

"When this is all over, Marcia and I perhaps might go abroad for a week or two," she thought.

A swift step approaching—a peremptory knock at the door.

"Come in!"

Arthur entered, and with his back against the door stood surveying his mother. She waited for him to speak, expecting violence. For some moments—in vain. Except in so far as his

Mrs. Humphry Ward

quick-breathing silence, his look of dry, hollow-eyed exasperation spoke—more piercingly than words.

"Well, Arthur," she said, at last, "I have been expecting you for some time."

"I have been trying to put the mischief you have done me straight," he said, between his teeth.

"I have done you no mischief that I know of. Won't you come and sit down quietly—and talk the whole matter over? You can't imagine that I desire anything but your good!"

His laugh seemed to give her physical pain.

"Couldn't you take to desiring something else, mother, than my 'good' as you call it? Because, I tell you plainly, it don't suit my book. You have been meddling in my affairs!—just as you have always meddled in them, for matter of that! But this time you've done it with a vengeance—you've done it *damnably*!" He struck his hand upon a table near. "What right had you"— he approached her threateningly—"what earthly right had you to go and see Enid Glenwilliam yesterday, just simply that you might spoil my chances with her! Who gave you leave?"

He flung the questions at her.

"I had every right," said Lady Coryston, calmly. "I am your mother—I have done everything for you—you owe your whole position to me. You were ruining yourself by a mad fancy. I was bound to take care that Miss Glenwilliam should not accept you without knowing all the facts. But—actually— as it happens—she had made up her mind—before we met."

"So she says!—and I don't believe a word of it—*not—one— word*! She wanted to make me less mad with you. She's like you, mother, she thinks she can manage everybody. So she tried to cram me—that it was Glenwilliam persuaded her against me. Rot! If you hadn't gone and meddled, if you hadn't treated her like dirt—if you hadn't threatened to spoil my prospects, and told her you'd never receive her—if you hadn't put her back up in a hundred ways—she'd have married me. It's you—you—*you*—that have done it!"

He threw himself on a chair in front of her, his hands on his knees, staring at her. His aspect as of a man disorganized and undone by baffled passion, repelled and disgusted her. Was this her Arthur?—her perfect gentleman—her gay, courteous, well-behaved darling—whose mingled docility and good breeding had, so far, suited both her affection and her love of rule so well? The deep under-sense of disaster which had held her all day, returned upon her in ten-fold strength. But she fronted him bravely.

"You are, as it happens, entirely wrong, Arthur. It's not I who have done it—but Miss Glenwilliam's own good sense—or her father's. Of course I confess frankly that I should have done my best—that I did, if you like, do my best, to prevent your marriage with Miss Glenwilliam. And as for right, who else had a right, if not I? Was it not most unkind, most undutiful on your part!"—her tone was a tone of battle—"was it not an outrage on your father's memory—that you should even entertain the notion of such a connection? To bring the daughter of that man into this family!—after all we have done—and suffered—for our principles—it's you, who ought to ask *my* pardon, Arthur, and not I yours! Times without number, you have agreed with me in despising people who have behaved as if politics were a mere game—a trifle that didn't matter. You have told me often, that things were getting too hot; you couldn't be friends in private, with people you hated in public; people you looked upon as robbers and cheats. And then—*then*—you go and let this infatuation run away with you—you forget all your principles—you forget your mother, and all you owe her—and you go and ask this girl to marry you—whose father is our personal and political enemy—a political adventurer who is trying to pull down and destroy everything that you and I hold sacred—or ought to hold sacred!"

Mrs. Humphry Ward

"For goodness' sake, mother, don't make a political speech!" He turned upon her with angry contempt. "That kind of thing does all very well to spout at an election—but it won't do between you and me. I *don't* hate Glenwilliam—*there*! The estates—and the property—and all we hold sacred, as you call it—will last my time—and his. And I jolly well don't care what happens afterward. *He's* not going to do us much harm. England's a deal tougher proposition than he thinks. It's you women who get up such a hullabaloo—I declare you make politics a perfect devilry! But then"—he shrugged his shoulders fiercely—"I'm not going to waste time in arguing. I just came to tell you *what I intend to do*; and then I'm going up to town. I've ordered the motor for seven o'clock."

Lady Coryston had risen, and stood, with one hand on the mantelpiece, looking down upon her son.

"I shall be glad indeed to hear what you intend to do, Arthur. I see you have missed two or three important divisions lately."

He burst out:

"And they won't be the last either, by a good way. I'm going to chuck it, mother! And if you don't like it—you can blame yourself!"

"What do you mean?"

He hesitated a moment—then spoke deliberately.

"I intend to leave Parliament after this session. I do! I'm sick of it. A friend of mine has got a ranch forty miles from Buenos Ayres. He wants me to go in with him—and I think I'll try it. I want something to distract my mind from these troubles."

Lady Coryston's eyes blazed in her gray-white face, which not even her strong will could keep from trembling.

"So this, Arthur, is the reward you propose for all that has been done for you!—for the time, the thought, the money that has been showered upon you—"

He looked at her from under his eyebrows, unmoved.

"I should have remembered all that, mother, if you—Look here! Have you ever let me, in anything—for one day, one hour—call my soul my own—since I went into Parliament? It's true I deceived you about Enid. I was literally *afraid* to tell you—there! You've brought me to that! And when a man's afraid of a woman—it somehow makes a jelly of him— altogether. It was partly what made me run after Enid—at first—that I was doing something independent of you— something you would hate, if you knew. Beastly of me, I know!—but there it was. And then you arranged that meeting here, without so much as giving me a word's notice!—you told Page *before you told me.* And when I kicked—and told you about Enid—did you ever come afterward and talk to me nicely about her?—did you ever, even, consider for one moment what I told you?—that I was in love with her?—dead gone on her? Even if I was rude to you that day when you dragged it out of me, most mothers, I think, would have been sorry for a fellow—"

His voice suddenly broke; but he instantly recovered himself.

"Instead of that, mother—you only thought of how you could thwart and checkmate me—how you could get *your* way—and force me to give up mine. It was *abominable* of you to go and see Enid, without a word to me!—it was *abominable* to plot and plan behind my back, and then to force yourself on her and insult her to her face! Do you think a girl of any spirit whatever would put herself in your clutches after that? No! —she didn't want to come it too hard on you—that's her way!—so she made up some tale about Glenwilliam. But it's as plain as the nose in your face! You've ruined me!—you've ruined me!"

He began to walk furiously up and down, beside himself again with rage and pain.

Lady Coryston dropped into a chair. Her large, blanched face expressed a passion that even at this supreme moment, and under the sense of doom that was closing on her, she could not restrain.

"It is not I who have ruined you, Arthur—as you put it—though of course you're not ruined at all!—but your own wanton self-will. Are you really so lost to all decency—all affection—that you can speak to your mother like this?"

He turned and paused—to throw her an ugly look.

"Well—I don't know that I'm more of a brute than other men—but it's no good talking about affection to me—after this. Yes, I suppose you've been fond of me, mother, in your way—and I suppose I've been fond of you. But the fact is, as I told you before, I've stood in *fear* of you!—all my life—and lots of things you thought I did because I was fond of you, I did because I was a coward—a disgusting coward!—who ought to have been kicked. And that's the truth! Why, ever since I was a small kid—"

And standing before her, with his hands on his sides, all his pleasant face disfigured by anger and the desire to wound, he poured out upon her a flood of recollections of his childhood and youth. Beneath the bitterness and the shock of it, even Lady Coryston presently flinched. This kind of language, though never in such brutal terms, she had heard from Corry once or twice. But, Arthur!—She put up a trembling hand.

"That's enough, Arthur! We had better stop this conversation. I have done the best I could for you—always."

"Why didn't you *love* us!" he cried, striking a chair beside him for emphasis. "Why didn't you *love* us! It was always politics—politics! Somebody to be attacked—somebody to be scored off—somebody to be squared. And a lot of stupid talk that bored us all! My poor father was as sick of it often as we were. He had enough of it out of doors. Damn politics for women, I say—damn them!"

Lady Coryston raised her hand.

"*Go*, Arthur! This is enough."

He drew a long breath.

"Upon my soul, I think it is. We'd better not excite each other any more. I'll speak to Sir Wilfrid, mother, before I go, and ask him to report various things to you, which I have to say. And I shall go and see the Whips to-night. Of course I don't want to do the party any harm. If there is a general election in the autumn, all that need happen is that I sha'n't stand again. And as to the estates"—he hesitated—"as to the estates, mother, do as you like. Upon my word I think you'd better give them back to Coryston! A certain amount of money is all I shall want."

"Go!" said Lady Coryston again, still pointing.

He stood a moment, fiddling with some ornaments on a table near him, then caught up his hat with a laugh—and still eying her askance, he walked to the door, opened it, and disappeared; though he closed it so uncertainly that Lady Coryston, until, after what seemed an interval, she heard his footsteps receding, could not be sure that he was really gone.

But he was gone; and all the plans and hopes of her later life lay in ashes about her. She sat motionless. After half an hour she heard the sound of a motor being driven away from the front of the house. Through the evening air, too, she caught distant voices—which soon ceased.

She rang presently for her maid, and said she would dine in her room, because of a bad headache. Marcia came, but was not admitted. Sir Wilfrid Bury asked if he might see her, just for a few minutes. A message referred him to the next morning.

Dinner came and went down untouched. Whenever she was ill, Lady Coryston's ways were solitary and ungracious. She hated being "fussed over." So that no one dared force themselves upon her. Only, between ten and eleven, Marcia again came to the door, knocked gently, and was told to go away. Her mother would be all right in the morning. The girl reluctantly obeyed.

The state of terrible tension in which Lady Coryston passed that night had no witness. It could only be guessed at, by Marcia, in particular, to whom it fell afterward to take charge of her mother's papers and personal affairs. Lady Coryston had apparently gathered all Arthur's, letters to her together, from the very first to the very latest, tied them up neatly, and laid them in the drawer which held those of her dead husband. She had begun to write a letter to Coryston, but when found, it was incoherent, and could not be understood. She had removed the early photographs of Arthur from her table, and a larger, recent one of the young M.P., taken in London for the constituency, which was on her mantelpiece, and had placed them both face downward in the same drawer with the letters. And then, when she had found it impossible to write what she wished to write, she seemed to have gone back to her arm-chair, taking with her two or three of Arthur's Eton reports—by what instinct had she chosen them out from the piles of letters!—and a psalter she often used. But by a mere accident, a sinister trick of fate, when she was found, the book lay open under her hand at one of those imprecatory psalms at which Christendom has at last learned to shudder. Only a few days before, Sir Wilfrid Bury had laughed at her—as only he might—for her "Old Testament tone" toward her enemies, and had quoted this very psalm. Her helpless fingers touched it.

But the night was a night of vigil for others also. Coryston, who could not sleep, spent the greater part of it first in writing to Marion Atherstone, and then in composing a slashing attack upon the High Church party for its attitude toward the divorce laws of the country, and the proposals recently made for their reform. "How much longer are we going to allow these black-coated gentlemen to despise and trample on the laws under which the rest of us are content to live!—or to use the rights and powers of property for the bare purpose of pressing their tyrannies and their superstitions on other people?"

Meanwhile, in the beautiful chapel of Hoddon Grey, Edward Newbury, worn out with the intolerable distress of the preceding forty-eight hours, and yet incapable of sleep, sat or knelt through long stretches of the night. The chapel was dark but for one light. Over the altar there burnt a lamp, and behind it could be seen, from the chair, where he knelt, the silk veil of the tabernacle. Reservation had been permitted for years in the Hoddon Grey chapel, and the fact had interwoven itself with the deepest life of the household, eclipsing and dulling the other religious practices of Anglicanism, just as the strong plant in a hedgerow drives out or sterilizes the rest. There, in Newbury's passionate belief, the Master of the House kept watch, or slept, above the altar, as once above the Galilean waves. For him, the "advanced" Anglican, as for any Catholic of the Roman faith, the doctrine of the Mass was the central doctrine of all religion, and that intimate and personal adoration to which it leads, was the governing power of life. The self-torturing anguish which he had suffered ever since the news of the two suicides had reached him could only endure itself in this sacred presence; and it was there he had taken refuge under the earlier blow of the breach with Marcia.

The night was very still—a night of soft showers, broken by intervals of starlight. Gradually as the darkness thinned toward dawn, the figures, stoled and winged and crowned, of the painted windows, came dimly forth, and long rays of pale light crept over the marble steps and floor, upon the flowers on the altar and the crucifix above it. The dawn flowed in silently and coldly; the birds stirred faintly; and the white mists on the lawn and fields outside made their way through the open windows, and dimmed the glow of color on the walls and in the apse.

In those melancholy and yet ardent hours Edward Newbury reached the utmost heights of religious affirmation, and the extreme of personal renunciation. It became clear to a mind attuned for such thoughts, that, by severing him from Marcia, and, at the same time, and by the same stroke, imposing upon him at least some fraction of responsibility—a fraction which his honesty could not deny—for the deaths of John and Alice Betts, God had called him, Edward Newbury, in a way not to be mistaken and not to be refused. His life was henceforth forfeit—forfeit to his Lord. Henceforth, let him make of it a willing sacrifice, an expiatory oblation, perpetually renewed, and offered in perpetual union with the Divine Victim, for their souls and his own.

The ideas of the Conventual house in which he had so lately spent hours of intense religious happiness closed upon him and possessed him. He was not to marry. He was reserved for the higher counsels, the Counsels of Perfection. The face and talk of his friend Brierly, who was so soon going to his dangerous and solitary post in Southern India, haunted his mind, and at last seemed to show him a way out of his darkness. His poor father and mother! But he never doubted for one moment that they would give him up, that they would let him follow his conscience.

By the time the sun was fairly up, the storm of religious feeling had died down in Newbury. He had taken his resolve, but he was incapable of any further emotion concerning it. On the other hand, his heart was alive to the thought of Marcia, and of that letter she had sent him. Dear, generous Marcia! Once more he would write to her—once more!

"DEAREST MARCIA,—I may call you so, I think, for the last time, and at this turning-point of both our lives. I may never see you again; or if we do meet, you will have become so strange to me that you will wonder in what other and distant life it was that we loved each other. I think you did love me for a little while, and I do bless and thank you that you let me know you—and love you. And I bless you above all for the thought of consolation and pity you had toward me, even yesterday, in those terrible hours—when you offered to come back to me and help me, as though our bond had never been broken.

"No, dear Marcia!—I saw the truth in your face yesterday. I could not make you happy. I should set jarring a discord in your life for which it was never meant. You did right, absolutely right, to separate yourself from one whose inmost and irrevocable convictions repelled and shocked you. I may be narrow and cold; but I am not narrow enough—or cold enough!—to let you give yourself back to one you cannot truly love—or trust. But that you offered it, because you were sorry for me, and that you would have carried it out, firmly, your dear hand clenched, as it were, on the compact—that warms my heart—that I shall have, as a precious memory, to carry into the far-off life that I foresee.

"I cannot write much about the terrible thing at Redcross Farm. Your great pity for me implies that you think me—and my father—in some way and in some degree, responsible. Perhaps we are—I do not wish to shirk the truth. If so, it is as soldiers under orders are responsible for the hurt and damage they may cause, in their King's war—as much, and as little. At least, so far as the main matter is concerned. That I might have been—that I ought to have been—infinitely more loving, wiser, stronger to help them—that I know—that I shall feel as long as I live. And it is a feeling which will determine all my future life.

"You remember what I told you of Father Brierly and the Community of the Ascension? As soon as I can leave my father and mother—they are at present in deep distress—I shall probably go to the Community House in Lancashire for a time. My present intention is to take orders, and perhaps to join Brierly eventually in mission work. My father and mother are splendid! They and I shall be separated perhaps in this world, but in that mysterious other world which lies all about us even now, and which is revealed to us in the Sacraments, we shall meet at last, and forever—if we are faithful.

"Good-by—God be with you—God give you every good thing in this present time—love, children, friends—and, 'in the world to come, life everlasting.'"

* * * * *

About the hour when the letter was finished, when the July sun was already high over the dewy new-shorn fields, Coryston, after an hour's sleep in his chair, and a bath, left Knatchett to walk to Coryston. He was oppressed by some vague dread which would not let him rest. In the strong excitements and animosities of the preceding day he had forgotten his mother. But the memory of her face on the sofa during that Sunday reading had come back upon him with unpleasant force. It had been always so with him in life. She no sooner relapsed into the woman than he became a son. Only the experience had been rare!

He crossed the Hoddon Grey park, and then walked through *a* mile of the Coryston demesne, till he reached the lake and saw beyond it the Italian garden, with its statues glittering in the early sun—and the long marble front of the house, with its rococo ornament, and its fine pillared loggia. "What the deuce are *we* going to do with these places!" he asked himself in petulant despair. "And to think that Arthur won't be allowed to sell it, or turn it to any useful purpose whatever!"

He skirted the lake, and began to mount the steps, and flagged paths of the formal garden. Suddenly as he approached the garden front he saw that two windows of his mother's sitting-room were open, and that some one—a figure in black—was sitting in a high-backed arm-chair beside one of them. His mother!—up?—at seven o'clock in the morning? Yet was it his mother? He came nearer. The figure was motionless—the head thrown back, the eyes invisible from where he stood. Something in the form, the attitude—its stillness and strangeness in the morning light—struck him with horror. He rushed to the garden door, found it open, dashed up the stairs, and into his mother's room.

"Mother!"

Lady Coryston neither moved nor spoke. But as he came up to her, he saw that she was alive—that her eyes opened and perceived him. Nothing else in her lived or moved. And as he knelt down by her, and took her tenderly in his arms, she relapsed into the unconscious state from which his entrance had momentarily roused her.

*   *   *   *   *

What else there is to tell had best be told quickly. Lady Coryston lived for some eight months after this seizure. She partially recovered from the first stroke, and all the organization of the great house, and all the thought of her children circled round the tragic death-in-life into which she had fallen.

Arthur had come rushing back to Coryston after the catastrophe, restored by it, like a stream which has wandered in flood, to the older and natural channels of life. Bitter remorse for his conduct to his mother, and a sharp resentment of Enid Glenwilliam's conduct toward himself, acted wholesomely. He took up his normal occupations again, in Parliament and on the estates, and talked no more of Buenos Ayres. But whether his mother's darkened mind ever forgave him it would be difficult to say. She rarely noticed him, and when she spoke it was generally for Coryston. Her dependence upon her eldest son became a touching and poignant thing, deepening the souls of both. Coryston came to live at Coryston, and between his love for Marion Atherstone, and his nursing of his mother, was more truly happy for a time than his character had ever yet allowed him to be. The din of battle, political and religious, penetrated no more within a house where death came closer day by day, and where weakness and suffering had at last united these differing men and women in a common interest of profoundest pity. Lady Coryston became strangely dear to her children before she left them forever, and the last faint words she spoke, on that winter morning when she died, were for Coryston, who had her hand in his. "Corry—Corry darling"—and as he came closer—"Corry, who was my firstborn!"

On the night of Lady Coryston's death Reginald Lester wrote:

"Coryston has just taken me in to see his mother. She lies in a frowning rest which does not—as death so often does—make any break with our memories of her when alive. Attitude and expression are characteristic. She is the strong woman still, conscious of immense power; and, if that shut mouth could speak, and if health were given back to her, ready no doubt still to use it tyrannously. There is no weakening and no repentance in the face; and I like it better so. Nor did she ever really reverse, though she modified, the exclusion of Coryston from the inheritance. She was able during an interval of comparative betterment about Christmas-time, to make an alteration in her will, and the alteration was no mere surrender to what one sees to have been, at bottom, her invincible affection for Coryston. She has still left Arthur the estates for life, but with remainder to Coryston's son, should he have one, and she has made Coryston a trustee together with Sir Wilfrid Bury. This will mean practically a division between the brothers—to which Arthur has already pledged himself, so he tells me—but with no power to Coryston to make such radical changes as would destroy the family tradition, at least without Arthur's consent and Sir Wilfrid's. But Coryston will have plenty of money and plenty of land wherewith to experiment, and no doubt we shall see some strange things.

"Thus she kept her flag flying to the end, so far as the enfeebled brain allowed. Yet the fact was that her state of dependence on her children during her illness, and their goodness to her, did in truth evoke another woman with new perceptions, superposed, as it were, upon the old. And there, I think, came in her touch of greatness—which one could not have expected. She was capable at any rate of *this* surrender; not going back upon the old—but just accepting the new. Her life might have petered out in bitterness and irritation, leaving an odious memory. It became a source of infinite sweetness, just because her children found out—to their immense surprise—that she *could* let herself be loved; and they threw themselves with eagerness on the chance she gave them.

"She dies in time—one of the last of a generation which will soon have passed, leaving only a procession of ghosts on a vanishing road. She had no doubts about her place and prerogative in the world, no qualms about her rights to use them as she pleased. Coryston also has no doubts—or few. As to individuals he is perpetually disillusioned; as to causes he is as obstinate as his mother. And independently of the Glenwilliam affair, that is why, I think, in the end she preferred Coryston to Arthur, who will 'muddle through,' not knowing whither, like the majority of his kind.

"Marcia!—in her black dress, beside her mother, looking down upon her—with that yearning look!—But—not a word! There are things too sacred for these pages."

* * * * *

During the months of Lady Coryston's illness, indeed, Reginald Lester entered, through stages scarcely perceived by himself and them, upon a new relation toward the Coryston family. He became the increasingly intimate friend and counselor of the Coryston brothers, and of Marcia, no less— but in a fresh and profounder sense. He shared much of the estate business with Mr. Page; he reconciled as best he could the jarring views of Coryston and Arthur; he started on the reorganization of the great Library, in which, so far, he had only dealt with a fraction of its possessions. And every day he was Marcia's companion, in things intimate and moving, no less than in the practical or commonplace affairs of ordinary life. It was he who read poetry with her, or played accompaniments to her songs, in the hours of relief from her nursing; it was he who watched and understood her; who guided and yet adored her. His love for her was never betrayed; but it gradually became, without her knowing it, the condition of her life. And when Lady Coryston died, in the February following her stroke, and Marcia, who was worn out, went abroad with Waggin for a few weeks' rest, the correspondence which passed between her and Lester during the earlier days of her absence, by the more complete and deliberate utterance which it permitted between them, did at last reveal to the girl the depths of her own heart.

During her travels various things happened.

One chilly afternoon, late in March, when a light powdering of snow lay on the northern slopes of the hills, Coryston went up to the cottage in the hopes of finding Marion Atherstone alone. There had been a quiet understanding between them all the winter, more or less known to the Coryston family, but all talk of marriage had been silenced by the condition of Lady Coryston, who indeed never knew such schemes were in the air.

About six weeks, however, after his mother's death, Coryston's natural *fougue* suggested to him that he was being trifled with. He burst into the little sitting-room where Marion was just making tea, and sat down, scowling, on the further side of the hearth.

"What is the matter?" Marion asked, mildly. During the winter a beautifying change seemed to have passed upon Atherstone's daughter. She was younger, better looking, better dressed; yet keeping always the touch of homeliness, of smiling common-sense, which had first attracted a man in secret rebellion against his own rhetoric and other people's.

"You are treating me abominably!" said Coryston, with vehemence.

"How? My conscience is as sound as a bell!" Wherewith, laughing, she handed him his cup of tea.

"All bells aren't sound. Some are flawed," was the prompt reply. "I have asked you twice this week to tell me when you will be good enough to marry me, and you haven't said a single word in reply."

Marion was silent a little; then she looked up, as Andromache looked at Hector—with a laugh, yet with something else fluttering behind.

"Let's ask ourselves once more, Herbert—is it really a wise thing to do?"

Nobody else since his father died had ever called Coryston by his Christian name; which was perhaps why Marion Atherstone took a peculiar pleasure in using it. Coryston had mostly forgotten that he possessed such a name, but from her he liked it.

"What on earth do you mean by that?"

"In the first place, Herbert, I was never intended by nature to be a peeress."

He sprang up furiously.

"I never heard a more snobbish remark! All that you are asked is to be my wife."

She shook her head.

"We can't make a world for ourselves only. Then

Mrs. Humphry Ward

there's—father."

"Well, what about him?"

"You don't get on very well," she said, with a sigh.

Coryston controlled himself with difficulty.

"For your father, the Liberal party is mostly Jahve—the hope of the children of light. For me the Liberal party is mostly Dagon—either made a god of by Philistines, or groveling before a stronger God—Mammon. But that don't matter. I can behave myself."

Marion bent over her work.

"Can't I behave myself?" he repeated, threateningly, as he moved nearer her.

She looked up at last.

"Suppose you get bored with me—as you have with the Liberal party?"

"But never with liberty," he said, ardently.

"Suppose you come to see the seamy side of me—as you do of everybody?"

"I don't invent seamy sides—where none exist," he said, looking peremptorily into her eyes.

"I'm not clever, Herbert—and I think I'm a Tory."

"Heavens, what do I care? You're the woman I happen to love."

"And I intend to go to church."

"Edward Newbury's kind of church?" he asked her, uneasily.

She shook her head.

"No. I'm an Evangelical."

"Thank the Lord! So am I," he said, fervently.

She laughed.

"It's true," he insisted. "Peace on earth—goodwill to men—that I can understand. So that's settled. Now then—a fortnight next Wednesday?"

"No, no!" she said, in alarm, "certainly not. Wait a minute, Herbert! Where are you going to live, and what are you going to do?"

"I'm taking over the Dorset estates. Lots to do on them, and not much money. Arthur washes his hands of them. There's an old farm where we can live. In six months I shall have quarreled with all the neighbors, and life will be worth living again."

She lifted her eyebrows.

"A charming prospect for your wife!"

"Certainly. You'll have the life you were born for. You'll go round after me—whitewashing the scandals I cause—or if you like to put it sentimentally—binding up the wounds I make. But if I'm anything I'm a sociologist, and my business is to make experiments. They will no doubt be as futile as those I have been making here."

"And where shall I come in?"

"You'll be training up the boy—who'll profit by the experiments."

"The boy?"

"The boy—our boy—who's to have the estates," said Coryston, without a moment's hesitation.

Marion flushed, and pulled her work to her again. Coryston dropped on his knees beside her, and asked her pardon with eyes whereof the male audacity had passed into a steady and shining tenderness.

When Coryston returned that night to the big house, he found his brothers Arthur and James arrived for the week-end. Arthur was full of Parliamentary gossip—"battles of kites and crows," of which Coryston was generally intolerant. But on this occasion he took it silently, and Arthur rambled on. James sat mildly beaming, with finger-tips joined, and the look of one on the verge of a confidence. But he talked, after all—when Arthur paused—only of music and the opera, and as his brothers were not musical, he soon came to an end, and Arthur held the stage. They were gathered in the smoking-room on the ground or garden floor, a room hung with pictures of race-horses, and saddened by various family busts that had not been thought good enough for the library. Outside, the March wind rattled through trees as yet untouched by the spring, and lashed a shivering water round the fountain nymphs.

"Whoever could have dreamed they would have held on till now!" said Arthur, in reply to a perfunctory remark from James. Coryston looked up from a reverie.

"Who? The Government? Lord!—what does it matter? Look here, you chaps—I heard some news in Martover just now. Lord William Newbury died last night—heart failure—expected for the last fortnight."

Arthur received the news with the lively professional interest that one landowner feels in another, and tied a knot in his handkerchief to remind himself to ask Page when the funeral was to be, as the Member for the division must of course attend it. James said, thoughtfully:

"Edward, I saw, was ordained last week. And my letter from Marcia this morning tells me she expects to see him in Rome, on his way to India. Poor Lady William will be very much alone!"

"If you make a solitude and call it religion, what can you expect?" said Coryston, sharply. His face had darkened at the Newburys' name. As always, it had evoked the memory of two piteous graves. Then, as he got up from his chair, he said to Arthur:

"I've fixed it up. Marion and I shall get married next month."

The brothers looked a little embarrassed, though not at all surprised. Corry's attachment to this plain, sensible lady, of moderate opinions, had indeed astonished them enormously when they first became aware of it; but they were now used to it.

"All right, Corry!" said Arthur, slapping his brother on the back. "The best chance of keeping you out of a madhouse! And a very nice woman! You don't expect me to chum with her father?"

"Not unless you wish to learn a thing or two—which was never your strong point," said Coryston, dodging a roll of some Parliamentary paper or other, which Arthur aimed at him. He turned to James. "Well, James, aren't you going to congratulate me?—And why don't you do it yourself?"

"Of course I congratulate you," said James, hastily. "Most sincerely!"

But his expression—half agitated, half smiling—betrayed emotions so far beyond the needs of the situation, that Coryston gave him a puzzled glance. James indeed opened his mouth as though to speak. Then a bright, pink color

Mrs. Humphry Ward

overspread his whole countenance from brow to chin; his lips shut and he fell back in his chair. Presently he went away, and could be heard playing Bach on the organ in the central hall. He returned to London the same evening carrying a cargo of philosophical books, from the library, and a number of novels, though as a rule he never read novels.

The next morning, in a letter to Coryston, he announced his engagement to a girl of nineteen, an orphan, and a pupil at the Royal College of Music. She was the daughter of his Cambridge tutor—penniless, pretty, and musical. He had paid her fees it seemed for several years, and the effect on him of her charming mezzo-soprano voice, at a recent concert given by the College, had settled the matter. The philosopher in love, who had been too shy to tell his brothers *viva voce*, was quite free of tongue in writing; and Coryston and Arthur, though they laughed, were glad that "old James" had found the courage to be happy. Coryston remarked to Arthur that it now remained for him to keep up the blue blood of the family.

"Or Marcia," said Arthur, evading the personal reference.

"Marcia?" Coryston threw his brother an amused, significant look, and said nothing for a moment. But presently he dropped out:

"Lester writes that he'll be in Rome next week looking after that Borghese manuscript. He doesn't expect to get back here till May."

For Lester had now been absent from Coryston some three or four weeks, traveling on matters connected with the library.

Arthur made no comment, but stood awhile by the window in a brown-study, twisting his lip, and frowning slightly. His nondescript features and boyish manner scarcely allowed him at any time to play the magnate with success. But his position as master of Coryston Place, the great family house with its pompous tradition, and the long influence of his mother, had by now asserted, or reasserted themselves; though fighting still with the sore memory of Enid Glenwilliam. Was he going to allow his sister to marry out of her rank—even though the lover were the best fellow in the world? A man may marry whom he will, and the family is only secondarily affected. But a woman is absorbed by the family of her husband.

He finally shrugged his shoulders over it.

"Marcia is as stiff-necked as Coryston," he said to himself, "if it comes to that."

* * * * *

April followed. Amid a crowded Rome, alive with flowers and fountains under a life-giving sun, Marcia Coryston became sharply conscious again of the color and beauty interwoven with mere living, for the sane and sound among men. Edward Newbury passed through on his way to Brindisi and Southern India; and she saw him for an hour; an interview short and restrained, but not to be forgotten by either of the two persons concerned. When it was over Marcia shed a few secret tears— tears of painful sympathy, of an admiration, which was half pity; and then threw herself once more with—as it were—a gasp of renewed welcome, into the dear, kind, many-hued world on which Edward Newbury had turned his back. Presently Lester arrived. He became her constant companion through the inexhaustible spectacle of Rome; and she could watch him among the students who were his fellows, modest or learned as they, yet marked out from most of them by the signs he bore—signs well known by now to her—of a poetic and eager spirit, always and everywhere in quest of the human—of man himself, laughing or suffering, behind his works. The golden days passed by; the blue and white anemones bloomed and died in the Alban woods; the English crowd that comes for Easter arrived and departed; and soon Marcia herself must go home, carrying with her the passionate yet expectant feeling of a child, tired out with happy days, and dreaming of more to come.

These were private and personal affairs. But in March a catastrophe happened which shook the mind of England, and profoundly altered the course of politics. An American yacht with Glenwilliam on board was overtaken off the Needles by a sudden and terrific storm, and went down, without a survivor, and with nothing but some floating wreckage to tell the tale. The Chancellor's daughter was left alone and poor. The passionate sympathy and admiration which her father's party had felt for himself was in some measure transferred to his daughter. But to the amazement of many persons, she refused with scorn any pecuniary help, living on a small income, and trying her hand, with some prospect of success, at literature. About six weeks after her father's death Arthur Coryston found her out and again asked her to marry him. It is probable there was some struggle in her mind, but in the end she refused. "You are a kind, true fellow!" she said to him, gratefully, "but it wouldn't do—it wouldn't do!" And then with a darkening of her strong face: "There is only one thing I can do for *him* now—to serve his causes! And you don't care for one of them! No—no! Good-by!—Good-by!"

At last, in May, Marcia came back again to live—as she supposed—at Coryston with Arthur, and do her duty by her own people. A wonderful spring was abroad in the land. The gorse on the slopes of the hills was a marvel, and when the hawthorns came out beside it, or flung their bloom along the hedgerows and the streams; when far and near the cuckoo's voice made the new world of blossom and growth articulate; when furtive birds slipped joyously to and fro between the nests above and a teeming earth below; when the west winds veering between south and north, and driving the great white clouds before them, made, every day, a new marvel of the sky—Marcia would often hold her breath and know within herself the growth of an answering and a heavenly spring. Lester finished his scholar's errands in Rome and Naples, and returned to Coryston in the middle week of May, in order to complete his work there. He found much more to do than he supposed; he found his friends, Coryston and Arthur, eager to capture and keep him; he found in every field and wood the kindling beauty of the year; he found Marcia!—and a bewildering though still shy message in her dark eyes. Through what doubts and scruples, through what stages of unfolding confidence and growing joy their minds passed, and to what end it all moved on, let those imagine, to whom the purest and deepest of human emotions has ever spoken, or is speaking now.

ABOUT THE AUTHOR

 **Mary Augusta Ward** (née Arnold; June 11, 1851 – March 26, 1920), was a British novelist who wrote under her married name as Mrs. Humphry Ward.

Mary Augusta Arnold was born in Hobart, Tasmania in 1851. She was the daughter of Tom Arnold, a professor of literature, and Julia Sorrell. Her uncle was the poet Matthew Arnold and her grandfather had been Thomas Arnold, the famous headmaster of Rugby School. Her sister, also called Julia, married Leonard Huxley, the son of Thomas Huxley and their sons were Julian and Aldous Huxley. As a young woman, Mary married Humphry "Thomas" Ward, a writer and editor.

Mary Augusta Ward began her career writing articles for magazines while working on a book for children that was published in 1881 under the title Milly and Olly. Her novels contained strong religious subject matter relevant to Victorian values she herself practised. Her popularity spread beyond Great Britain to the United States. According to the New York Times, her book Lady Rose's Daughter was the bestselling novel in the United States in 1903 as was The Marriage of William Ashe in 1905. Her most popular novel by far was the religious "novel with a purpose" Robert Elsmere, which portrayed the religious crisis of a young pastor and his family.

Choose from Thousands of 1stWorldLibrary Classics By

A. M. Barnard	Booth Tarkington	Edward Everett Hale
Ada Leverson	Boyd Cable	Edward J. O'Biren
Adolphus William Ward	Bram Stoker	Edward S. Ellis
Aesop	C. Collodi	Edwin L. Arnold
Agatha Christie	C. E. Orr	Eleanor Atkins
Alexander Aaronsohn	C. M. Ingleby	Eleanor Hallowell Abbott
Alexander Kielland	Carolyn Wells	Eliot Gregory
Alexandre Dumas	Catherine Parr Traill	Elizabeth Gaskell
Alfred Gatty	Charles A. Eastman	Elizabeth McCracken
Alfred Ollivant	Charles Amory Beach	Elizabeth Von Arnim
Alice Duer Miller	Charles Dickens	Ellem Key
Alice Turner Curtis	Charles Dudley Warner	Emerson Hough
Alice Dunbar	Charles Farrar Browne	Emilie F. Carlen
Allen Chapman	Charles Ives	Emily Bronte
Alleyne Ireland	Charles Kingsley	Emily Dickinson
Ambrose Bierce	Charles Klein	Enid Bagnold
Amelia E. Barr	Charles Hanson Towne	Enilor Macartney Lane
Amory H. Bradford	Charles Lathrop Pack	Erasmus W. Jones
Andrew Lang	Charles Romyn Dake	Ernie Howard Pie
Andrew McFarland Davis	Charles Whibley	Ethel May Dell
Andy Adams	Charles Willing Beale	Ethel Turner
Angela Brazil	Charlotte M. Braeme	Ethel Watts Mumford
Anna Alice Chapin	Charlotte M. Yonge	Eugene Sue
Anna Sewell	Charlotte Perkins Stetson	Eugenie Foa
Annie Besant	Clair W. Hayes	Eugene Wood
Annie Hamilton Donnell	Clarence Day Jr.	Eustace Hale Ball
Annie Payson Call	Clarence E. Mulford	Evelyn Everett-green
Annie Roe Carr	Clemence Housman	Everard Cotes
Annonaymous	Confucius	F. H. Cheley
Anton Chekhov	Coningsby Dawson	F. J. Cross
Archibald Lee Fletcher	Cornelis DeWitt Wilcox	F. Marion Crawford
Arnold Bennett	Cyril Burleigh	Fannie E. Newberry
Arthur C. Benson	D. H. Lawrence	Federick Austin Ogg
Arthur Conan Doyle	Daniel Defoe	Ferdinand Ossendowski
Arthur M. Winfield	David Garnett	Fergus Hume
Arthur Ransome	Dinah Craik	Florence A. Kilpatrick
Arthur Schnitzler	Don Carlos Janes	Fremont B. Deering
Arthur Train	Donald Keyhoe	Francis Bacon
Atticus	Dorothy Kilner	Francis Darwin
B.H. Baden-Powell	Dougan Clark	Frances Hodgson Burnett
B. M. Bower	Douglas Fairbanks	Frances Parkinson Keyes
B. C. Chatterjee	E. Nesbit	Frank Gee Patchin
Baroness Emmuska Orczy	E. P. Roe	Frank Harris
Baroness Orczy	E. Phillips Oppenheim	Frank Jewett Mather
Basil King	E. S. Brooks	Frank L. Packard
Bayard Taylor	Earl Barnes	Frank V. Webster
Ben Macomber	Edgar Rice Burroughs	Frederic Stewart Isham
Bertha Muzzy Bower	Edith Van Dyne	Frederick Trevor Hill
Bjornstjerne Bjornson	Edith Wharton	Frederick Winslow Taylor

Friedrich Kerst	Hayden Carruth	James Branch Cabell
Friedrich Nietzsche	Helent Hunt Jackson	James DeMille
Fyodor Dostoyevsky	Helen Nicolay	James Joyce
G.A. Henty	Hendrik Conscience	James Lane Allen
G.K. Chesterton	Hendy David Thoreau	James Lane Allen
Gabrielle E. Jackson	Henri Barbusse	James Oliver Curwood
Garrett P. Serviss	Henrik Ibsen	James Oppenheim
Gaston Leroux	Henry Adams	James Otis
George A. Warren	Henry Ford	James R. Driscoll
George Ade	Henry Frost	Jane Abbott
Geroge Bernard Shaw	Henry James	Jane Austen
George Cary Eggleston	Henry Jones Ford	Jane L. Stewart
George Durston	Henry Seton Merriman	Janet Aldridge
George Ebers	Henry W Longfellow	Jens Peter Jacobsen
George Eliot	Herbert A. Giles	Jerome K. Jerome
George Gissing	Herbert Carter	Jessie Graham Flower
George MacDonald	Herbert N. Casson	John Buchan
George Meredith	Herman Hesse	John Burroughs
George Orwell	Hildegard G. Frey	John Cournos
George Sylvester Viereck	Homer	John F. Kennedy
George Tucker	Honore De Balzac	John Gay
George W. Cable	Horace B. Day	John Glasworthy
George Wharton James	Horace Walpole	John Habberton
Gertrude Atherton	Horatio Alger Jr.	John Joy Bell
Gordon Casserly	Howard Pyle	John Kendrick Bangs
Grace E. King	Howard R. Garis	John Milton
Grace Gallatin	Hugh Lofting	John Philip Sousa
Grace Greenwood	Hugh Walpole	John Taintor Foote
Grant Allen	Humphry Ward	Jonas Lauritz Idemil Lie
Guillermo A. Sherwell	Ian Maclaren	Jonathan Swift
Gulielma Zollinger	Inez Haynes Gillmore	Joseph A. Altsheler
Gustav Flaubert	Irving Bacheller	Joseph Carey
H. A. Cody	Isabel Cecilia Williams	Joseph Conrad
H. B. Irving	Isabel Hornibrook	Joseph E. Badger Jr
H.C. Bailey	Israel Abrahams	Joseph Hergesheimer
H. G. Wells	Ivan Turgenev	Joseph Jacobs
H. H. Munro	J.G.Austin	Jules Vernes
H. Irving Hancock	J. Henri Fabre	Julian Hawthrone
H. R. Naylor	J. M. Barrie	Julie A Lippmann
H. Rider Haggard	J. M. Walsh	Justin Huntly McCarthy
H. W. C. Davis	J. Macdonald Oxley	Kakuzo Okakura
Haldeman Julius	J. R. Miller	Karle Wilson Baker
Hall Caine	J. S. Fletcher	Kate Chopin
Hamilton Wright Mabie	J. S. Knowles	Kenneth Grahame
Hans Christian Andersen	J. Storer Clouston	Kenneth McGaffey
Harold Avery	J. W. Duffield	Kate Langley Bosher
Harold McGrath	Jack London	Kate Langley Bosher
Harriet Beecher Stowe	Jacob Abbott	Katherine Cecil Thurston
Harry Castlemon	James Allen	Katherine Stokes
Harry Coghill	James Andrews	L. A. Abbot
Harry Houidini	James Baldwin	L. T. Meade

L. Frank Baum
Latta Griswold
Laura Dent Crane
Laura Lee Hope
Laurence Housman
Lawrence Beasley
Leo Tolstoy
Leonid Andreyev
Lewis Carroll
Lewis Sperry Chafer
Lilian Bell
Lloyd Osbourne
Louis Hughes
Louis Joseph Vance
Louis Tracy
Louisa May Alcott
Lucy Fitch Perkins
Lucy Maud Montgomery
Luther Benson
Lydia Miller Middleton
Lyndon Orr
M. Corvus
M. H. Adams
Margaret E. Sangster
Margret Howth
Margaret Vandercook
Margaret W. Hungerford
Margret Penrose
Maria Edgeworth
Maria Thompson Daviess
Mariano Azuela
Marion Polk Angellotti
Mark Overton
Mark Twain
Mary Austin
Mary Catherine Crowley
Mary Cole
Mary Hastings Bradley
Mary Roberts Rinehart
Mary Rowlandson
M. Wollstonecraft Shelley
Maud Lindsay
Max Beerbohm
Myra Kelly
Nathaniel Hawthrone
Nicolo Machiavelli
O. F. Walton
Oscar Wilde

Owen Johnson
P.G. Wodehouse
Paul and Mabel Thorne
Paul G. Tomlinson
Paul Severing
Percy Brebner
Percy Keese Fitzhugh
Peter B. Kyne
Plato
Quincy Allen
R. Derby Holmes
R. L. Stevenson
R. S. Ball
Rabindranath Tagore
Rahul Alvares
Ralph Bonehill
Ralph Henry Barbour
Ralph Victor
Ralph Waldo Emmerson
Rene Descartes
Ray Cummings
Rex Beach
Rex E. Beach
Richard Harding Davis
Richard Jefferies
Richard Le Gallienne
Robert Barr
Robert Frost
Robert Gordon Anderson
Robert L. Drake
Robert Lansing
Robert Lynd
Robert Michael Ballantyne
Robert W. Chambers
Rosa Nouchette Carey
Rudyard Kipling
Saint Augustine
Samuel B. Allison
Samuel Hopkins Adams
Sarah Bernhardt
Sarah C. Hallowell
Selma Lagerlof
Sherwood Anderson
Sigmund Freud
Standish O'Grady
Stanley Weyman
Stella Benson
Stella M. Francis

Stephen Crane
Stewart Edward White
Stijn Streuvels
Swami Abhedananda
Swami Parmananda
T. S. Ackland
T. S. Arthur
The Princess Der Ling
Thomas A. Janvier
Thomas A Kempis
Thomas Anderton
Thomas Bailey Aldrich
Thomas Bulfinch
Thomas De Quincey
Thomas Dixon
Thomas H. Huxley
Thomas Hardy
Thomas More
Thornton W. Burgess
U. S. Grant
Upton Sinclair
Valentine Williams
Various Authors
Vaughan Kester
Victor Appleton
Victor G. Durham
Victoria Cross
Virginia Woolf
Wadsworth Camp
Walter Camp
Walter Scott
Washington Irving
Wilbur Lawton
Wilkie Collins
Willa Cather
Willard F. Baker
William Dean Howells
William le Queux
W. Makepeace Thackeray
William W. Walter
William Shakespeare
Winston Churchill
Yei Theodora Ozaki
Yogi Ramacharaka
Young E. Allison
Zane Grey